TOUCHED BY THE LIGHT

TOUCHED BY THE LIGHT

Linn B Halton

Book Guild Publishing
Sussex, England

First published in Great Britain in 2011 by
The Book Guild Ltd
Pavilion View
19 New Road
Brighton, BN1 1UF

Typesetting in Baskerville by
Keyboard Services, Luton, Bedfordshire

Printed in Great Britain by
CPI Antony Rowe

A catalogue record for this book is available from
The British Library

ISBN 978 1 84624 531 2

Author's Note

I realise that writing about the 'afterlife' as an integral part of a story involves a level of sympathetic imagination in return from the reader. Some information has to be presented as if it were factual and not necessarily as just an interpretation or even a personal belief. I mean no disrespect whatsoever to either religion or spiritualism for anything presented as a part of this piece. This is just a story that I hope you will enjoy in the spirit (no pun intended here) in which it's written.

Acknowledgements

I have always loved the phrase 'No man is an island'* and I have come to realise that this is probably never truer than when writing one's first book. So a big hug and grateful thanks to a few very special people in my life:

My husband Lawrence, for his unwavering love, support and guidance

My late mother, Lilian Elsie Wilkins, for inspiration every step of the way both sides of life

Lawrence and Jane for caring enough to give me their honest feedback

Jonathan Cainer, whose daily horoscopes have kept me going for a very long time and gave me the reassurance I needed to finally give up work and write

And last (but not least) Book Guild Publishing for making my dream come true!

---

*John Donne (1572–1631) from *Devotions upon Emergent Occasions*, Meditation XVII, 1624.

Contemplation

How much time do I spend
Contemplating what I do not know,
Trying to find some logic
Or even some common thread
That will explain it all?

I cannot quite conceive
The idea that
There isn't always an answer,
Not always a solution,
And that some things
Were just
Never meant to be.

I just cannot accept
Defeat,
For that is what it feels like to me
When I cannot solve a problem,
Find the perfect solution
Or even an answer that will
Get me where I want to be.

And yet I have spent my life
Battling with the impossible
The improbable and often
The un-do-able,
Because something inside
Just won't allow me
To give in and accept I'm beat.

Have I made my life hard? Yes.
Have I won all my battles? No.
Have I cried tears of frustration? Yes.
Would I change anything? No.

Why? Because this is who I am.

Suddenly, I see the light

Dying was, quite frankly, incredibly easy. One minute I was there and the next minute I was 'here', wherever 'here' is. If someone had asked me what my thoughts were about how life 'ends', I can't say this is necessarily how I would have pictured it. I probably would have imagined more drama, but the truth is, I had never given it any considered thought. I've come to think that that's probably a good thing, because it might be easier not to have any pre-conceptions, as in my case. One thing I can say for sure is that the possibility of dying at a young age had never crossed my mind.

Up to that point I'd only been confronted by the deaths of two people who were really involved with my life. Andy was only eighteen years old and we worked together. I took him through his induction programme and on-the-job training, when he joined the company where I was employed as a marketing executive. We spent a large part of that time laughing while we worked. He was a fun-loving guy and suddenly it was just that little bit easier getting up each morning and getting myself into work. Not that there was even a hint of romance between us, but we just sort of 'clicked' in a 'friends for life' kind of way. He was out one night with the guys and managed to fall out of a slowly moving train, with fatal consequences. It was only a few months later that my Great Aunt Elspeth died and I felt I had lost someone who had really understood me, in a way a lot of other people just didn't. Both were very real tragedies to me – Andy had a quality

1

about him that made him special and Elspeth was just the best person ever to be with. Both were people who made me feel very happy whenever I spent time with them. My reaction to their deaths was not to contemplate my own future demise, but to feel bitterly cheated by theirs.

Anyway, back to the present – and this will probably sound *so* predictable, but there really *was* a bright light. No, I'm not joking. It entered my vision before I was technically 'dead' and I remember it vividly, because it felt strangely comforting. At the point at which it appeared, I really wasn't feeling too good, well obviously because (I suppose) I was dying. I think I'd developed pneumonia but I was only semi-conscious and it was difficult to understand what exactly was going on. The panic around me seemed to be focused on my temperature and I was painfully aware that the things they were doing to cool me down weren't pleasant. They also weren't making me feel any better. I remember odd words here and there and lots of different faces peering down at me, but none of it made any sense. And then that was it! Easy. I just followed the path into the light and I was suddenly pain-free.

Rewind three months

Hitting twenty-five was a real turning point for me. Waking up that morning, I distinctly remember looking into the mirror and thinking 'now comes the grown-up bit of my life'. In some ways I was more than ready and looking forward to a more thoughtful, considered and responsible me!

My friends and family were going to be astounded by the new Mya Coles. However, the reflection that came back to me in the mirror that morning was clearly a person who had partied too hard and for too long the night before. I remember leaning in closer to the mirror to inspect the bags under my eyes and thinking 'suitcases' would be a more appropriate description. I grimaced a 'squint' as a flash of glinting sunlight made me recoil sharply and remember muttering, 'Never, ever, again...' I like to think that there was a new, mature sincerity in the tone of my voice that day.

Life was looking pretty good – I think my boyfriend Sam was on the brink of suggesting we move in together. We'd had the usual jokey conversations about it and laughed at friends who had gradually stopped partying and started inviting us around to 'dinner'. Grown-up stuff! We'd progressed to the hesitant, serious stage – neither wanting to be the first to admit it was time and neither sure quite how to approach it. Sam does everything in a considered way.

To my utter amazement (being the self-sufficient, Amazonian woman I was extremely proud to have become),

I found that it was very important to me that Sam made the first move. I know! I should be ashamed of myself, equality of the sexes, feminism, and all that. But it might as well have been the Neolithic period, because I wanted – no, needed – Sam to grab me lovingly by the hair, in a very possessive way and drag me off into his cave. Not literally of course, just symbolically: let's just say his flat wasn't 'co-ordinated' and mine had the additional advantage of being much bigger. And perfect.

So, we were *there*, teetering on the edge and it felt hugely exciting – a bit like waiting for Christmas when you're five years old.

Work was also going extremely well. After a succession of bosses who ranged from useless (as in chocolate teapot) to annoyingly sanctimonious (God help me!), I finally found myself working with someone who understood my enthusiasm and who was forging ahead, dragging me happily in his wake. We made a good team and although Chay (as he liked to be called, well Charles sounds so *old*) was only twenty-nine, his marketing talent was revitalising Masonbury's Town and Country Homes.

Property development was a difficult market to be in after the credit crunch and Masonbury's in Bristol, like many other developers, were struggling. Before Chay started, my boss Martin just wasn't interested in any of the fresh ideas I put before him. I was concerned that we needed to develop a more aggressive approach to marketing. The traditional format wasn't bringing in the business, it seemed clear to me that we had to make more of what the company could offer to have any chance of surviving the downturn. It was a hard market and there was no doubt about that, but there were still discerning purchasers out there with money to spend. Companies just had to re-think their strategies and no one could afford to waste time moaning about the situation or

4

hesitating about what to do next. Day one with Chay and everything changed – management didn't know what had hit them! He reviewed my ideas and, with a few fairly minor tweaks, he pressed the 'go' button. People were seeing me in a new light. My ideas were out there for all to see and getting results.

So, all in all, I think I was justified in feeling that life's apprenticeship was over for me at last and the payback was about to begin. So WHY? Why me, why now?

OK, back to the light

So, here I am. It's the weirdest thing but I seem to be watching someone else's life – I just don't know how else to describe it. I'm not sure where I am – and this is going to sound even weirder – I feel 'here' but there's no physical presence to this feeling. I still feel 'me' – same thoughts, same memories but it's almost like I'm floating and seeing only through my mind's eye. I know, it sounds insane but I need to try to explain, to make some sense of it. When I stop panicking and relax, what I see and feel is what is going on in someone else's life. Yes, I know, *I know* how it sounds but just because it sounds unbelievable that doesn't mean I'm not experiencing it.

Perhaps it would help if I explain what happened after 'the light'. The truth is, actually, not a lot, but it was so much more than just a light. Imagine the warmest of spring afternoons following a long, dark and, at times, very damp winter. You know the feeling, short hours of daylight and we all feel like we need a holiday. Suddenly the sun shines and it reminds you that spring is coming and summer will follow on behind it. Well, it was like that, a really good feeling of promise and anticipation of what's coming, almost euphoric. Then nothing. Well not exactly *nothing*, but no colour or light – more like being suspended in fog. The problem is, I don't know for how long, but I felt like I was resting and enjoying a sense of calm way beyond any yoga class.

You know the way you wake up sometimes, slowly drifting

in and out of a dream you're trying to leave behind, but you keep dozing and falling back into it? Well, I'm feeling full of energy now, revitalised even, but whenever I want to start engaging my brain, all of the thoughts coming my way seem to relate to someone called Laurel. How do I know this? I can hear you thinking. Well, and this is the scary bit, she keeps trying to communicate with me.

I know it sounds ridiculous but it's a bit like picking up the phone and dialling a number, except my phone doesn't have a dial so I can't choose who to ring. Laurel clearly has a very busy life going on, so why would she choose to communicate with someone who (let's face it) can't really be of much help?

I so wish I had read up on the subject of the afterlife. Is this the way it's supposed to be, or am I doing something wrong? Whatever happened to angels and clouds? I ask myself. Wasn't I supposed to have a helper to greet me and show me the ropes?

Anyway, I've made a decision – although I acknowledge that I don't really seem to have any choice in the matter. I'm going to chill, communicate with Laurel and see what happens next.

Laurel and me

As I float lazily in my cosy little haze, I can hear a voice that's becoming increasingly familiar to me.

'For goodness' sake Dan, Lennie's on her way over and there isn't an inch of floor space that doesn't have your clutter all over it.' Laurel is giving Dan 'the stare' and just the one look is enough to get him on the move and clearing up his paperwork.

Laurel and Dan's very stylish, three-bed flat is smart and spacious, although I get the feeling it's not the first time Dan has managed to hide this under a layer of papers covered with sketches. However, he knows her well enough to see when she means business and a girls' night in with Lennie (Leanne), her best friend, is not to be jeopardised.

It's amusing watching them inter-react; Dan is sexily broody, very tall and lanky with a dark, Mick Jagger look. In contrast, Laurel is a 'wisp', small and almost fragile-looking with naturally blonde hair and big, pale blue eyes. However, she has a steely strength and determination enough to take on the world *if* she has a mind to. Thankfully, her normal mode of operation seems to be reasonably relaxed, in an energetic sort of way. Dan isn't saying much as usual, but just seems to be very relaxed and content to be around her.

What is becoming more and more obvious as I'm watching them, is that they complement each other really well. Dan's height clearly makes him feel awkward at times and his stance often reflects a sense of embarrassment, like he's in the way. Laurel moves around quickly, almost running circles around him. However, the warmth and charm that emanates from him is almost magnetic, both comforting and reassuring at the same time. I can see he is very protective of her, almost as if he's afraid she's so fragile she'll break, despite the fact that she's a frenetic ball of energy. The contrast of his almost jet-black hair and rangy bulk, against her feather-light frame and quick intensity, is strangely harmonious. I'm suddenly feeling very emotional and wonder, if I was earth-side, whether my eyes would be watering. Well, I've always been a girlie girl and what is life without an appreciation for romance?

I'm not sure if I'm speaking out aloud – I don't seem to be able to 'hear' myself other than in my head – but I'm laughing as I watch the diminutive Laurel physically pushing the towering Dan into the bathroom.

'If you shave and shower now, you can be dressed and out the door before Lennie arrives – I'll tidy up.'

'But Babe, I'm not meeting the lads until eight and it's only six thirty!' he whines and I must admit it's a heartfelt plea, delivered with boyish appeal.

'Fine by me. Everyone here at seven pm gets a full-on facial. Cucumber slices, the lot. I can probably find some black nail polish...' You just have to admire that woman!

'OK, OK, you win. Give me five and I'll be out of your hair. What time do you want me back?'

Laurel walks up to him, putting her hands flat against his chest and, on tip toe, plants a little kiss on his neck. 'Ten o'clock with pizza,' she says with a silly grin on her face.

'Ah,' he calls over his shoulder from the bathroom, 'you're only after me for my money. You women are all the same.' He turns to the mirror and starts singing while he runs some hot water into the sink and I can't help but notice that he has the most heart-warming smile on his face.

I'm entranced watching Dan, but suddenly I feel a real pang of sadness, like a wave and I'm being physically 'sucked' into another room. Laurel is bent over, tidying up and I suddenly realise I can see tears plopping down on to the cushion she has in her hands. Damn it! I can't read her thoughts, I think she's blocking me out.

Dan and Lennie literally pass in the doorway.

'Thank goodness you're going out. Saves me the energy of flirting with you – totally wasted on someone as attached as you,' she says, smiling up at him, 'but it's such a *shame.*'

'Behave yourself,' Laurel calls from the kitchen, clinking wine glasses. 'Have a good time with the lads, hunky.' Hunky? Now I'm really laughing, that is perfect, he really is a hunk.

Her mood is different now, lighter but still nothing – no voice in my head or stream of thoughts. I sort of drift off, half-listening, half caught up with little memories of my own floating in and out of my head. Suddenly, a sharp twist and I'm next to Laurel on the sofa, looking across at Lennie. It's almost as if I'm really here, physically, and hearing Laurel talking at normal volume. Real, live. I just can't believe that neither of them can see me.

'We've tried and tried and yet another month goes by and I'm still not pregnant. Dan won't talk about it, he just says I need to be patient, but I think about having a baby all the time. A year ago I wouldn't even have given it a passing thought, but now... It gets me down.' Laurel is absentmindedly twisting the wine glass in her hands.

'Dan's right, Laurel, you just gotta be patient. You can't live in a permanent state of anxiety – that probably doesn't help the process either. Anyway, are you *sure* you want a baby with Dan? Giving birth to a six foot six baby isn't going to be exactly easy...'

Laurel, laughing, chokes on her wine and wipes her mouth with her sleeve.

'Idiot – have you ever even seen a baby? They start off as tiny little things and don't get to six foot six until they're at least twelve, if they take after Dan, that is!' They both lay back laughing, and for the moment I feel the lift in her mood and see her start to relax.

Suddenly I'm above them, looking down and Laurel is lying back against the sofa cushions looking directly up at me, as if she can actually see me. The question in her mind surprises me.

'What do you think? Any advice?'

I look across at Lennie to see if she's heard but she's caught up, singing along to the background music and doesn't appear to have heard anything.

'Laurel, this isn't fair,' I retort, our minds connecting.

'You must see things I can't see, can't you help at all?' she asks and I can hear the disappointment in her voice. I'm clearly way out of my depth here.

'I'm just struggling – with all of this.'

Silence. Is it possible to have a headache in the afterlife?

'Look,' she says edgily, 'this gift isn't something I asked for. Have you any idea how disruptive this is to my life? I don't mean to be difficult and it's not your fault that you don't understand what it's like. Some people are able to pick up on vibes and some can't or decide it's not for them. The vibes I experienced as a young child were just too strong and too vivid to ignore, so I had no choice. Besides, I didn't know I was seeing or talking to dead people so I wasn't at all afraid. It was a long time before I realised, quite suddenly, that this didn't happen to everyone and that came as a real shock at the time. I think my mother suspected, although she never picked up on it until I broached the subject. Her attitude was that it was best not to encourage "experiences" and it would all eventually go away, as it had done for her. But it was too real for me to ignore and eventually I realised that I had one 'visitor' who was more frequent than all the others. I read up on it a bit and came to understand that 'Oratam' is my spirit guide. He's a Hackensack Indian who was born in the 1600s. I Googled his name when he first started coming through to me, just because it seemed a bit odd not knowing anything about him. He brings through other spirits who don't have the strength to communicate on their own, so he becomes the channel or link for them. I stopped encouraging messages a few years ago because I don't want to become a medium and besides, people don't take well to being given messages from the dead, believe me!'

What I found truly shocking was the fact that Laurel was clearly comparing her visitors with me, whereas in my mind, I'm still an earthly person like her. Wow, no wonder she's fed up. I'm starting to understand why Laurel is so upset that I'm just assuming she is happy to accept me being around.

'So why isn't your spirit guide here with us now?' Simple question, I'm thinking. Why is she frowning? That's not a good sign.

'Look – this is obviously traumatic for you, but you have to understand that the connection between you and me is, well, different yet again. So this is a first for me too.' I *so* wasn't expecting that.

'How? How is it different – you said you saw things all the time. I just need to understand what's going on here.' My words begin to have a ring of desperation to them and Laurel is looking uncomfortable.

'I know, but let me try to explain. I "see" or sometimes "feel" a presence and it's not like seeing a person in the flesh, OK? It's usually a shadow or a slight movement of the air that you could miss in a nano-second. The sort of thing you could easily convince yourself you didn't actually see at all. On the other hand, messages usually come via Orrie, as I call him. He also acts as a filter now, so it's more controlled and that means I only have contact if I want to be receptive. He tells me who he's bringing and tries to find out what they want to pass on. That way at least I get a choice. It's not like that with you.'

'Sorry, I'm beginning to understand. Do you *see* me?'

'No. Since you first arrived, about a week ago, I can feel when you're here and our thoughts are linked but you don't actually appear.'

'Laurel, I don't scare you, do I?' She's smiling now and shaking her head. I'm looking across at Lennie, who is smiling back at her, totally unaware that Laurel and I are having this conversation.

'No, as I said, I don't see you, just sometimes you're there, in my head and we're talking. It's a bit like talking to yourself in your thoughts, except since you've appeared I seem to spend a lot of time "talking" to you now.'

The realisation that I really have 'passed over' and that this is it from now on is a pretty hard fact to face.

Suddenly, just as if we're talking on the phone and Laurel has put down the handset, we aren't linked any more and I'm back inside my cosy, foggy little zone.

Fuck – I'm dead, I'm *really* dead!

OK, so let's look at the positive side of things

I've decided to wallow for a bit, regain my composure and fill my 'zone' with nice cheerful things – happy memories. As my mood lifts, I'm starting to think about the positive side of being 'here' instead of 'there'. Well, no more credit card bills, no more running on the treadmill at the gym, I'm feeling great and there isn't really anything to complain about. Good start. So, the only thing *missing* is a point to all of this. Why didn't everything just end, there, after the 'light' experience? Why am I here, seeing all this, getting involved in things? There must be a point to it all. It doesn't seem to be linked into heaven or hell – I'm certainly not suffering in any way, just a bit frustrated I'm not in control, but neither do I feel like I'm being rewarded. The answer must lie with Laurel. Why can't I link with Sam or my sister Sadie or Mum and Dad – all people I dearly love and would like to help, or at least be able to tell them that I'm OK.

It feels incredibly indulgent to just laze and think, with no feeling of pressure, concern about time or responsibility to, or for, anyone else. So unlike being alive, where it felt like I was constantly 'running late' on the things that had to be done or that other people were relying on me to do for them. I was one of life's 'do-ers' as in, if you want something done, give it to a busy person ... because they are the people who do, actually, get things done. My mobile was never out of my hand and work was like a whirlwind, although in a good way. So, I guess you can say this new state of being is growing on me. I can sort of 'feel' Laurel's thoughts turning over in the background, but I don't feel like getting pulled back in. At least not just yet, anyway.

I'm thinking about what life is like for Sam now. Is he missing me? How is he coping? What was my funeral like? Aren't I supposed to be able to see all that?

The worst thing about dying so suddenly, I have decided, is that you can't prepare. What was the last thing I said to Sam? Being the romantic I am, I sincerely hope it was a passionate and memorable 'I love you'. I bet it was something like, 'You've left a disgusting ring around the bath again, I hope you don't think I'm going to clean it!'. Not exactly words to treasure for the rest of time and that's making me feel a bit sad now.

Anyway, I obviously don't have all the answers, but I'm thinking about what Laurel said and if she can pass on messages from an old Indian Chief (she did say he was a Chief, didn't she?) then surely she can pass on a message from me. That's it! As they say, every cloud has a silver lining and I think I've just found the one in mine, figuratively speaking of course.

I'm really enjoying what I assume is the afterlife equivalent of a Sunday morning lie-in, when suddenly I'm back into Laurel's space. So real, just like when she was talking with Lennie, that I feel sure they must be able to see me now. Except this isn't a pleasant situation. Laurel is going off on one and Dan is looking like he's going to walk out. I'm desperately trying to stop her talking and at the same time trying to catch up with what is going on here. However, the jolt that dragged me here was so fierce and sudden, that everything is just too loud and too bright. In the seconds it's taking me to adjust, it's too late and Dan walks out, slamming the door behind him, leaving just the two of us and a horrible, stunned silence.

'What did I just miss?' I ask Laurel but either she can't

hear me or she doesn't want to hear me – but which? I'm trying to work out what has happened when suddenly I'm not there any more.

Where am I *now*? I feel so disorientated, like I've just stepped off the waltzer at the fairground – and I *really* hate rides with a passion. OK, I'll try closing my eyes – which feels a bit like withdrawing, and now I've opened them again, I'm at the beach! Hey, this is really great. I can hear seagulls and waves lapping onto pebbles. It's so bright and I can hear kids laughing. Hang on – this is *not* funny! I'm back with Laurel again and it's clear she knows I'm here.

'What's wrong?' she asks and it's barely a whisper.

'I don't know. Things are happening that I can't control. You're going to think I'm mad,' I say hesitantly.

'No, I won't – you can share it with me – I'll understand.'

'OK. I've been to the beach.'

'Great! I'm having the worst crisis of my entire life and you're complaining because you've been to the beach?' I knew it was going to sound odd.

'But Laurel, I'm dead.' I'm expecting some sort of reaction here, but she just skips over my words as if they aren't relevant.

'You've probably been shown some link to your next life,' she tells me with a slight sniff, while she dabs at her eyes with a soggy tissue.

'Next life? What "next life"? You didn't say anything about that before.' There's only so much earth-shattering news I can take in at any one time and this is all becoming a little over-whelming.

'Look, sor-reee. It's just that I think Dan is going to break up with me and I don't know what to do or why things are going so wrong. I thought you were sent to help me but you're really hard work. You keep distracting me when I need to have my mind free to think about

16

what's going wrong with my life and what I'm going to do about it.'

Wow, now I feel selfish. After all, I'm only dead and Laurel and Dan might be *splitting up*! Great, I can still be sarcastic in the afterlife!

'Look, I'm the novice here, but I think we've been put in touch for a reason. If we're going to have to share "mind" space (does that sound freaky or what?) perhaps we need to focus ourselves.' I sound practical, sensible even, and it's certainly having a calming effect on Laurel. There's a delay as she thinks it through.

'Right ... so what exactly does that mean?' she asks.

'Well, call it women being intuitive or something–'

'You're a WOMAN?'

'God – you thought I was a MAN? You really can't see me, can you?'

I don't know what Laurel is thinking at this exact moment, but I'm beginning to see how I'm going to have to start looking at things in a whole new way. She thought I was a MAN! Cool – perhaps there are other ways spirits can create an impression. This fact hasn't occurred to me so far. I guess I'm starting to learn there's a whole new experience ahead of me and I've only just scratched the surface.

Let's not panic, there has to be some logic here somewhere

I'm increasingly finding that having no concept of time is really making things difficult. At first, 'down time', as I've started to think of the time when I'm not linked to Laurel, was peaceful, tranquil even. Thinking of the things that happened in my life, I wasn't sad, but happy and I laughed a lot. In fact, it was great. Now things are getting complicated and I seem to be spending whatever time I have 'unlinked' trying to work out what's going on. Then, when we do link up again, I have absolutely no idea how long it's been since the last time I saw her, or what has happened in between, it's really diff– hell!

With no warning at all, once again I'm somewhere else. I'm getting used to the movement – it's more like an adrenalin rush than a physical jerk I suppose. Hey, I'm back at the beach again! I'm walking along and the waves are lapping on to the sand, barely three feet away from me. There's a young boy ahead, he's very thin and quite tall and he's flying a kite, he looks like a young version of Dan. A young couple have just walked past me, hand in hand and I think they're his parents. I can take a deep breath and smell the sea and … chips. Spinning around, I spot a little hut back up near the road selling burgers and chips and the obligatory candyfloss. It all smells great, very nostalgic, and it triggers a whole flood of memories from my own childhood – but here I go again!

It's now pitch black and I've left the beach. It might

just be the contrast from light to dark, but I can't see a thing at the moment. Hang on, I can hear something, it's a soft moaning – eeuuww! I'm in a bedroom and Laurel and Dan are making out – get me out of here NOW! Shit, nothing's happening.

'I love you Babe. I love you so much, my heart feels like it's going to explode.' I'm trying so hard not to listen but I'm shocked by the strength of feeling in Dan's words – the air is electric.

'Don't ever leave me Dan, *ever*,' Laurel whispers. Suddenly I'm 'fading' back into my zone.

Why is all of this happening? What's this beach thing all about? Am I supposed to be doing something about Laurel and Dan? What if I don't work it out in time and they split up for good?

OK, I'm going to try to apply some logic. This is like a jigsaw puzzle, so I just need to start putting the pieces together – you don't need all of them to get a rough idea of the final picture, do you? However, I just don't have enough pieces yet to get a meaningful glimpse, so perhaps I should start with a list.

1. Laurel loves Dan.
2. Dan loves Laurel.
3. Dan and Laurel both want a baby.
4. No baby yet.
5. No mention of marriage – does anyone care?
6. Likely complications (sub-list):

   Money – no problems, both working
   Previous partners causing trouble – no problems there
   In-law disputes – none have come to light yet (that always gets thrown up in an argument if it's a problem)

Oh great, here I go again! Now *that* really hurts. I have a dragging sensation that isn't very pleasant to say the least. It's really dark again, I can make out the shapes of people around me and it feels ... intense. The atmosphere is heavy in an unpleasant way. Two guys are having a conversation, but keeping their voices very low, so it's hard to make out what they're saying. They're watching a small bank of monitors on a large control panel and one of them is sliding levers up and down. It's like he's editing something, but I can't see what they're watching.

Something is spinning me around and I can hear a voice, very clear and very chilling saying, 'If anybody's there, please make your presence felt'.

'What the–?' I'm trying to turn back around, so that I can focus on the two guys as somehow I feel it's important. I'm sure I heard one of them mention Dan's name just now, but I'm not even sure they're in the same room – which is huge – and something is stopping me every time I try to look. I think it's this woman with the 'voice' that seems to be pulling me back each time. OK – she's not giving up so I'm going to have to see what she wants.

Now that my eyes have adjusted to the darkness I scan around the room. I can see there are seven or eight people sitting around quite a large table. The woman who's speaking is telling the group to put their fingers on a glass in the centre of what I can see now is a Ouija board – for Christ's sake!

Suddenly I'm being dragged up to the ceiling, directly above them. It's like I'm pinned up here and these people are doing this to me. Un-be-liev-able and I'm starting to feel really, really angry. My eyes are searching out the two guys at the monitors. I can't see them, so I don't know if they're a part of all of this, but I can hear them talking quite clearly now. They *are* talking about Dan.

'His title graphics are great, he's got some innovative

ideas – it's just a pity he works for Jupiter Live, their management are such a pain. I heard from the boss this morning that we're pulling the plug on their contract – they're lucky they aren't being charged penalties for the delays they've caused.'

'If anybody's there, please tell me your name.' The voice is at it again and I'm still pinned to the ceiling. Go away, damn you!

Looking down at the table I can hear the voice spelling out my message and the glass is moving rapidly around the letters on the board – did I really do that?

'G ... O ... A ... W ... A ... Y ... D ... A ... M ... N ... Y ... O ... U ...' She trails off and the silence is really heavy now, like they're all holding their breath.

'We're here to receive any messages you would like to pass on,' she's saying. I don't want to say anything, what does she expect from me? Back to the guys in the background, who I now realise are recording this 'experience' live and that is what they're watching on the monitors.

'These titles of Dan's work well but it's probably the last chance we'll get to use him once the contract is pulled. Pity the company can't afford to take him on but there's just not enough work until we get a bit bigger. Just hope this series doesn't fall flat.'

My eyes are being drawn back to the table again. There's a lot of muttering going on below me and I can feel that some of the people are very uncomfortable with my unintentional message. I didn't ask to be dragged here and I really don't like the way they're talking to me like I'm just a ghost, it's freaking me out.

Almost as if she's heard me, which I doubt, she starts speaking again.

'If you're trapped,' she's saying, 'talk to us. We'll try to help you.'

My mind is now screaming several obscenities I *know* she won't let the glass repeat and I'm right. Makes you wonder just how the glass actually moves, doesn't it? Not that I'm sceptical of course. I think she's beginning to get the real message that I don't want to play. However, just as I'm thinking that I've beaten her into submission, suddenly I'm literally 'dropping' towards the table! Concentrate, concentrate – wow, that is close. I'm hovering and … oh my God.

One of the people around the table is my sister.

What's Sadie doing here, at a live Ouija board session that's being recorded for late night re-runs on the telly? It's so not her style. Seeing her now though, she looks very uncomfortable with what's going on around her. She shouldn't be here and it makes me want to give her a hug, let her know she's not alone. I don't feel sad, I actually feel happy to see her. Suddenly I'm standing behind her and I can smell the shampoo in her hair and I long to hug her. It wouldn't hurt to just touch her shoulder would it?

As I gently lay my hand on her shoulder, she screams and jumps up. We sort of 'bump' but then Sadie's body continues on through me and she just stops short of bouncing off the wall behind me. I'm shaking and everyone around is wide-eyed with terror.

'Something touched me, something touched me,' she's shrieking.

Guess that wasn't the smartest thing to have done, because now everybody is spooked. Looking over at the guys in the corner recording the live action, they're both bent over the monitors pressing buttons and frantically moving levers up and down.

'Guess it's going to be a good show after all!' one of them is saying amidst the noise. Great, I've just provided live footage that has freaked everybody out, including me, and I don't even know what I'm doing. I've probably broken some afterlife code or something; can I get into trouble for that?

I just can't get my head around the fact that Sadie is here and she seems to be on her own, as I don't see any of her friends. One of the group is comforting her now and she seems to have calmed down. I know we both went to a clairvoyant a few years ago, but that was for a laugh with a group of friends on a hen night and no one really took it seriously. Neither of us were into this sort of thing, although I'm now beginning to wish ... anyway, I digress. So, by a process of deduction, my sister is here for one reason and one reason only. Because I'm dead.

Suddenly even 'the voice', which is trying to bring some order back to things, doesn't seem quite so irritating. After all, perhaps I should give her the benefit of the doubt – I'm a novice after all, and she's probably been doing this for years and might be able to help me.

Now Laurel's voice is in my head.

'What are you doing?' she's asking, quite casually as if she's on the phone and ever so slightly bored, so decided to give me a call.

'I'm at a séance, well, there's a Ouija board thingy.'

Her voice changes immediately. 'Get back here *now!*' and her tone starts to panic me. 'What are you playing at?' she's literally hissing at me.

'It isn't like I've got a choice,' I say in my defence. 'I don't *want* to be here.'

'OK, don't worry – I'll call on Orrie, see what he can do.' It may have been minutes later or seconds – I just don't know – but suddenly, here I am, back in Laurel's flat. I must admit, I'm impressed. He must really know his stuff, because I don't think the group had quite finished with me.

I'm beginning to feel as if I'm at everyone's beck and call and my 'sanctuary zone' is starting to feel like a place to hide. Instead of it being a restful, contemplative experience, it's starting to feel like hard work. The jigsaw is expanding rather than the pieces fitting together, so I haven't made any progress at all.

And now I have a new concern. Sadie. Why would she take part in a live TV programme contacting spirits? I'm also really worried about the Ouija board, I don't know much about it, but common sense tells me you don't mess with things you don't fully understand. Getting a reading from a clairvoyant is not that unusual. I must admit our visit did throw up a few interesting things – my youthful demise not being one – but calling up spirits like this? That's something else. I was certainly dragged in reluctantly, but whether that was because of Sadie's presence or the link with those guys and Dan, I can't be sure.

Clearly, I'm going to have to do something about Sadie and the only route I have is Laurel.

Sometimes if I concentrate on Laurel it seems to work in opening our link. I'm trying really hard now but nothing at all is happening. I'm not sure, but something is in front of me and it's growing. Well, not growing but appearing, right in front of my eyes.

He's an Indian Chief all right. From the feathers in the headdress, the beads around the neck and the distinctly musky smell of his animal skins, this must be Orrie. Freaky thing is, he's fully visible now, but I can only see him from his head down to about his mid-calf area, where he appears to end hazily. I'm trying not to laugh as I wonder what he's wearing on his feet. His arms are crossed and I can't make out whether he's looking miserable or just very old and wrinkled.

'Huh,' he says, looking at me, 'you girl not man!' His voice is heavily accented and deep, with a gruff, almost gritty quality to it. What is it with everyone thinking I'm a man for Christ's sake? I'm beginning to get a complex.

Literally, before my very eyes, he starts fading away. There's a hazy sort of movement in the air where he was and I can smell wood smoke and a strong earthy, animal scent. I may not be able to see him now, but his presence is tangible and I feel that if I reach out my hand, I'd be able to touch him. The silence between us is growing and I'm trying to think of something to say, but my mind is completely blank. I wonder if Laurel brought him here?

I'm desperately trying to think of something suitably profound yet respectful, but something is blocking my thought processes. There, right in front of me, I can now see a teepee! It's totally amazing, a picture is appearing and it's in colour.

'Me ... home,' he's saying. There's no emotion in his voice, but looking at this picture is making me feel very emotional indeed. It's beautiful; as the picture expands I can even see wisps of smoke rising from a group of teepees. It's a large settlement, but I can just about make out the shapes of people and animals milling around. In the background there's a river and a forest of trees – they must be very old, as the trunks are huge. The word 'Hohokus' literally jumps into my head – where did that come from? There's a smell in the air that reminds me of November and fireworks. I feel very honoured and don't know what to say, I can't seem to find any words, but I think it's because Orrie is trying to connect with my mind.

Clearly, from what I saw when he first appeared, he's a very old Indian and the magnificence of his dress would probably have meant he was the chief of chiefs or something. All of this is making me feel so nervous, I can't relax my mind and I can feel his impatience. I'll close my eyes and see if that helps.

It's Dan I see now and he's holding a baby, but there are no clues as to where he is or whose baby he's holding.

Now I'm seeing Dan walking along the beach, my beach! Then I'm seeing Dan and Laurel's flat, but as an outsider – I'm not actually there and I'm looking at two people, but they're not Dan and Laurel. It's gone as quickly as it appeared. I'm too scared to say anything because the power I'm sensing around me is terrifying.

Just as I'm starting to relax slightly, something touches my arm and in my ear I can hear the word 'beach' low and clear. I hear the same word again, but it's more like an echo now. Then nothing. The air around me feels lighter and I know he's gone.

OK, the time to panic has arrived

Time isn't relative to me any more, but I can tell from Laurel's thoughts that it's been a while, quite a while. I'm suddenly with her again, but she looks different. She's had her hair cut into a short, flicky style that really suits her and she looks relaxed. I'm looking around the flat and it's tidy, everything in its place and I know that something is wrong.

'Where's Dan?' I ask.

'He left a few weeks ago, a lot has happened since the last time you were here.'

I'm dumbstruck. 'Why?' is all I can think of saying.

'He said it was work, that they were struggling to survive and he had to go to Brighton for a couple of months for a project they were involved in. I know he was just looking for a way to make the break, because he wouldn't discuss it – couldn't wait to go actually, so I ended it. It's OK, I'm fine – I'm over him.' I must admit she does look fine, but I'm finding this incredibly hard to believe. Our link is a bit different, her mind isn't as open as it usually is, or perhaps I'm being a bit paranoid.

I suddenly realise there's someone in the kitchen and, to my horror, a young guy I haven't seen before is walking into the living room. He swaggers in as if he owns the place, with a wine glass in each hand. I admit I can't control where and when I go, but the shock is enough to sever our link and for once I'm glad. I need to think about all of this.

Right, what was Orrie trying to show me? I saw Dan

27

holding a baby then he was on his own walking on the beach – Brighton beach perhaps? Then Dan and Laurel's flat and two complete strangers were there, then the word 'beach' – and that had been *very* clear.

Perhaps Dan was meant to go to Brighton and they really are supposed to split up. The vision of the flat might have been a confirmation that they didn't have a future together. So why then am I involved, if there's nothing I can do? It doesn't make any sense.

As usual, I can feel Laurel's thoughts in the background and I know she wants to speak to me. I let myself slide into contact and I'm right, she's on her own and I can see her curled up on the sofa in the flat.

'I'm sorry,' she says. 'You've been gone a long time again – it's been a few weeks. I just want to try to explain. After you left I thought about what I'd said and how difficult things are for you. You weren't around when it all happened, so I must have seemed dismissive when you reappeared and I told you about Dan as if it was not a big deal. Of course it would be a bit of a shock because you'd missed all the initial anguish so that wasn't fair of me.' Her words aren't quite what I was expecting to hear, but to be very honest, I'm relieved.

'Look Laurel, I'm really trying to make sense of things at the moment. Why am I here, why am I getting information I don't know what to do with? It's so confusing; you just can't imagine what it's like. Then you tell me our link isn't the way it's supposed to be, then Orrie rescues me and gives me other whacky bits of information. It's all … well, very heavy, to say the least!'

'I've been wondering whether you're just a figment of my imagination and not a spirit after all. I could be the one doing this to you and making all this happen.'

Now I'm scared. I feel real, I go through the thinking processes. I surely can't be a figment of someone's imagination, but she's unsettling me. The Laurel I've been watching is gentle but tough, knows her own mind and what she wants. Suddenly she's doubting everything. I decide I'll ignore her last comment for the moment and try to steer clear of talking about Dan.

'Thanks for asking Orrie to rescue me from the séance. It wasn't a great experience – I don't know who was more spooked – them or me. I need to ask you a favour though.'

'OK,' she says but she sounds hesitant.

'My sister Sadie was at the séance and she was there on her own. I can only assume she's looking to make some sort of contact with me and she must have felt desperate to take part in a live, televised ghost hunt!'

Laurel is looking directly at, or possibly, through me. 'That's not the programme Dan's been involved with is it? *Connections* – he's doing the title graphics, but I think he had some problems because he was very moody when he was working on that job. He wouldn't talk about it at the time.'

Whoops – I walked into that one. I didn't know Laurel would make the link, so I need to move quickly on if I'm going to get her to help me.

'I don't know, but Sadie was really scared and I want to make sure she doesn't get involved in anything like that again. The thing is, the only way is to get a message to her from someone who can explain – and you're the only person I can connect with.' I know it's a lot to ask Laurel. She's already told me she hasn't passed on any messages for a few years now, because of the experiences she had before.

'Look, I understand how you feel but—'

'Just hear me out, please. Think about what it would be like if our situations were reversed. If you were here – wherever I am – and, say, Lennie was desperately trying to make contact. It's not a nice world, there are lots of unscrupulous people out there. If Sadie ends up getting involved with people who dabble and don't know what they're doing, it could be dangerous. You know that.' I can tell from her body language that she's growing more receptive and she swings her legs over the side of the sofa to sit up.

'What exactly do you want me to do?'

'Find her and tell her you have a message from Mya. Just explain that I've been in touch with you and I'm all right, she's not to worry, but I don't want her going to any more séances.'

'Your name is Mya – that's pretty. I feel really sad for you and bad that I can't be of much help, but I'll try to talk to her and see if it does any good. She might not listen and she might not believe me. You'll need to give me some validation – some bit of information only known to you both, it'll help.'

My mind is flooded with disjointed memories like movie clips, but what will mean something to Sadie? I'm trying to think of a secret, something we shared perhaps, but never talked about because it was too embarrassing ... got it!

'I kissed a girl and Sadie caught us. We were practising for our first kiss with a boy and decided we would rather die of embarrassment in front of our best friend, than mess up with a boy. Sadie was still very much a kid and said she'd tell Mum, so we had to explain and then she said it was very funny. I had to buy her sweets for a month and we never, *ever* talked about it afterwards.'

Laurel's laughing. 'Brilliant. Where does Sadie live?'

I'm opening my mouth, but there aren't any words to come out – I can't remember where we live. How can I forget?

'Laurel, this is going to sound strange, but I don't know. I can see the house in my head, but there's a blank when I try to think of the address.' Now I'm really puzzled.

'OK, what's your surname?' Another blank.

'Er ... I can't remember that either. Perhaps I've got amnesia.'

'Selective amnesia when you can remember other detailed things? I doubt it. Mya, I think this is a part of what is happening to you. OK, describe the house and what you see.' I try to relax and let the picture of my family home grow in front of me.

'It's an old stone lodge. There's a pretty garden all the way around and we've got a fishpond. There isn't a proper front path, so you can miss seeing the front gate if you don't know what you're looking for. It's partly hidden by a low-hanging holly tree. I know it's quite close by, because I recognise the view from your bedroom window. You can see up to the hills from here and we have the same view from the garden. It's on the edge of town and it was a hunting lodge for the Manor House. That's it! Find the Manor House and it's close by.'

'I hope this is going to be the right thing to do. I've seen so many different reactions when trying to pass on a message. Some people are horrified and won't listen, others want to latch on to every word and you have to be so careful what you say and how you say it. People can be very, well, fragile sometimes and other times they think you're just a troublemaker. It's hard either way.' I can see how sad she's feeling and that makes me feel really awful, but I need her help to do this and it's not as if I have any other options.

'I can't sit by and do nothing after what I witnessed, because I'm scared for Sadie. If I had any other way to do this I wouldn't ask, so please, just do your best, that's all I ask. Oh, just one more thing, can you Google Hohokus?'

'OK – but just remember there are no guarantees and what the heck is Hohokus?'

'I don't know, that's why I need you to Google it.'

I've never felt so useless and incapable before and it's painful. To be stuck here and be able to see the problems, but not the solutions and have no way of influencing things, is the hardest thing I've ever had to bear. Perhaps I'm here to learn a lesson that I couldn't learn in life – I can't always make things happen just because I want them to.

Life sucks sometimes, but from where I am now, it seems that the afterlife sucks even more.

My name is Laurel and I see dead people

When I was very young I started talking to my 'friends'. At first the spirits were mostly children like me. Sometimes they were older, but it was usually just a fleeting glimpse or sometimes they would show me things about their lives. I would talk to them, they didn't often talk back, but that was OK.

Eventually I came to understand that I see dead people and now Orrie, my spirit guide, is my protector. I call him that, because for a while I felt swamped and bewildered. I just didn't know how to handle what felt like an onslaught of messages from dead people I didn't know, for living people I also didn't know. I didn't want to develop the 'gift' I'd inherited because that's my right, but it's pretty strong and it's not something you can just walk away from. So Orrie helps me as a 'filter' and from time to time I do get involved, but since he's been around it's becoming less and less frequent thankfully.

Then Mya appeared. Or rather, she doesn't actually appear, but our minds link. It happens in a way that hasn't happened to me before, so I don't quite know how to 'handle' her as a spirit. She seems to be a very nice, caring person and her thoughts, when we are linked, are vivid. At first, I assumed she was a man and then one day when we were chatting, she revealed she was a woman. I don't know why it was such a surprise at the time, but it was and it certainly explained a few things. How can I put this? She's very *intense*. She's also quite impatient and she seems to think I've got all the answers. However,

I've never ever met a spirit like her before and even Orrie can't seem to act as a filter between us. He did manage to get her out of a spot of trouble with a Ouija board, but it was only a brief contact.

She seems to feel she was meant to save my relationship with my ex, Dan. I still miss him, although it's been a few months now and, as they say, life goes on. I really thought Dan was 'the one' for me and I genuinely believed I was 'the one' for him. We wanted to have a baby and it didn't happen, but I don't think that affected our relationship. The problem was that Dan just wouldn't talk – about anything. He went off to Brighton and I don't know if the real reason was work, or because he was fed up because we'd been arguing. Perhaps he'd met someone who lives in Brighton, how was I to know what was really going on? It hurt having to ask questions when surely, if it was innocent, he should have been open about it? He said his company were probably going to go bust and he would lose his job, so he didn't have a choice. That was about all he would say. It came out of the blue and it was odd, why hadn't he mentioned anything before? Things like that don't just suddenly happen and even if it was the truth, if he was hiding that from me, what else had he hidden? Anyway, I don't want to go there – so let's just say that, for self-preservation reasons, I told him it was over.

Right, back to Mya. With Orrie, contact is always difficult. His English isn't very good; he can't do sentences, just short strings of words or single words. For instance, if the message involves someone's birthday he might say 'born' or 'birth' if I'm really lucky. Sometimes I just can't interpret what he's trying to tell me, so he'll show me a picture instead. With Mya it's like I'm chatting to my best friend Lennie, a normal conversation, but it's in my head! It's weird.

Anyway, now I have a problem. She's asked me to give a message to her sister – nothing heavy, just to say she's OK, because her sister was at a Ouija board session. I can't imagine what it must be like to die young, although I don't know how old Mya is, but I sort of feel she's about my age. She's also very confused. But she doesn't understand that passing on a message is the hardest thing to do for a million different reasons. Most people don't believe you or get angry. Some want more than you have to give and won't accept that you're only a messenger. Whatever reaction, it's seldom just a delivery.

What would you do if you were in my position? It's easy to stand back and say 'no', but hard to do it when you feel really sorry for someone. I think she passed fairly recently and can't comprehend what's going on. She's worried about her sister and I can understand that, so I feel like I just don't have a choice. So, I'm going to do it and I guess I knew that as soon as she asked. I just hope it doesn't cause more problems than it solves.

I'm a workaholic and my life's a mess

I'm trying really hard to hold things together since Laurel threw me out. Man, that was the worst day of my life and it felt like my whole world was crashing down around me.

I wasn't honest with her, I realise that now. But I couldn't even admit to myself what a mess my life was becoming, so how was I supposed to admit it to her? She was so happy when we first decided to try for a baby and life seemed sweet, because everything was going really well. The flat was perfect and it was great to finally find a place that felt like home, we were so excited to be living there. Yeah, I'm messy when I work, but Laurel was cool with it most of the time and I tried really hard to make her happy. She made it easy to make her happy, that's why she's special. Then the baby thing – great, I couldn't wait and I just know it was gonna happen when she just stopped stressing and relaxed. That was the easy bit.

Work had become a nightmare. Jupiter Live was (in the past tense) going through a tough time, all because the two brothers who ran it just couldn't grow up. The daily battles had become monumental, there were times when they wouldn't talk to each other. We missed deadlines because information didn't get through. There was a team of six of us trying to cover a workload that could keep twice as many people busy. Everyone thinks it's cushy when most of your work is done from home. But add in two bosses who can't agree, too many deadlines and handling customers who get angry when you can't tell them why things are going wrong, and it's stressful, man! Beyond belief. So many deadlines were missed and a lot of my work was just wasted. If Jupiter failed to meet their contractual obligations, that meant no payment and I knew I was getting close to having to tell Laurel we couldn't afford the flat. I was actually scared she would come home and say she was pregnant, because I knew I couldn't support her. She deserves more than the mess I've made of things and I know she's better off without me – so that's that!

Except life isn't that easy, is it? I don't think I can survive without her. She thought I was the strong one – physically I was – but the truth is Laurel was always the one with the real strength. I think of her all the time and I will always remember the hurt in her eyes when she told me to go. She loathed me, man, really loathed me. She knew there were things I hadn't said and I realised then that basically, I'm just a coward.

So, where am I now? The guys needed me in Brighton, a lot of work is done there for two small production companies trying to make a name for themselves. One is doing really well at the moment making, believe it or not, live 'hunt the ghost' programmes. We nearly lost their contract a couple of months ago and that would have meant shutting the doors forever. Sean and Chris asked me to come down here for a while to try to get things back on track. I think that was the final straw for Laurel, when I told her I had to work in Brighton for a few months. Perhaps she suddenly woke up and saw the real me, I don't know because she didn't tell me why it was over. It's not like I don't try and I'm good at what I do – I know that much. But Laurel deserves someone who can take away all her worries, look after her and I guess I'm just not good enough. See – everything for me revolves around Laurel and I just can't let it go.

At least I'm busy. The guys finally realised that going bankrupt just isn't an option and although they owe all of us a fair chunk of money still, enough is coming in to keep the bills paid. Three of us are sharing a flat about twenty minutes from the office and about half an hour from the two main recording studios we go between for the two production companies.

I guess you could say professionally I'm doing great – Sean told me I'm always the first choice for several of our top clients. Most of the assignments I get take my first offering with only minor changes, so I'm cost effective. If Sean and Chris can keep it together, this time next year we could all be reaping the benefits, but a year is a long time.

The titles I'm working on now are for the next six episodes of the ghost show. The credits start really smoky in the distance and slowly float to the front, becoming darker and darker until they can be read for an instant and then suddenly disappear.

'Hey Dan,' Sean is walking across the room towards me, 'good news, mate. Just had a big cheque in from SC, we're going to be able to clear quite a few debts and you'll get two months' pay on Friday.' He's smiling as if he's won the lottery and I suppose after what we've all been through, it's great news.

'Cheers Sean,' and hearing my own voice even I know it lacks enthusiasm.

'Look Dan, it can't just be all work and no play. It's not healthy, you need to get out a bit, move on with things.' He's looking at me sympathetically, but I can feel the awkwardness because he hasn't acknowledged the situation before. Guess I must look really terrible for Sean to feel sorry for me.

'I'm good mate, honest. Just grappling with these credits, I want them to be just right and I promised I'd have it ready for tomorrow.'

'OK. OK. Just remember to take some time off when you can. A couple of days would do you the world of good – you could go back home for a bit, see what's happening.'

'Yeah, perhaps. I'll let you know,' I say, but as he walks away he knows it isn't going to happen. So, back to the credits.

I've been sitting in front of this Mac for three hours now without a break, but I would swear there's something in the corner of the room. I keep telling myself it's just screen glare or that I'm not focusing properly because I'm tired. It keeps catching my eye, whenever I sit back a bit from the screen to get the wider picture. It's like a movement. I think I might need to get my eyes checked or perhaps I've spooked the ghosts and they don't like my graphics for the show. They've come to haunt me to get their revenge. Heh, heh – guess that's enough for today anyway!

Don't shoot the messenger

'Hi, look, I know this is going to sound strange, but I've got a message for Mya's sister.' The young man in front of me has opened the door very wide and I can see inside. It's a beautiful old stone lodge and the decoration is tasteful and simple. He's looking at me as if he's seen a ghost, so I guess this is the right place after all. I decide to let it just sink in, so I'm standing here trying not to look embarrassed and trying to look like a trustworthy person and not a deluded nutter.

'S … s … s … sorry,' he says and I can see he's really trying to pull himself together, but he's not sure how to react. OK, let's try to make this a bit easier.

'This will be a shock, I really understand that and no one has to listen to me if it's too distressing.' He seems taken aback by my statement but makes a movement with his hand to allow me inside.

It's so cosy, all white walls and lovely pieces of rustic furniture that look almost contemporary in their setting. It feels homely, loved and I can see that Mya's family are very close. One whole wall in the hallway is devoted to pictures spanning probably thirty years. I follow the guy into a sitting room that isn't large, but has two sofas facing each other across an old, wooden coffee table of enormous proportions. Amidst a scattering of magazines and a couple of coffee mugs, is a large bronze centre-piece standing a foot high, Rodin's 'The Kiss'. The naked lovers look perfectly natural and comfortable sitting here in this room, clearly the heart of the house. This is a loving family.

40

The guy excuses himself and leaves me, gesturing for me to take a seat on one of the sofas. It's as if he can't speak, or perhaps that stutter of his makes conversation with strangers difficult. I sit down on the edge of one of the sofas. I don't want to look like I'm making any assumptions that they'll welcome me with open arms, but I need to look approachable and sincere. I was hoping Mya would be with me, but she hasn't been around for a while and there's no sign of her today again.

The door is opening and in comes the guy followed by a girl, who looks to be in her early twenties. She has a beautiful face with a trendy, dark, very short and choppy haircut and is about five foot two with a 'cuddly' build. There are dark smudges beneath her eyes though and she looks very, very tired.

They both walk in and sit down on the sofa opposite me. There's an awkwardness between us. I decided not to stand up when they came in and now I'm regretting it, it might have broken the ice to shake hands. They're waiting for me to say something.

'Are you Sadie?' I ask, trying to keep my voice soft and natural. Instead of responding instantly, she looks at the guy for a few seconds until he nods and now she's turning back to look at me.

'Yes,' and that's it. Clearly not going to make it easy for me, but why should they? The seconds are ticking and I need to fathom out the right approach. I don't know enough about them and the longer the silence continues, the more nervous I'm becoming. OK, here I go.

'I'm really sorry to just knock on your door like this and I understand that you have no reason whatsoever to believe anything I might say.' I pause to judge what sort of reaction the direct approach is having and other than a brief glance between them, they're still listening. Good!

41

'Believe me, it isn't my idea to come here, so I need to explain. I don't want to offend you at this difficult time, but I sometimes get messages from people who can't deliver them themselves. I've received a message from your sister, Mya.' The moment I finish speaking Sadie bursts into tears, I feel like a monster.

'I'm so sorry – of course you don't want to hear this, I'll just go–' the guy is raising his hand to stop me and, to my surprise, gives me a warm smile.

'Please, just give Sadie a minute. She's been waiting for some sign from Mya, we all have. It's such a shock, you see. I'm Sam by the way–'

Before he even has chance to finish, I start speaking. 'Mya's boyfriend, she told me about you!'

'Did she now? I trust it was all good.' Sadie is smiling now and Sam gives her an encouraging pat on the arm. 'There you are, Sadie. I said Mya was with us! Sorry,' he says, turning to face me, 'I didn't ask your name?'

'I'm Laurel. Laurel Prentis.' I'm feeling so nervous, partly from having tied myself up in knots before I'd even knocked on the door, but also partly from their reaction. This is too easy. It's not a typical reaction by any means.

'Thank you for coming, Laurel. It's all been too much to cope with and we both had this very strong feeling that Mya has something to say. Sadie's been to several clairvoyant evenings but no messages, nothing. It's been a while and we still can't get our heads around all this. We think she might have been around us here, because Sadie's noticed the cat acting very strangely sometimes. Almost as if he's seeing something we can't see. Parsley is Mya's cat you see. Sorry, I'm waffling but it's just great, great that you're here.' Oh dear, this is going to be bad, they're going to want to know way more than I'm going to give them. They're going to hang on my every word, I'm going to have to be *so* careful.

'Yes,' Sadie is saying as she sits forward on the sofa, as if trying to get closer to me, 'you've seen her?'

'Not exactly, but she's been in contact and wanted me to come to see you. Look, it's just a message she needed to give to you so you wouldn't worry. She's fine, but she's worried about you. You went to a Ouija session and she was there. She doesn't want you dabbling with things like that and she thought that if I came to let you know she's OK, you could well … relax.' It wasn't flowing and it sounded lame, but sitting here looking at two people who are bright eyed and beaming at me as if I have just saved the world, isn't something I feel comfortable with.

'Sam, she was there! At the Ouija session, I knew she'd come and it must have been Mya who touched me! Did she say anything else? I have to know.' I shift uncomfortably, this is exactly how it starts – you give them a little and they just have to have more.

'To prove it's her I asked for something personal, a secret that you two shared. She said to remind you about "THE kiss".'

Sadie looks at the statue on the coffee table for a brief moment, her eyes open really wide and I hear her sharp intake of breath. 'Wow. Thank you so much, Laurel, you don't know what this means to us … both.' She's smiling now and wiping away tears and I see that Sam is holding one of her hands. Is that a normal thing for a dead sister's partner to do? The more I look at them, it would be easy to mistake them for a couple and that was the last thing I was expecting. But I suppose, as Sam said, it has been a while and things move on. I'm doing my best to shake off my feelings and trying to focus, when Sam starts questioning me.

'When did she first get in contact, how often does she talk to you? If she can talk to you, could she come through to us? I'm not sure how it works and what if—'

I have to stop this now. 'Look, Sam, it's just a message. Probably a one-off. You have to take this as a sign to start moving on. Mya probably won't contact me again. This will give her the peace of mind that she's been seeking.' Yuk! I can't believe I'm saying these stupid words, but these are desperate people and the more I say, the more I'm in danger of opening a floodgate in their need for more. More information, more contact – but more doesn't bring the person back and they need to draw a line now and get on with their lives.

'I was going to ask her to marry me, you know,' Sam says, flushing slightly. 'I waited too long.' It's the saddest statement I think I've ever heard.

Enough! As I stand up they both follow my lead, but an anxious look is passing between them. This isn't closure as I was hoping and I need to get out quickly, before they start asking even more questions. 'Look, give me your telephone number and if I get anything else I'll be in touch. Please, don't expect anything though because it's highly unlikely.' Sadie grabs my hand and looks into my eyes, almost pleading. It's heartbreaking to see the depth of her sadness.

'Please, please leave your number for us too, just in case we see anything. Mya obviously chose you because she trusts you and it will only be "just in case", I promise.' She won't let go of my hand, so I give her a brief nod. Sam produces a pen and paper and I give them my number. Sam hands me Sadie's number in return.

At the door I turn to say goodbye and am shocked as Sam suddenly gives me the briefest of hugs. Sadie is still blotting tears, but smiling through it as if she's the happiest person alive.

As I'm walking down the street I'm cringing inside. I could have told them all of it, as it is, but I just know they couldn't take it. They would want more, want to be there when she was with me and start living on expectations. The reality is that Mya is dead and they have to move on – you can't live your life based around séances, it's too morbid.

In the hallway there was a photo, the sort proud parents take of their two daughters, taken on a bright, sunny day. Mya and Sadie, arms around each other, laughing as if they didn't have a care. I would say Sadie was about sixteen years old at the time the photo was taken and, even at a glance, you can tell they are sisters as the likeness is startling. Mya is just a slimmer, slightly taller version of Sadie, with long, straight, very dark hair but her eyes and mouth are unmistakably the same.

As I'm walking away from the front door, I start thinking about what I'm going to say to Mya about how it went. I think I should keep it short and I won't tell her about exchanging phone numbers. She needs to start letting things go herself and move on – it happens in the afterlife too. She just hasn't been there long enough yet to recover her energies to allow her to do this, but she will.

My phone keeps bleeping and, as I pull it out of my pocket, I realise it must have been pressed up against the sofa when I sat down. A text message is already open and I scroll quickly down in disbelief.

Hi Babe, running late coz we over shot the deadline. I'll bring pizza – see u one hour. Luv ya loads xxxxx

For one moment my heart misses a beat and I'm standing here shaking my head. Then it hits me, it's an old message – probably the last one Dan sent me before we finished. I don't know why I'm crying, all that's behind me now. As I slip my phone into my handbag, I cross the road and head home.

Shoot the messenger, PLEASE!

I arrive home to find Josh in the kitchen (my kitchen) making dinner. Nice thought, I hear you thinking, but let's get this straight: I didn't invite him and we've only seen each other a dozen times. It's all been very low-key, friendly dating, nothing serious.

George on reception didn't even forewarn me that Josh had talked him into letting him into my flat. I suspect Josh said it was a surprise and George had seen him around a few times, so I suppose I can't get really mad. He's the only guy I've invited here since Dan. But I *am* mad. I feel my privacy has been invaded and that's nothing to do with the fact that Josh is Josh and not Dan. I really don't feel as if Dan should be here any more and I don't miss him now in the way I did at first. I admit it was tough to begin with. Everything I touched, everywhere I turned, I could picture Dan. His smile, his presence ... anyway, I just don't want another man permanently in my life at this moment in time.

Josh beamed when I walked into the kitchen just now, poured me a glass of wine as if nothing was unusual, and pushed me gently back into the lounge. I'm sitting here on the sofa now, trying to pretend I'm not angry and resentful, but suitably grateful for this 'wonderful' surprise. Josh has just got to go! Anyway, I've been thinking about taking a break and having a holiday. Lennie's been on at me to think about doing a girl thing together and perhaps I need to give this some serious thought.

The kitchen door swings open and Josh is standing

there in the doorway, naked except for my best butcher's apron, just about covering the bare essentials (well, it's a very small apron). That's it!

'Josh.' Oops, too severe. 'Josh, darling. I'm really sorry, but I can't do this. My ex has been in touch and we're thinking of giving it another go, I'm so sorry.' Not exactly the truth, but I'm trying to spare Josh's feelings. Dan has sort of been in touch today, it's just that the message happened to be an old one.

It takes Josh ten minutes to finish his wine. I hold his hand (he's dressed now, I might add) and we commiserate about why we had to meet now, when I'm still not over my ex. I think I've managed to sound very sympathetic and disappointed, whilst acting confused and irrational enough to convince him it's all real. He's a great guy, but very young for his age – bit of a Mummy's boy if you ask me. I think he lives off Daddy's money. He just doesn't seem to understand how life is for those of us out here in the real world, having to stand on our own two feet.

As I'm closing the door, I decide I'm going to sit and think of Mya. I don't want to keep mulling over in my head what I'm going to say to her. I just want to get it said. Suddenly the light on the side table changes from a bright white light to a low, yellowish hue, as if it's on a dimmer switch. It stays like that for a few seconds and suddenly I know Mya is here. She hasn't been able to do this so far and this means she's gaining back the strength she lost whilst she was dying. It's a good sign, it means she's progressing.

'Was he naked?' she's asking, sounding quite shocked by what she witnessed just now.

'Yes, he was naked and no, it wasn't my idea. He wasn't even supposed to be here, George must have let him in, but he definitely won't be coming back!' I think Mya can tell I'm serious. She's different somehow, I can't explain how exactly, but there's definitely something – different. She laughs.

'Sorry, I'm not prying. How long is it since I've been here?' She certainly hasn't asked that before in such a pointed way. Actually, she sounds a bit stressed. Is it possible to be stressed in the afterlife?

'It's been a fortnight. You sound a bit worried. Everything OK?'

'It's not easy, you know, having no control over things. Did you have any luck finding Sadie?' Ah ha, she's probably still worried about what's happening to her sister, so perhaps this will cheer her up. It's just that I'm not sure just how much to tell her.

'I saw her today actually.'

'You *did*? I mean, you did? Great, great – how was she?' Truth or diplomatic? I wish I had a coin I could flip.

'She ... looked tired. She's been trying to get in touch with you and I think it was the right thing for me to go and see her.' I've decided on the softly, softly approach.

'Great, good. What did you say?'

'Just what we agreed. That you were OK and you didn't want her going to any more séances. She appreciated the validation – it meant a lot to her to know it was really you sending the message.' There, short and sweet and simple.

'Yes, but how was she, really? Were Mum and Dad there?' Great, here we go.

'No, but Sam was there.'

'Really, how strange. Perhaps he's taken a few days off after the funeral to be around the family. Give Sadie someone to sit with while Mum and Dad sort things, I suppose.' Oh God!

'Yes, possibly.' I wish that had sounded more convincing.

'What? What is it you're not telling me? I need to know.' Oh how I *hate* that phrase – they *all* say it.

'Well, not exactly.'

'Not exactly *what*?'

'You've been dead a little while.'

'You're joking. I've only just got here. I know I've got this problem with time at the moment but even so—'

'Look Mya, you can't stress about things. Time in the afterlife isn't supposed to be like time here. What does it matter how long? You're doing OK and now they're going to be fine. They just needed to know, you know. That you ... arrived safely on the other side.' Nicely put Laurel, if I say so myself.

The silence is, I assume, because Mya is taking this all in and, I have to say, I would probably be acting much the same if I was in her position.

'Yes, but it's disorientating losing chunks of time. I can't keep up with everything that's going on.' It sounds very much like she's struggling to hold it together. Just my luck that a spirit I can really communicate with happens to be unravelling emotionally at the same time.

'So what? You just need to feel comforted that they were very happy to listen to the message. You've given them what they needed to start moving on.'

'I've done something right then.' Thank goodness.

'But did Sam say anything? How was he? What did he look like? Is he missing me?' Oh no, here we go again.

'Mya, please, just relax a little. Sam looked fine, but of course he misses you and he said they've been waiting and hoping for a sign from you. I think they've both found it very hard and the two of them have been trying to give you every opportunity to get through to them. He said Sadie had been to a few séances, but they can now put that behind them, can't they? You all need to move on now. You have to think of where you're going and not where you've been.' I think that sounds pretty good, believable and positive.

'OK, so that's it now then, is it?' she's saying, but her tone is hesitant. I think she's hoping I've got something up my sleeve that will make all this – I don't know – easier, go away, make sense? Who knows what she's thinking?

'Yep. Time to chill and move on, the way you're supposed to now.' Firm, positive, rational.

'Right. Fine. Good. By the way, I've been seeing Dan.'

'What the f–? Mya, what exactly do you mean?' I think I've just gone deathly pale.

'Not talking to him, like I do with you. I've just seen him places – work, home, walking along the street. He doesn't see me, so he doesn't acknowledge I'm there.' Now it's my turn to be confused and, my God, I'm shaking.

Getting to know Dan

The first time I 'saw' him after he'd gone to Brighton was shortly after I asked Laurel to contact Sadie with my message. Nothing in particular was happening, I just suddenly found myself watching Dan sitting in front of a computer screen. I was shocked at how awful he looked. I would say 'haggard' was a pretty accurate description. He was wiry before, but his face looked hollow now and although his chest and arms still looked honed and muscular, I'd say he'd lost a stone in weight easily. It made me feel sick to my stomach to see him looking so dreadful and I knew I should have been able to do something to prevent the split. For goodness' sake, I can 'talk' to Laurel directly, so why hadn't I tried to make her see some sense?

He was editing some title credits and I was watching him from the corner of the room. He couldn't see me and there was no contact between us – I wasn't able to talk to him or read his thoughts. Since then I've seen him quite a bit, I see him more frequently than I see Laurel now and it makes me sad to see how his life has changed. All he does is work, but I can see how talented he is and I'm not sure even he understands his full potential. Laurel needs to understand how single minded he has to be and what possibilities there are ahead for him if he continues as he's going. His friends are clearly worried about him, because he's pushed everyone away and all he does is drink too much coffee, eat the minimum he needs to keep working – and he's smoking weed to relax. Not a good sign. I suppose it could be even worse – he could be drinking heavily as well. His mother keeps leaving polite little prompts on his voicemail for him to give her a call, but he's avoiding her too.

I'm watching him now and he really is damn cute, even though he's pale, tired and clearly in need of a slap up dinner or two! The guys at work have dragged him out to a restaurant, it's Friday night and they're all on a high because it's been a good week for the business. They're clearly in the mood to celebrate and poor Dan is doing his best not to spoil their fun, but I can see he just doesn't want to be here. A guy called Sean has just brought three ladies across to the table.

'Steve, Dan, Hamish – this is Karen, my wife. This is Karen's sister Sally and this gorgeous young lady is my niece, Steffy.' They're all shaking hands and bantering. I think Sean is Dan's boss. He looks about forty and his wife, Karen, is a bubbly, very cuddly sort of lady, with at least three chins that wobble as she laughs. Her sister looks a few years younger and is a bit slimmer. In total contrast, Steffy's probably late twenties, very thin but with generous proportions, if you get my drift. Judging by her clothes she's a bit of a Goth, dressed in black with immaculate make-up, chalk-white skin and dark, kohl-lined eyes. Sean is steering Steffy around the table so she can shake hands with Dan.

To everyone's surprise – and my horror – as soon as Dan stands up, Steffy is throwing her arms around his neck and kissing him. He's smiling from ear to ear.

'Hey dude,' she's saying, 'you don't look so hot – have my uncles been over-working you? I didn't know you were working for Jupiter Live. It's been a long time.' Sean is looking totally bewildered and Dan is grinning at him over Steffy's shoulder.

'Kingston Uni – Graphic Design – we graduated in the

same year,' he whispers to Sean and then picks Steffy up and swings her around. I guess he's pleased to see her. 'You're looking good, girl. Still in black I see,' actually both Dan *and* Steffy are in black and I have to admit they look like a matching pair. This is *so* not the time for Dan to be meeting up with someone so, so ... interesting and, damn it, why is she so attractive?

I watch Dan and Steffy as they're walking towards the bar to get a drink. They sit on the high bar stools and Dan orders two 'Brass Monkeys'. As they start talking I'm watching the barman pour rum, vodka and orange juice into two tumblers of ice. He gives a quick stir with a long twizzle stick and places their drinks on the bar.

Steffy is laughing as she picks up her tumbler and chinks her glass against Dan's. 'To old times,' she says and he's chuckling as if she's said something really funny, but I just don't get it. To look at them you'd think they were a pair of teenagers, all giggly and matey – it's obscene.

'So,' Dan's looking right into her eyes, 'you're Sean and Chris's niece – I just can't take it in. No family resemblance whatsoever. It's good to see you, kid.' He's really made up about seeing her, so whatever they shared must have been good.

'I'm just trying to remember whether I'm still speaking to you or not – wasn't the last time we were together when you decked Phil?' Dan stops mid-sip and is looking sideways at her, raising an eyebrow.

'Phil deserved it, if I remember rightly. That guy was bad news and you deserved better. What's happening now? Don't tell me you married him.'

'No, no, God no. You were right, he was an ass. I've only just come back from the States, I've done some work in Hollywood – low budget stuff, but I've had a great time. Things are a bit sticky over there at the moment so I thought, time to go home and see what's happening.

Uncle Sean has offered me a job, which I have no intention of accepting, but I had no idea you were working for him. I should have known he would have snapped you up – number one student at Kingston for our year – he doesn't miss a trick does Uncle Sean.'

Dan's blushing! I don't believe this. Steffy turns her head to the right and the barman is there, as if he's been killing time just until he can have the pleasure of serving her again. It's incredible.

'Two more, dude, nothing like a Brass Monkey when you're celebrating.' As she's saying it, she's giving him a really sexy little intimate smile. Now I don't know her at all, but I *hate* women who act as if they can wrap men around their little fingers, even if they actually can. Do I sound jealous?

Dan is just sitting back on his stool, basking in the little cloud of happiness that seems to be surrounding Steffy. Part of me feels glad that something has finally happened to get Dan thinking of something other than work, but I haven't given up on Laurel and Dan. I admit though, this is a problem I hadn't even considered. I have no idea what exactly they shared in the past and I wish I understood why Dan had hit Steffy's boyfriend. I wonder what that was all about?

As I'm watching them both finishing their drinks, toasting the future and downing the remains, I'm seeing a side of Dan I haven't seen before. I want to leave, but it's just my luck that nothing's happening and I hate not having a choice over where I am and what I see. Steffy is leaning heavily on Dan's leg and laughing, suddenly they're both getting up and shouting out goodbyes as they head for the door, together.

I'm closing my eyes to see if I can sever my link, but I open them and I'm sitting in the front of a taxi watching them both in the vanity mirror. It's sickening.

'I can't believe you're working here in Brighton. How do you get on with Sean and Chris? I'm amazed my uncles are still in business together,' Steffy's talking to Dan and their eyes are glued to each other.

'Hm, gotta be careful here, girl. My bosses you're talking about. Let's just say that I think they've learnt a thing or two over the last six months that might see their relationship handled in a slightly different way from here on in.' He's letting her hold his hand now. 'It's really good to see you again and you look like life's been treating you pretty well.' Yuk!

'Thanks, I wish I could say the same for you ... don't you have some little woman to look after you? When was the last time you ate anything?' At least she sounds concerned and she's stopped doing the sexy 'bat the eyelashes' thing at last.

'Long story, alas. Lost my woman 'cause I'm a jerk, so it's all my own fault. Thing is, I've made a mess of things – I just let life carry on, even though I knew deep down I had things to sort. I guess I lost sight of the big picture and got bogged down with the detail.'

'If by detail, you mean Uncle Sean and Uncle Chris's insanity, then I can't believe you're still with them, putting up with it. I wouldn't work for them if they paid me double what I'm worth and I'm really surprised at you. Or, on reflection, perhaps not. You've got too big a heart, Dan, that was always your downfall. You care too much about other people.' She's reaching out and brushing his cheek with her hand. Even I feel touched.

'Hey girl, don't feel sorry for me 'cause it's nobody's fault but my own. I should have been thinking about Laurel and not my career. I'll be fine, it's just early days yet.'

'Well,' she says, half turning in her seat, 'I've finally found the solution to picking the wrong men! You'd be really proud of me,' and she's chuckling. I can see Dan raising his eyebrows in mock disbelief.

'Oh yes,' he says, 'the girl who just loves the bad guys suddenly turns over a new leaf?'

'Exactly. Instead of dating men, I now date women.'

Thank the Lord! I'm so tense I feel like I've finally exhaled after holding my breath for a long time, and I'm really surprised neither of them suspect I'm sitting here, listening. Even the taxi driver hasn't sensed a thing. However, as I'm looking out of the window, I'm realising that Dan is telling him to pull up and we're outside Dan's flat. My mind is going into over-drive, when suddenly I'm not here with them any more. I'm not in my usual space either and it's eerily light all around me. At first it's quite nice to be in this tranquil place, where I'm getting a feeling of great warmth – not heat exactly, just a sort of a glow.

Now it's dark, so I'm somewhere else and there's moonlight coming in through a window. The curtains are only part drawn and I can hear breathing. I'm looking across at a bed and I know what I'm going to see. Yep, knew it! Dan and Steffy are both laying on top of the bed covers, sound asleep. The sort of sleep you get after drinking alcohol and it smells like a brewery. They aren't undressed as such, just a few items missing and I really haven't got a clue what might have happened here. Enough to say I'm worried – she may say she prefers 'ladeez' but I'm not so convinced and Dan is just too vulnerable at the moment. I'm going to have to think strategy before this gets out of hand!

Is that strange, or is it just me?

Waking up this morning, I turned over to snuggle into Laurel and found myself looking at Steffy! Now don't get me wrong, Steffy is gorgeous, but you can't imagine my disappointment as, for just a split-second, I forgot about everything that's happened over the last few months. Before my brain had time to kick in and load up, there was just this familiar feeling of knowing someone's in bed with you. It just wasn't the person my mind, which was on auto-pilot, thought it was going to be. It felt like being kicked in the balls. I jumped straight into a cold shower and the misery came back like a cloud that just won't go away.

Steffy's a laugh and it's great to see her, but so much has happened and she's not the sort of girl who takes things seriously. She was always a good mate and she's the life and soul of a party. But she's not good at listening to problems and although I do sort of wish there was someone I could pour it all out to, Steffy wouldn't be the one.

After three strong cups of coffee this morning, she was on her way and I had to duck and dive a bit to avoid getting caught up in her plans. She thinks I need cheering up – that's her solution. She just can't comprehend where I'm at and I think she'd be shocked if she knew what was really going on in my head. I'm not saying I'm ready to end it all, but if it wasn't for work, it might be a different story.

The thing is, strange things have started happening. I

seem to have become paranoid and I feel I'm being watched – not all the time, just sometimes. When I get that feeling, it can last for twenty minutes or several hours. It passes and then everything feels normal again. At first I thought it was my imagination. Then the table light blew up. That was the start of it. For instance, when Steffy was here last night, I know we'd had a few to drink, but it was weird, man. Twice during the night things fell off the bookshelf. For no apparent reason. Steffy thought it was funny, but at the time I had that feeling again, of being watched, and it gave me the creeps.

Sometimes when I lay in bed at night, I can feel my heart pounding as if it's going to burst. I want to be alone, but when I am alone I'm starting to feel isolated. It's a nightmare making the effort to have simple conversations if it's not work-related. It's like I don't care about what's going on around me any more and I know it's not healthy to brood about my own problems and push people away. But they don't understand and I guess a part of me is ashamed that I had it all and I wasted it, man, really wasted it.

See, I'm sitting here now, in the kitchen drinking coffee and suddenly I feel like someone's here, watching me. How bloody paranoid am I, that I even think I know it's in the corner by the window? I can clearly see there's nothing there at all and yet I'm convinced someone is standing there watching me.

OK Danny boy, what does that tell you? Yep, I think it's time to go see the Doc!

What's happening NOW?

I'm really worried about Dan. Not just because Steffy's timing is so unfortunate, with her appearing out of the blue and with him being particularly vulnerable, but he's so ... edgy. Every time I see him it's like he's wired – high on coffee or whatever and he just can't seem to relax. It's wearing him out and I don't know what I can do to help. My heart goes out to him and I just want to give him a big hug.

It feels like a long time since I saw Laurel, but I'm guessing because I just can't judge – I never thought I'd miss having a clock! I seem to know a lot about Dan's daily life now, whereas I'm not sure what Laurel's doing any more, so I'm assuming that means it's been a while.

Other things have been happening to me and I really want to ask her about them. I keep hearing voices – not in the way that I hear Dan talking to himself sometimes, or even how I 'hear' Laurel when we link. No, this is different. It's odd sentences that seem to come from nowhere and I don't see a person connected with the words, the words just seem to 'float' in. For instance, I was watching Dan and suddenly I kept hearing the same words over and over again: 'You know we love you, we're here'. It wasn't anything going on with Dan and it was a woman speaking in a tearful whisper.

It's happening now! I can clearly hear the words, 'You can do it, come on, stretch it out, that's a good girl!' What the heck does that mean? This afterlife thing is so complicated. Am I getting caught up in the middle of other people's messages now? Should it mean anything to me personally or should I be trying to do something about it?

Laurel said that it was 'time to move on' and she meant for me, as well as my family. Are all these odd things to do with that? I don't feel like I can think straight at the moment and the only time I feel really 'calm' is, ironically, when I'm watching Dan. Perhaps it's because his problems feel even bigger than mine. I think he really is losing the plot and I know that somehow or other, I've got to engineer some way of getting Laurel and Dan to cross paths again. I'm sure if they could just casually bump into each other, it would all come back and they'd remember how they felt about each other. So, when I'm not caught up in other people's conversations, I'm working on my master plan. Heck, here it is again. I can clearly hear someone saying, 'It's OK to let go, if you have to'. What's the point of giving a message that no one can understand? What the hell do these people think I can do with a message like that? I'm beginning to feel really sorry for Laurel, if this is what she has to put up with all the time!

Ciel sur la terre (heaven on earth)

When Lennie first suggested a girls' away trip for us both, I wasn't keen. I'd only just managed to get back into a routine that I felt comfortable with and I can now admit that I did fall apart a bit after I threw Dan out. I think it was Josh that made me realise, that getting away from it all could stop me rebounding into some relationship I didn't really want. So, in a way, it's Josh I have to thank.

Lennie and I packed up my new Hyundai Coupe SIII – a little present to myself for my birthday – and off we drove to the Channel Tunnel. Brighton was gorgeous, we stopped off and spent an hour or two walking along the beach and eating ice cream. Then down towards the Tunnel and within a couple of hours we arrived at Le Crotoy.

Whenever I visited France before, it was always to head further south, usually beyond the Loire Valley. As soon as we arrived here, Lennie couldn't wait to dump our stuff and take me out to show me how beautiful the Somme estuary is, close up.

I wasn't prepared for the breathtaking sunrise and sunset, or the tranquillity in watching the tide come in and go out. At high tide, watching the sailing boats filling the horizon with their multi-coloured sails just reaffirms your faith in the positive side of life and what it has to offer.

Lennie's been a star and let me wander off by myself at times without making me feel awkward, so I can just chill and think. You know, someone told me once that you only truly appreciate a high point in your life when

61

you're coming out of a particularly low one. I didn't understand at the time, in fact I think I remember saying I thought it was rubbish. Suddenly though, I understand exactly what it meant. Under normal circumstances, I just wouldn't have enjoyed the simple things here, unless I had some testosterone-filled guy alongside me. Essentially, I tend to think of nature and romance as things that go together. Holding hands and walking in the rain, holding each other and being windswept, gazing up at the stars – it goes on and on. You can't be romantic on your own very easily, can you? But here I am, really enjoying myself – whether I'm walking with Lennie next to me chatting away and laughing, or walking on my own, deep in thought.

It's been cathartic and I feel like I can let go of a few things. It's also made me think about the future and whilst I don't really know what I'm looking for, I'm getting a clear picture of what I don't want. I don't want any man, I want *the* man – Mr Right for me. And do you know what? If there isn't a Mr Right out there, I've decided it's not the end of the world. There, I've said it.

I'm running along the beach now, shouting it as loud as I can and watching the sun in its final seconds, before it slips over the horizon. It's good to be alive, to be healthy and not to be afraid of what's ahead. I'm young and I can do whatever I want and all I have to do is decide what's going to make me happy. Looking back towards the flat, I can just about make out the shape of Lennie, walking towards me carrying something. Along the entire length of the sandy beach, which stretches as far as the eye can see around the bay, there are probably not more than a dozen people to be seen. As the daylight has faded, a crystal clear sky, full of twinkling stars and a three-quarter moon, bathes us in a dusky hue. There's no wind and the evening is balmy; life couldn't get much better than this.

'Hey girl! Was that you I heard shouting? I brought you a glass of the best *vin de maison*.'

'Cheers.' We clink glasses and I give Lennie a careful hug, not wanting to spill a drop.

'What's that for?' She's smiling in a puzzled way.

'Oh, just for being there. For not saying the obvious things and for knowing this was what I needed. It's so peaceful and it's opened my eyes to the way I'm living my life as if there isn't any alternative. Think about it, I could move to France if I wanted to, or go off travelling around the world. What's to stop me?' I realise she's frowning and looking at me in a very concerned way.

'What's brought all this on? I thought the purpose of this break was to chill out and relax, not fill your head with wild ideas!'

We both sip our wine in silence.

'I know. I don't mean I'm going to go off and do something totally mad, but the point is, I'm free to change things if I want to. Look at you – since you've gained your CCT in Intensive Care Management, you've become one of the best nurses on the unit. It suits you – you don't get bogged down like some do, you seem to be able to light people up with your energy and it makes a difference! Perhaps I need to think about my career in a slightly different way now. It's just that I've always assumed I would get married fairly early in my life (like now!) and have kids. Nursing is great, but I saw it as a role that would fit around my life and I guess now I'm thinking perhaps that was a mistake.'

'You don't enjoy nursing?' Lennie seems shocked.

'It's not that. If I'd been thinking of a career for life, I probably would have gone into midwifery, specialised. What do you think?'

We walk along in silence for a little while and I'm surprised at Lennie's reaction. I thought she might be pleased I was thinking of the bigger picture for a change.

'I don't know how to say this, so I'll just come out with it. I thought you needed a break to think and I *thought* you'd maybe want to consider giving Dan a second chance. Please don't be mad at me, but on our way back next week we're meeting Dan for a drink at a pub in Brighton.'

Gob-smacked. I'm gob-smacked.

'What on earth made you arrange that? Lennie, you never get involved, you're usually the listener and the hand-holder. I'm the one who meddles and tries to sort out the problems. How did all this happen?' I'm too shocked to be angry and because it's so out of character for Lennie, I can't actually believe she's done this.

'It's a long story,' she's muttering.

'OK and we've got all night. Come on, we'll walk back and you can tell me everything that's happened.'

'Well, don't think I'm trying to pass the buck, but I feel like it wasn't my idea at all. Except, it was.'

'Lennie, that makes no sense whatsoever.' I realise my wine glass is empty and I pinch the wine bottle out of Lennie's backpack to refill my glass. 'Go on.'

'It was like, everywhere I turned there were things pointing me to Brighton and Dan. Coincidences that were odd because, I don't know how to explain it, but it didn't feel natural.' I start to get goosebumps and I don't think it's the chill coming in from the sea.

'In what way?'

'I Googled a route at work for a colleague and every time I typed in Birmingham, Brighton would come up! We all had a go, several of us and it was always the same. The route to Brighton – didn't matter what we put in. Sally went off and tried it on her PC and Birmingham came up first time!'

'OK, keyboard freeze. You must have used the word

Brighton at some point and it stuck in the system.' Hmm, long-shot but possible?

'Yeah, right. Then I had this picture of you and Dan, after the split I put it in a book on my dressing table. I couldn't bring myself to throw it away, but I didn't want it hanging about in case you saw it. So I hid it. Every morning when I woke up it would be there, on the dressing table – just as if someone had taken it out of the book and laid it out for me to see.'

'Oh come on Lennie, you could have knocked the book over whilst doing your make-up and then put it back and not noticed the loose picture falling out. That can't count as an "odd coincidence".' I'm starting to relax now and thinking perhaps Lennie's adding up two and two and making five.

'Laurel – this was *every* day for a week!'

'Oh.' That took the wind out of my sails. 'Is there anything else?'

'Let's see – there was a message kept coming up on my phone. It was a text you sent me ages ago, saying you weren't coming out 'cause you were meeting up with Dan. He'd been working late, so you wanted to skip drinks with the girls. For a couple of days, every time I looked at my phone, your text was there. At first I laughed because I thought, you know, I'd been leaning on my phone or it was pressing up against something in my bag. But I began to feel like my phone was possessed. Really. I started adding everything up and I felt a bit, spooked.'

The hard bit here is, close as we are, I've never told Lennie (or anybody else) about my 'sensitivity'. Not a word. About anything. What do I do now? Do I tell her about Mya? Do I just laugh it off?

'Laurel, it's starting to worry me. Do you think I'm having bad dreams while I'm awake? You don't think it's the start of schizophrenia do you?' Lennie sounds serious and is clearly looking for some sort of reassurance from me. I need to lighten the moment but I can't seem to raise a light-hearted laugh, all I can think of is Mya.

'Course not. You're fine, you've just been pulled into my little pit of unhappiness and your mind has been looking for ways to make things better. It just shows you're a true friend and subconsciously you've linked bits together that you wouldn't normally do. Perhaps deep down you feel I wasn't fair to Dan.' At least the last part of that is probably based on the truth.

'Yeah, you might be right. I like Dan, he was a good one. I'm just sorry he hurt you and I bet he's missing you like crazy. You were his world, so I guess I just don't understand what went wrong. Sorry if I sound a bit crazy and I'm sorry I went behind your back.' She's looking at me and, even in the gloom, I can see the glint of tears filling her eyes.

'Come here you,' I say as I give her a big hug. 'Don't worry about me, I'll be fine. We'll meet up with Dan, I don't hate him, I just don't want to be with him any more. It'll be OK, it's only a drink after all.'

'Thanks ... sorry!'

'Nothing to be sorry about. You went with your heart and what you thought was right.'

Walking back to the flat I am mad, but I'm mad with Mya, not Lennie. Mya's over-stepped the mark and started interfering. I can't imagine what this has been doing to Lennie – this could really mess up someone's mind. Can you imagine? The presence of a spirit is probably the last thing most people would suspect. In my case it's usually the first. I suddenly realise that I have to talk to Lennie about it, so she won't think she's been going crazy, but not tonight.

*   *   *

The last week has flown, we're packing up to leave and still I haven't had the talk. It's been bliss and ironically we've talked about practically everything else in our lives – but I can't seem to start the conversation in the right way. Lennie's jittery this morning and I'm not sure what that's about. As she's slamming the car boot shut she's smiling at me, but it's a worried smile.

'What? What's up?'

'Nothing, c'mon let's get going. I know it's only a couple of hours to the Tunnel, but we may want to stop off on the way. One last croissant or something.' We both instinctively turn around to get one last look at the beach and the bay. It's so hard to leave all this behind and not want to just stay here forever, hiding from the reality of our normal day to day lives. But that's the wonder of a truly good holiday I suppose and we just need to be grateful for what we've been able to enjoy.

'Onwards and upwards, Lennie,' I say and she giggles as she turns the key in the ignition.

'Can't believe you're letting me drive back. Are you sure you're OK about stopping off at The Lion to meet Dan?'

Looking at her troubled expression I feel so guilty. As she heads the car out of town I realise this is crunch time. 'Look Lennie, I should have told you this before. We've never had secrets and that's why our friendship has lasted. I've shared everything with you, my deepest thoughts, my fears, but there's one thing I just haven't been able to talk about.' I turn to face her and she gives me a two-second glance before turning her attention back to the road.

'This sounds heavy.'

'Yep. Pretty much. The only reason I haven't talked to you about this is because it's not something most people feel comfortable with. Once you know, it might change things between us.'

'God, Laurel. We've blubbed together, got pissed together and were partners in crime when we stole that traffic cone after Tom's party – what can there possibly be that we haven't shared?'

'Do you believe in ghosts?' As I look across at her, she frowns.

'I don't know. Do you?'

'Yes.'

'OK, that's not unusual – lots of people do. It's no big deal, Laurel.'

'It is when you see them all the time and you can talk to them.'

'What do you mean?'

'They talk to me – often. Sometimes I see them and sometimes I just hear them.'

'You're joking. You've never said a thing, not a thing about it.'

'I know. It's not something I'm proud of and it's not something I asked for.'

I'm looking out of the window, watching the countryside whizz by and looking at huge fields full of wheat.

'That's creepy. But why didn't you ever mention it before, it might have helped to talk about it. How do you cope with it?'

'It's not easy and it's not something I ever want us to talk about again. I get messages for people I've never even met and that's difficult. Sometimes a secret is so dark, you don't want to acknowledge it by talking about it.'

She's shaking her head as she's driving. 'I guess most people have something in their lives that they can't or don't want to face up to, so don't feel bad. Wow, Laurel this is so hard to take in. God! Do you see dead people when we're at work?' There is a sudden hint of alarm in her voice and it's making me feel uncomfortable.

'Sometimes. Some parts of the hospital are worse than others. I hate the Intensive Care Unit corridor and I always avoid it if I can.'

Lennie splutters. 'Shit, Laurel. Everyone thinks you've got mild OCD, did you know that?'

'What – obsessive compulsive disorder? What are you talking about?'

'Well, you know you've got this "thing" about always tidying, straightening, cleaning – you know how you do it, you can't help yourself. No one ever tidies up in the Staff Room because they know you'll do it at the end of your shift. Well, when you're at work people notice you don't always go the direct route between wards and, well, people think it's because of the OCD.'

I'm shocked and I don't quite know what to say.

'No, of course I haven't got OCD. I'm just a tidy freak, that's all. It's just sometimes I see some poor soul in the corridor and I don't want to get involved, so I take a different route. I feel a bit stupid now I know people have noticed.'

'It's no biggy. Honestly. Just an occasional joke – people don't mean any harm by it and it's not as if they think you're strange, just a bit compulsive sometimes. Bit like everybody expects me to arrive one minute late every day, that's just me. But poor you! How terrible to be surrounded by death at work and then have to see the spirits, hear their messages.' She actually shudders.

'I'm used to it, it started when I was a kid. I don't listen now like I used to, I just switch off or walk another route,' and we both start laughing.

'I guess I won't be in such a hurry to walk with you in future!'

'Lennie, that's a bit insensitive!'

'So why are you telling me all this now?'

'Because I don't want you to feel guilty about the Dan

thing. It wasn't you, you were right when you said it wasn't your idea.'

'Now you really are freaking me out! Was it one of your ghosts visiting me? Why would they do that?'

'She's a bit disorientated at the moment, they often are at first. She died young, I think she was about our age and she's struggling to come to terms with it all. She's convinced that her 'mission' is to get Dan and me back together, because the only person she's been able to talk to is me. I delivered a message to her family in the hope that this would allow her to move on, but it seems she's been trying to engineer things through you recently. I'm only telling you all this because I don't want you to think it's anything to do with you or your mind. I don't want you feeling guilty about something you've been pulled into. The chance of this sort of thing happening is so remote and I'm just so sorry she's put you through this without thinking what the effect was going to be on you. We'll meet Dan and hopefully she'll see that she's done all she can and leave it up to fate. She means well, she was obviously a lovely, caring person, but she's just confused at the moment.'

'God, you talk about it as if it's normal. How do you sleep at night?'

'I don't let it bother me. They can't hurt you unless you dabble – there is a dark side, but when you're a 'receiver' like I am, it's all just sad, lonely souls passing through. They usually just want to let their loved ones know they're OK.'

'Wow. And you've kept all this to yourself all these years? What a brave little girl you must have been – most of us would have had the screaming ab-dabs.'

'I wasn't brave, I didn't know they were dead then, so there was nothing to fear. I just don't want you to think strange things will happen around you again, it's a one-off and this spirit will move on soon if it hasn't already.'

'So, the Dan thing is over then? Really?'

'Yep, I think so. I suppose I won't know for sure until I see him again tonight, but even then, who knows? It's not easy when you think you have exactly what you want and then suddenly someone surprises you. You start to realise you don't know everything about them, when you thought you did. It's like the baby thing. I really wanted a baby so badly, but since splitting with Dan, it's gone completely out of my head. Guess I didn't want one so badly after all.'

'So what's next?'

'I can't believe I'm saying this, but I'm going to enquire about specialising – I want to be a midwife. I think I had this obsession about being a couple and settling down, like it was all I could think about. Perhaps it's because Mum and Dad split up when I was so young and I was looking for security. That was the thing about Dan, he always made me feel safe.' I start laughing and I can't help it.

'What?' Lennie gives me a quick look.

'A bit like having my own bouncer!' Now she's laughing as well. 'But Lennie, I want you to promise me not to mention this conversation to anyone and we won't be talking about it again, ever.'

She nods. 'OK, I understand. So, what are you going to say to Dan?'

'I have absolutely no idea.'

All's fair in love and war

Watching Laurel and Lennie walking into the pub is surreal. Partly because it's been months and I can't believe they're actually here and partly because this pub sort of represents my 'new' life. It's like the two different worlds are colliding and it feels strange. I realise my hands are sweating, so I wipe them on my jeans and stand up. My mind's in a whirl – should I hug? Kiss? Man, this is harder than I thought it was going to be.

Our eyes meet and Laurel's face screws up into one of her beaming smiles and I feel like it's going to be OK.

'Hi big man,' Lennie hugs me and I hug back. Laurel is hesitating, but as I put Lennie down she's stepping up to me and we hug as we used to do. It feels so good.

'Good to see you, girls. How was the trip?' We sit down and I'm glad it's a round table, because there's no awkwardness about who sits where. They both look tanned and relaxed.

'Right guys, I'm buying – the usual?' Lennie's up and off to the bar before we can even consider our answers and Laurel's smiling at me.

'She's being diplomatic. She wants us to talk. You OK with that, Dan?' Laurel puts her hand out across the table and I guess I'm a bit surprised, but I put my hand out and touch hers.

'I'm so sorry,' I say. 'Sorry for the mess I've made of everything. Lennie told me you didn't know anything about this, so I guess you've only just found out. It must have been a shock, but thanks for coming anyway, I know it isn't easy for either of us.'

She pats my hand and then withdraws hers. 'You look tired.' She's sitting back and I'm noticing how different her hair looks cut short, it suits her.

'Yeah, well, been working quite a bit. Doc says I'm anaemic and gave me a couple of jabs yesterday – says I'll be jumping around in no time. Gave me a lecture about eating properly, getting my iron and vitamins and all that stuff. I've been a bit of an idiot and I realise that now. Just joined the local gym as well. How about you? You're looking great, I love the new hairstyle.'

Lennie appears and puts a bottle of wine and two glasses on the table.

'There you go guys, I'll see you in a bit,' and she's gone. Laurel's watching me, I pour the wine and pass her a glass.

'Thanks. Yeah, the hair – spur of the moment thing. Bit like you, things went a bit haywire for a little while but, as they say, life goes on. Lennie meant well but this, it doesn't mean anything. I wouldn't want you to think there was any ulterior motive here...'

This is painful, I bet she thinks I look really pitiful.

'No, course, I know that. We didn't conspire, it was just a thought, you know, in Lennie's head and she told me it was something she would regret if she didn't do it. She said there were things that had been left unsaid. She was right but, man, all of the things I wanted to say have just ... disappeared!' We both laugh, I raise my glass and Laurel raises hers back.

'I know. That's fine, it's the same for me. All of the things I thought about saying just don't seem to be right any more. It's funny, I was so sure that you were cheating on me but you weren't, were you?'

I'm a bit shocked at this – why would Laurel have

thought I was cheating on her? I don't understand. 'Why would I cheat on you? I loved you. Babe, you were my world.'

'You said "loved".'

'No, no, I don't mean it that way. Being apart, I'm just ... afraid of the distance between us now. I don't know what's been happening to you, I don't know how you feel. You hated me, I could feel that. I didn't cheat, I didn't want to cheat. Why would you think that?' She's beautiful, so beautiful and I know I've lost her. But I think I still love her, only I'm not as sure now as I was, because I'm not feeling the love back. She's changed.

'Look Dan, I'm not trying to be mean, this isn't about scoring points off each other. I didn't hate you, I just, well, I suppose I just couldn't understand why you weren't talking to me. I was open with you about everything, I talked to you about how I was feeling, I laid my soul open to you. It was like you were somewhere else when we were together and I couldn't get to the real you, your feelings. You didn't want to share the things that were hurting you, causing you pain and that was hurtful to me. I guess I became a bit paranoid about the reason and whether it was work or another woman, the thing is, you were choosing not to share your innermost thoughts with me any more. You were my security blanket and suddenly I felt like I was alone, even though we were still a couple. I still don't understand what went wrong.'

I wish I could explain, I wish I could find the right words but my head's empty, there's only this sense of panic, this realisation that maybe it's already too late. She's moved on and I'm starting to think that anything I say tonight isn't going to make any difference at all.

'I'm sorry, I let you down. Things were getting on top of me and I couldn't cope with the pressure of everything starting to unravel. So I just shut everything out. It's like, every day I just got out of bed and did things automatically. I swear there was no one else, there *is* no one else. There was only you, Babe. Always. It sounds stupid, but work fills my head sometimes and blocks everything else out. I knew I was no good to you in the state I was in, but coming to Brighton wasn't running away, not from us, I swear. I can see now what you must have thought and I'm ashamed to say I think I was having some sort of breakdown.' I'm watching her wipe away some little tears that are falling slowly down her left cheek.

'Sorry,' she says.

'No, no, it's not you, Babe. You've nothing to be sorry for.'

'But I am, Dan. I was bossy, I pushed you away because all I could think about was my disappointment about not getting pregnant and if I'd just stepped back... You must have been in hell, I know how hard you work, but I didn't realise how badly wrong things were going. I let you down and I'm ashamed to say that I think it was because I was punishing you.' She pulls a tissue out of her bag.

'You weren't punishing me – that's nonsense.'

'I was punishing you because you were supposed to be my tower of strength, you were my protection from the world. When you withdrew from me, I felt like I was all alone and vulnerable. I guess we failed each other.'

'Is it over?' I'm looking at her and trying to show her that I can take the answer, whatever she says. She's looking back and I can see the same honesty in her face.

'The truth is, I just don't know. I don't think either of us know. Getting away these last two weeks, has made me realise that it's not fair of me to rely on someone else all the time in order to feel secure. Perhaps I need to spend some time working on my own problems, instead of trying to bluster through and convince people I'm strong. The thing is, I'm organised and methodical because that's how I cope, but I'm not strong, it's just a façade.'

We both look up as Lennie is approaching the table and I think we both feel there isn't anything else that needs to be said tonight.

'You two OK?' she says brightly.

'We're fine. We just need a bit of personal space for a while, some time to sort ourselves out. We're still buddies. Perhaps Dan could come up for a visit some time soon? We could do a pub crawl, all the old haunts.'

'Good idea!' Lennie says brightly and we both hear the relief in her voice. She starts talking about Laurel's plans to think about midwifery and there's a sense of relief deep inside me as they start talking about their work.

I know the coming months are going to be hard for us, but if we ever get back together again, I know we'll both be better people by then. I wasn't expecting us to fall into each other's arms, I'm just grateful there's no sense of hatred. Laurel hasn't shut the door permanently and she wants to keep in touch. It's a start and it's enough to keep me going.

Keep taking the tablets

I told Laurel the truth, or at least part of the truth, about what the Doc had said. He said the blood tests showed I was very low on iron and a couple of other trace elements. I didn't realise that being low on things like potassium could have such a dramatic affect on your health and he read me the riot act. So, I'm shaping up and eating properly, back to the gym and I've stopped smoking – everything.

I felt really mental telling him about the 'being watched' feeling and he said that it could be a side affect of the vitamin deficiencies making me 'imagine' things. I felt like he wasn't taking me seriously, though, and he gave me a couple of jabs and a booklet about Healthy Eating. I felt a bit like a kid. Two days later I had this appointment come through in the post. He's sent me an appointment to see a 'Counsellor'. Looking through the booklet they sent with the letter, it seems people can have 'episodes' and sometimes it helps to talk about things. So, cutting to the bottom line, I might have had a bit of a breakdown or the split with Laurel may mean I need 'professional help' to move on. I think it's a load of rubbish and I decided not to go, but suddenly it's 2pm on Wednesday and I find myself sitting in a waiting room outside Dr Stein's consulting room. Guess deep down, I do feel like I need some help.

I'm the only one in the waiting room and that could be a good sign or a bad sign. It could mean they sort people out real quick or it could mean I'm nuts and there aren't many people around like me.

The receptionist calls my name and the consulting room door opens. A middle-aged woman appears and she smiles at me, holding out her hand.

'Mr Oliver, I'm Dr Stein. Do come in.' Her handshake is firm. I like that.

'Thanks Doc.' I follow her in.

I'm expecting a couch but there's just a desk and two armchairs around a coffee table. She indicates for me to sit down.

'Mr Oliver, what did your doctor tell you about this appointment?'

I don't know what to say really. 'He didn't – we just talked about, um, the feeling I was having.' I decide that I must remember in future that there are just some things you definitely shouldn't tell your doctor.

'What feeling is that? Please, just relax and tell me a little more. There's no need to feel uncomfortable – I'm not here to judge you!' We smile at each other.

'This does feel a bit weird. He didn't say he was going to send me to see someone and when the appointment arrived I wasn't sure I should turn up. It's not that I don't think this sort of thing works, obviously, it's just that it wasn't that big a deal, really.'

'What wasn't "a big deal"? You're here now so we might as well talk about it.'

I can see the logic and I'm thinking, what the heck. 'OK. I keep getting this feeling, like I'm being watched.'

'Does it happen all of the time or some of the time?'

'Some of the time.'

'Do you hear voices?'

I look her straight in the eye so she's clear about this. 'No, I don't hear voices – ever.'

'But it makes you feel uncomfortable?'

'Well, not really, it's not a bad feeling but it's not normal is it?'

'Define normal, Mr Oliver,' she says and she laughs.

'Please, call me Dan. OK, I get your point, let's just say it's not normal for me. It only started happening after my girlfriend split up with me.'

She's pouring two glasses of water and places one in front of me. I pick up the glass and down half of the contents in one. My throat's suddenly gone very dry. I realise she's seen all this before and if I want to get anything out of it, I have to be honest with her.

'Right Dan. So you've recently been through a traumatic event.'

'Yeah, I suppose you could say so. It's been a difficult year. My job wasn't going too well, the company looked like it was going bankrupt and I was working like crazy. Things just built up I suppose.'

'And your relationship. What did you feel when your girlfriend ended it?'

'Honestly? Like it was the end of my world,' and then do you know what happened next? I cried, man, I really cried. For me, for Laurel and for the great big mess this had all become.

Driving home I actually felt like a big weight had been lifted from my shoulders. Dr Stein explained that most men are brought up to hide their feelings, as if showing how they truly feel is a weakness. However, it's actually the other way around – failing to acknowledge you have feelings is being weak, because it means you're running away rather than facing up. I still felt bad crying because I'd only cried once before and that was when my Grandad died, when I was a kid. It was the only time I saw my Dad cry too. She said I must have had a strong relationship to be affected like I was and that bottling it up could lead to something like a breakdown. She thought I'd been lucky to get through everything and whilst she couldn't explain the 'being watched' feeling, she assured me she had no doubt whatsoever it wasn't a mental health problem.

She carried out a few tests and we did this 'word association' exercise, which I actually saw on TV once. Some of my answers (you're supposed to say the first thing that comes into your head) were off the wall, man, but she said it reassured her I was doing fine. She said your answers should partly reflect your personality and nature. She said if I had come up with safe, predictable words she would have known I was faking it.

So, I've got a clean bill of health, but shortly after I arrive back in the flat I'm getting that overwhelming feeling again that I'm being watched. OK, if it's not psychological then it's got to be 'spooky' and I know just who I'm going to consult next.

Before I can stop myself, I'm talking to the empty room as if someone is really there.

'I know I'm not nuts and I know you're there, 'cos I can feel you – you're giving out a vibe. I don't know what you want, but all of this is getting on my nerves now. I don't scare easily, so why don't you just show yourself? What have you got to lose?'

My eyes scan the place next to the open doorway, where I swear there's something like a 'movement' going on, but it's so faint my eyes just can't get a fix on it. The next thing I know, a shelf on the other side of the doorway crashes to the floor, throwing books and a jar full of small change flying everywhere. The noise is unbelievable, as small coins clatter on the wooden floor and the shelf splinters as it hits the floor. My heart feels like it's going to explode out of my chest but for some reason, I just start laughing.

'Pretty impressive! Perhaps we're going to get on after all!' I say to my invisible intruder and I wonder if people usually talk to their 'visitors' or whether they're too intimidated.

'Well, to date my life has been ruled by women and I just bet you're a female. I'm going to call you "Cupcake" and if you don't like it, you can find someone else to bother.'

As I'm walking into the kitchen to put the kettle on, I'm actually smiling. I seem to have found myself a new and unusual friend, someone it's going to be easy to talk to because she can't talk back. Sounds perfect to me!

A friend in need

I've come to the conclusion that Dan is the sort of guy that most women are really looking for. Watching him talking to Laurel in that pub in Brighton, I couldn't understand why she was holding back. I watched her bravely wiping away her tears while he talked and she couldn't even sense I was there. I've tried so hard to get through to her since then, but our link is severed, it's like I'm up against a closed door that won't budge.

It took a lot of energy to steer Lennie into arranging for Dan and Laurel to meet and I wonder now if that has drained me in some way. It's not that I feel tired, but I'm worried that it's taken away the only real channel of communication that I had. It's great being around Dan, but he only seems to be able to sense my presence, we can't talk as I was able to with Laurel.

In the very beginning when I saw Dan with Laurel, I really only caught glimpses of him around their flat. My impressions of him were really Laurel's thoughts on the sort of person Dan was. After their split, when I found I was able to watch him close up, I was able to see a different side of him and it scared me how badly he was doing. He really is one sensitive guy and he hides so much of what he's feeling. I can see now that Laurel steered both of their lives and Dan didn't really get a chance to have much input. It appeared to be working, but Laurel was trying to surround herself with a picture-perfect lifestyle to avoid confronting her insecurities. Dan thought loving someone meant doing anything they wanted, without question, so they would be happy. Dan didn't want to spoil anything for her, so when things were getting difficult at work and then Laurel started getting really stressed about not getting pregnant, he didn't know how to handle it. He would rather have risked having a nervous breakdown than disappoint Laurel – how committed and selfless is that? Of course it's totally stupid too, but that's the power of love. You see, Dan thinks he failed her. The crazy things is, Laurel now thinks she failed Dan. Why am I the only person who can see it all so clearly and why me, when it's virtually impossible for me to be able to do anything about it?

I've decided all I can do is befriend Dan. I'm concentrating all my energies on trying to make some sort of contact. I've found out I can move things – well, sometimes anyway. It's not very controlled and it's usually not very subtle. I could end up demolishing the flat Dan shares. I've already broken a shelf, smashed a glass jar full of loose change – oh, and melted the wire on his table lamp. Still, I've made an impression and even if he can't hear me or see me, he knows I'm there. He's given me a nickname – Cupcake.

At first he was upset about me and I can fully understand that. Before I 'saw the light' I would have been upset if this was happening to me. But I'm growing on him, he talks to me a lot, even though talking out loud when there's no one else visible in the room must make him feel like a bit of a weirdo. He never gets angry with me now, he treats me like a sort of 'agony aunt'. He often asks for my opinion and then ends up answering his own questions, which has been surprisingly good for him. You don't agree? You see, he needed to talk about things and learn not to keep things bottled up. That's just what he's been doing since I've been around him. I'm like one of those expensive therapists, all I do is listen and the patient heals himself!

So, things are relatively fine (all things considered) except for Steffy. I'd decided she was a designing, manipulative female, but now I know her better I can see it's more complicated than that. She has the naivety of a 60s flower child, the body of a sex goddess, a flighty mind that's all over the place and she's a compulsive flirt. She's actually very intelligent, I bet she'd be a good candidate for Mensa! She thinks she's gay but she isn't – it's just a phase that will pass, I'm sure of that. What is very clear, is that she has this enormous crush on Dan and he doesn't know how to handle it.

What scares me is that Laurel doesn't know anything about Steffy and things are happening that could be misinterpreted. I just hope the physical distance between Laurel and Dan now, means Laurel doesn't know the day to day happenings in Brighton. My other concern is that Dan works for Steffy's uncles. One of them, Sean, is making it clear he thinks Dan would be a good influence on her, calm her down a bit. He keeps asking Dan to do little favours for him, could he just 'pick Steffy up and drop her home', that sort of thing. Work's going great for Dan and for Jupiter Live, it would be just awful if something between Dan and Steffy spoilt it.

Also, I'm beginning to feel very protective of my favourite guy and I think he's really beginning to feel the healing and affection I'm trying to surround him with. He's eating well, working out and I notice he's been singing in the shower lately. If I can just keep trouble away from him, he'll be ready to pick back up with Laurel when she's sorted herself out. Sounds easy, doesn't it? And if I could just talk to him I'd be feeling quietly confident of achieving my goal. Instead I'm feeling concerned and the only thing I can do to exert some sort of 'control' is to try to spook Steffy. Thankfully nothing I do seems to faze Dan at all – no matter how much noise my efforts end up creating.

There's a kindness in Dan that overrides everything and, even though he doesn't really understand what's going on around him, he's giving me the benefit of the doubt. He's fundamentally a 'glass half full' guy and not the 'glass half empty' type. And what am I? I suppose you could say a frustrated control freak, being taught a really, really tough lesson.

So, what are friends for?

The last week or two I've started feeling more like my old self, so I'm guessing the Doc's diagnosis was right after all. I've also noticed I'm not getting the sympathy vote at work any more, so things are gradually returning to normal and I like that.

We're down to just the two of us in the flat now, so it means there's more space. Which is just as well, as Cupcake seems to be around an awful lot. She's noisy as hell sometimes and just loves being the centre of attention. I'm not sure if she comes with the flat, or if she's just latched on to me. I spoke to Grace Norris, the medium who works on the *Connections* programme and she was quite interested. She wants to come to the flat some time soon to see if there's anything she can do, but I must admit that Cupcake is growing on me. It's like having a friend you can really open up to, with a guarantee that they won't repeat a word or, for that matter, judge you. If she's not happy about something I do or say, she lets loose and my bin is always full of something or other she's broken. I share the flat with Karl from work and he complains about the noise sometimes, but I'm not sure he really understands what it's all about. I think he'd like to move out, but he's got the hots for Steffy, so while she's around I don't think he's going anywhere.

I'm actually solvent again and I'm also working on a side-deal with *Connections*, that Sean arranged for me. I know he feels partly responsible for my split with Laurel and even though I've told him it was just one of those things, he's really looking out for me. I'm a bit fed up of baby-sitting Steffy though, but it's hard to say anything to Sean. She's his favourite niece and she's a great girl, but she's really hard work to be around sometimes.

As I unlock the front door to the flat, I can feel Cupcake waiting and it's a bit like going home to the wife. I play this sort of game with her. I don't say a word until I've had something to eat and I've made a cup of coffee. Sometimes she moves things, just small things to get my attention, but I ignore her. Then, when I sit down with my coffee I talk to her. I tell her about my day, the lows and the highs, what the weather's like … everything, anything. I've changed a lot since the Doc sent me to see Dr Stein. I'm sleeping like a log now and I think it's because talking to Cupcake is really helping. It empties my mind of all the garbage that floats around and used to wind me up. Once I've talked to her about things, it's like suddenly it's not such a big deal. I don't lay there, going over and over things any more like I used to.

I'm also trying to exact my revenge on Cupcake. There must surely be times when she regrets picking me to spook, because she got a lot more than she bargained for. I don't think I'm going to be able to put Grace off for much longer and I don't know how I'd feel if, after her visit, Cupcake goes away. Grace said spirits usually hang around because they're unhappy or they can't let go of something – like they're stuck. Sounds pretty sad to me, so I'm trying to remember that when I'm talking to Cupcake and I'm not rude to her any more.

Oh great, Karl's just let Steffy in.

'Hi gorgeous, I didn't think you'd be home yet!' She's clearly been shopping and I've never seen so many bags. 'I've got food and a surprise.'

'Really? You should have said you were coming round, I'm going out in a bit,' I'm trying to look like it's inconvenient, but as usual Steffy's taking no notice whatsoever.

'Aw, come on, you can't spoil my surprise and I've got food from Marks and Sparks – sushi.'

Sounds good, my favourite in fact, but I'm not going to encourage her. Karl's hovering and follows Steffy into the kitchen, so at least I can get a few moments of peace and quiet.

I've been asked to come up with a 30 second advertisement for the new series of *Connections* and my mind is working through a series of frames. Their last ad was fine, but it had such an old-fashioned take and I want to do something new and exciting. The budget is small, but Sean has let me take this on as a personal project and I don't really care what they pay me. I'll just enjoy the challenge.

Karl and Steffy walk back in, carrying two large trays of food. It's a buffet to feed ten by the look of it.

'So, what's up?' Karl's asking, mouth full, looking directly at Steffy.

'I'm temping for one of the large TV production companies at the moment, the money's great but it's well hectic. How's your ad coming along, Dan?'

'Good. Slow but good. I'm kicking around a few ideas, but I don't want to get stuck in until the idea feels right, if you know what I mean.'

'Yeah, the best ideas are the ones you mull over for a while. How's your ghost?' Grief! She knows exactly what *not* to say. Karl looks murderous.

'She's fine. Hasn't broken anything at all today. Grace wants to come around soon to see if she can do anything.'

'I wondered what was going on! It's bloody ridiculous – he spends hours talking out loud and if he isn't talking, something's getting broken!' Karl's upset, I guess he understands more than I gave him credit for. I think I'd better change the subject.

88

'So, what's this surprise?'

'You've got to wait until Karl goes out,' she's smiling quite primly.

'That's not fair,' Karl turns to Steffy, 'why do I get to miss out on all the fun?'

I know that Steffy thinks Karl is a bit of a lech but that's unfair, she's an out-and-out flirt and he hasn't got a chance!

'OK, you asked for it.' She's grabbing a couple of carrier bags and heads off towards *my* bedroom. I can sense the mischief. I look at Karl and nod towards the door.

'Oh no, man. I gotta see this. She's up to no good, I can feel it,' he says.

When the door opens and Steffy walks in I think we *both* drop food that's halfway to our mouths, as our jaws drop in unison.

'I think my big boy has been bad, real bad and I've come to punish him,' she says. It looks like Miss Dominatrix has arrived, from the leather corset that barely covers ... well, never mind, to the little skirt that's hardly there, down to the six inch stilettos and the riding crop.

'Steffy, girl, you gotta stop doing that.'

'What? Surprising you? Lisa and I were talking about you and she thought it was just what you needed, she even offered to come over and join in.'

'You lucky git,' Karl says, standing up, but he still doesn't take his eyes off Steffy until he's the other side of the door.

'Steffy, join in what exactly?' I throw myself back against the sofa and give up on the sushi.

'I thought you needed some comfort sex,' she says, pouting.

'Having sex with you would be like having sex with my sister – if I had a sister, that is. If I want sex I'm perfectly capable of sorting it out for myself.' I realise I'm sounding a bit harsh, but I'm really pissed off. I don't care what Karl thinks, although he doesn't realise this is Steffy's way of having a laugh. We did make out once, first year at uni, but I knew straight away it was a mistake. Now I really do think about her as if she's my sister, an unruly one who's a bit too wild at times, I'm afraid.

'You know I've no intention of jumping into bed with you so I can only assume all of this was for Karl's benefit?'

Now she's sulking because I've rumbled her.

'What if it isn't for Karl at all?' she laughs wickedly, enjoying all of the fuss.

'You do know he'll never get this image of you out of his head now, don't you?'

'Serves him right for being a perv.'

'Steffy, he isn't a perv. He just fancies you! You're a very beautiful girl, I just wish you could behave yourself.'

'I'm bored. My life's boring since I've come back to Britain. I want to meet someone interesting, someone who sets me on fire.'

'So Lisa doesn't do it for you any more and you don't fancy Karl?'

'No, I still fancy you. I always have and all you do is humour me. Don't you find me at all sexy?' I'm looking at her and I have to admit she *is* the sexiest dominatrix I have ever seen.

'You're sexy as hell and you know it. Men and women can't help falling for you, but sex isn't just about, well, physical stuff, it's as much about what's inside your head.' The truth is, if this was anyone other than Steffy, here and now, I'd love to have sex. It's been a long time since Laurel. That, as they say, is the story of my life.

'So it's a "no" then.'

'It's a "no", and it always will be.'

'It was still worth it to see the look on Karl's face.'

'Come on, stick your jeans back on and we'll watch a

film,' I say and she turns on her very, very high heels
and does as she's told.

'Cupcake, I'm really sorry you had to see that,' I half-
whisper to the empty room. 'Believe me when I say it's
not what it looked like – Steffy likes to act crazy sometimes,
it's an attention thing. She knows she's safe with me, she's
not really wicked, honest.' I don't know why I'm explaining
anything to a ghost, but just in case she's a prim and
proper spinster, I feel I have to set the record straight.
As if in response, there's a loud crash suddenly in the
bedroom and Steffy comes sauntering back in.

'You just lost the vase off the window sill in your
bedroom – guess Cupcake didn't like the show,' she says
as she sits down, grabbing a packet of crisps from the
tray. I press play on the DVD and have to bite my lip to
stop myself laughing out loud.

And so to bed…

I'm beginning to feel that there's some sort of battle going on between Steffy and Cupcake. Steffy says she can't hear or feel my little spirit, but she does hear the little 'accidents' and they really seem to spook her. I suppose it's because she has no idea when they're going to happen. I seem to be able to sense when Cupcake is upset about something and I sort of know something is going to move or smash! Clearly though, they might not have direct contact with each other, but there is a sort of rivalry sparking when they're in the same room together. Steffy's presence seems to upset Cupcake and so she'll move something and then Steffy accuses me of not concentrating on her. It's almost like they're jealous of each other and fighting for my attention.

Taking Steffy home after the film, I can feel Cupcake is with us. It's like she's checking up on me or something. Steffy's leaning against my shoulder and her eyes are closed, so I'm surprised when she starts talking.

'Dan, you know how it feels to get your heart broken, don't you? It's the worst thing *ever*. Do you realise that if you don't give me a chance to convince you we could work, you'll be breaking *my* heart!' For a moment I'm speechless, because this is Steffy without the usual antics she uses as a smokescreen.

'So what's brought this on then? You are *not* in love with me, you just think you are. If we were going to work, then the magic would have happened back in uni, years ago. You've been away and coming home everything and everyone has moved on, so when we meet up again I'm instant comfort. You need to be honest with yourself, young lady. Your special partner is out there somewhere, I promise.'

She tilts her face towards me and I glance across at her, concerned.

'I wish I could believe you. I really do. It's just I feel so good when I'm with you.'

'I know, but feeling good isn't the same as being in love. I want it all – including the fireworks – don't you? I don't think anyone should settle for less, ever, because if you do you're cheating yourself as well as the person you're with.'

'You really are Mr Wonderful, do you know that? Laurel must be mad letting you out of her sight.'

'No, she's not mad. We just both need to be sure and sometimes spending time on your own is the only way you can really sort out your true feelings. Discover what you really want out of life.' She yawns and reaches out to touch my cheek. I feel really sad for her.

'But I will always love you a little, even though you don't love me back.' The temperature in the car suddenly drops a couple of degrees, but Steffy doesn't seem to notice it, she's too busy feeling sorry for herself.

As soon as I get back to the flat, I open the door and walk through to the bedroom without turning on the lights. I pull off everything so I can lay down on the bed in my boxers and T-shirt. I need to think. Do I really believe what I just said to Steffy? Have I got doubts about Laurel being the one? I'm feeling totally confused as I try to remember word for word what I said. My head is spinning or is it the bed? This is bad. I realise I'm in danger of hyperventilating, so I start controlling my breathing – long and slow, long and slow. My skin starts to feel slightly chilled and clammy, but I like it. Closing my eyes, I try to clear my mind by concentrating on what I can feel. The crisp, cotton pillow under my head, the raised pattern on the duvet cover. I trace the pattern with my fingertips and gradually I'm back in control and the panic sensation has passed. Perhaps it's because I'm concentrating so hard on my sense of touch, but suddenly I can feel the weight of another body lie down on the bed beside me. I even look to check, but there's nothing to see. But I know Cupcake is there.

'Bit of a panic attack there for a moment,' I say out loud. 'Guess I didn't know there were still things left buried inside me I hadn't confronted. Funny, I'm scared of facing up to these new feelings, but I'm not scared of you! No offence meant, Cupcake, I'm sure you don't want to scare me anyway. I think maybe you're feeling sad too and perhaps that's the thing we share. Lay here with me for a while, I don't want to be alone and I don't think you do either.'

This wave of sadness washes over me and I can't hold it back. Is this hitting rock bottom – when you ask a ghost to keep you company, I ask myself? Thankfully no one attempts to answer my thoughts.

To play charades you have to give us a clue

My name is Grace Norris and I'm a medium. What does that mean? Well, I believe that when people leave their bodies behind, what I like to think of as 'the essence' of the person moves on to the afterlife. I try not to use the word 'death' unless I absolutely have to, because it really upsets some spirits. Moving across into the new dimension can be very difficult, as some find it hard letting go of this side of life. Sometimes they hang back because their loved ones can't accept what has happened and I think they feel a sense of guilt. I also have a personal theory that spirits sometimes instinctively fight, without being sure exactly what it is they're fighting against or why. It's a pity, because what's to come is enlightening and they find a peace and purpose that gives a point to the life they had on earth. Well, that's true for most spirits, but there are, of course, those who suffer unfortunate deaths or have wronged others in this life and the transition is harder for them.

Dan's haunting sounds unusual and I must admit I'm a little curious. The trigger seems to have been the break-up of his last relationship. It's a time when emotions run high and often out of control. Spirits seem to be attracted to the intensity and unusually high energy levels surrounding traumatic events. Perhaps it mirrors their own activity levels and there is a comfort in being around people who are also fighting personal battles.

I've known Dan for about six months and it's obvious he's a lot happier now than he was, that's for sure. But there's still a general sadness about him and I feel a sense of intense loneliness that he's trying very hard to hide from the world. He's very popular at work because he has a wonderfully dry sense of humour, which is actually a part of his coping mechanism.

So, Dan tells me he has a ghost whom he refers to as 'Cupcake' and, whilst most people in his position would be coming to me to see if I can help make it all stop, Dan wants me to see if I can help the spirit. He told me he doesn't necessarily want her to go away, but he does want her to be happy and possibly prevent some of the breakages! He's a very unusual young man and there is an innate kindness in him that restores your faith in today's young people. The spirit seems to manifest herself mainly when Dan is at home and he's been unable to find out if the presence was there before he moved in. It seems she's becoming increasingly more active, judging by the diary Dan has been keeping for me for the past week. It shows fairly low-key stuff with activity levels varying from day to day. However, Dan's unusual approach in befriending and talking to this spirit may be encouraging it and I'm not sure that's a wise thing to do given Dan's current situation.

I'm just off to visit him now and, approaching the building, I realise he didn't tell me there were three floors. I bet he's on the top one – yes he is, flat 3b – and today my knees are really playing up. As my Mother would have said, 'Don't grow old, it's all aches and pains'. The flat is in a good area of Brighton and was probably built around the late 90s. I did a bit of research and it seems there were large storage warehouses here before the developers moved in.

Dan opens the door immediately I ring the doorbell and I'm still trying to catch my breath and wait for the shooting pains in my left knee to subside.

'Sorry Grace, I forgot to warn you about the stairs.'

'All right for you young people, I expect you run up here!'

'Tea? I'll just put the kettle on – go along into the sitting room,' he smiles and I can't help feeling a stab of sadness. I can feel the pain that he's going through and my senses tell me that this is probably one of the most difficult times that he will ever have to face in his life. He's scared of being alone. Without love. I lay my coat over the chair and limp out to the kitchen, where he's putting two very nice cups and saucers onto a tray – bless! He cares about things, the small things in life. He just lost his way for a while and now he has to re-invent himself. It's not easy.

'Do you mind if I have a wander around?'

'No, go ahead. I'm sure Cupcake can't wait to meet you,' he calls over his shoulder and I can hear his deep, throaty laugh. He's very like one of my nephews, but he's much too thin. I always want to take him home and cook him a meal whenever I see him. Usually he's behind a computer and often so deep in concentration, he's not aware of anyone else around him. He's very committed and loves his work, so people sometimes shy away from disturbing him and that hasn't been helpful during his recent crisis.

'Picking anything up?' he asks as he carries in the tea tray.

'I'm going to need a glass of water and I'll just go and wash my hands if that's all right. It's how I prepare to receive.' I can see he's anxious, it's written all over his face.

'Fine, fine. I didn't realise – I thought you'd just feel her presence like I do, the moment I walk in.'

I dry my hands and walk back into the sitting room. 'It varies. Sometimes a spirit will be around me all day when I have a sitting booked. As if they're excited and worried they won't have time to tell me what they want to pass on. Other times I don't get anything until the sitting begins or several spirits will come through in one session, all competing to be heard. Other times not a lot happens, so I might ask the client what information they are seeking and I try to focus on getting that for them. If I feel some sort of personal connection or empathy with the client, then I get a much clearer 'channel' and that either happens or it doesn't. Nowadays I don't take on new clients because of my involvement with the show. There are still a lot of people I see regularly though, who have had sittings for many years. OK, let's see if I can pick up anything.' I take five very long and very slow breaths in and out. I pick up the glass of water and take a few sips. It's a cleansing process and helps me to clear my mind of thoughts and to be open to absorb anything that comes along.

'It's strange, Dan. I'm picking up things from you and they're all connected with your recent problems, that's to be expected, but very little from your spirit friend.' It's a bit uncomfortable feeling some of the emotions Dan is giving off and I'm having to try quite hard to avoid them and try to pick up on anything else.

'My name is Grace and I'm a friend of Dan's. I'm happy to receive any messages you may have for him.' We sit in silence for several minutes before I get anything at all.

'Dan, I'm seeing an extremely pretty, younger woman. Probably about mid-twenties, she has a scar on her face. She's smiling, but I feel this is like a picture rather than a spirit presence. It's very strange. She's very close to you – is this someone you knew who passed recently?'

'No, I've never known anyone who died young – male or female.'

'For some reason she's not communicating with me.

It's still like I'm looking at a picture, although I'm feeling some very strong emotions here and they're all directly linked to you. Could you say something to her and let's see what happens?' He's looking very pale and nervous and I know we both hoped for some answers, but I'm just not getting any real information.

'Hi Cupcake. I'd like to know a bit about you – I think you're sad, but I don't know why. Is there anything you can share with us that might help?' Another few minutes pass in silence and the only change I can see in my head is the young woman in the picture has turned her head to the side. I can't get any impression at all of what she's looking at.

'Dan, all that's changed is she's moved her head to the side, as if she wants to show me something, but I can still only see her within a sort of frame and I can't see beyond the edge of that picture. However, instead of the emotional stuff that I was feeling just now, suddenly it's changed and now I can feel a tightness and pain in my chest. It's as if she's having difficulty breathing. She may be trying to tell you how she passed. But that's it I'm afraid.'

'Hey Grace, that's fine. I now know she's a woman, which is a heck of a comfort, as it would have been really weird if you'd told me it was a man! I like the thought that she's not just your average spirit, shows me she's here for a reason and there's nothing bad. Thanks Gracie.' He picks up one of my hands and gives it a squeeze. At that precise moment I get an instant flash of white light.

'What, what is it?' He feels me recoil, almost as if I've been hit by something.

'I don't know. The moment you touched me I saw this flash of light, it was very bright and there was lots of background noise. It was almost frightening, lots of faces peering down – just for a second and it was gone. Trouble is, I don't know what that flash is connected to, or whom, so it's not very helpful, is it?'

Dan helps me on with my coat, I give him a little hug and pat him affectionately on his back. I would have loved to have had a son of my own.

'I know someone who's doing research into telepathy, telekinesis, those sorts of things. I think we're looking at something a little unusual here – nothing to worry about, but if you really want some answers it might be worth us paying him a visit. What do you think?'

'Yeah, I'll give anything a try. You're a great lady, Grace, and I appreciate your kindness. My life at the moment seems to centre around trying to get some answers, I've got the list of questions – that was the easy part.' He laughs.

'I know, I know. Life isn't always going to be so tough, you know. The happiness will come, it's in your future all right, but there are a few things you need to experience first. Trust me, there's nothing bad to worry about – if there was I'd be warning you!'

He bends down to give me a kiss on the cheek and I blush. There really is something very special about Dan. He's rugged and interesting, but he also has a heart of gold. I wonder what went wrong with his relationship and whether the young lady concerned now regrets walking away from him. It's been a long time since a young man gave me a kiss. He's made my day – bless!

Being a slob isn't easy

It's funny how we don't always question the things we instinctively do, or choose not to do. Dan for instance, when he's working he's so absorbed he has to spread his paperwork everywhere. It's as if he needs to have sight of everything at the same time in order to keep his thoughts flowing. In nursing you learn to work tidily, everything has a place – you can't leave things hanging around for a patient to pick up or trip over.

I guess I was born a bit of a 'tidy' freak anyway, but what Lennie said about the OCD thing really hit home. It made me stop and think about how other people see me. Dan never complained about my constant need to have everything clean and tidy. At the end of each day he would automatically put everything away and didn't make me feel like I was being unreasonable. Except, thinking about it now, I wonder if he ever felt annoyed at having to lay everything out again each morning after I'd left?

So, I'm working on it. For instance, I'm sitting here now and Lennie's just left. Our coffee cups are still on the coffee table, I can see a piece of blueberry muffin Lennie dropped on the rug, and the cushions where she was sitting are all rumpled. Normally I'd see her to the door, come back and straighten everything up immediately. Not any more. I'm sitting back down to read my book and ignoring everything else. I'm reading about complications in pregnancy, a textbook a colleague lent me as I'm seriously thinking about midwifery. I keep reading and periodically I find myself glancing across at the mess, but I'm holding out.

I realise I'm sweating a bit, anxious almost and I guess a part of me is concerned about the fact that I might have mild obsessive compulsive disorder. OK, I need to put this into perspective. I just can't believe everybody who feels the need to tidy and clean is affected by OCD. Could it be that people who constantly live in a mess have a similar disorder at the other end of the scale? I rack my brains trying to think if I've ever heard of a medical term for what I call 'slob-itus'. Nothing springs to mind. Either way it's probably not good to appear even 'mildly obsessive'. It's funny, when I was making coffee earlier on, Lennie was standing next to me in the kitchen. 'Hey Laurel,' she said very matter-of-factly, 'you've left the tops off the sugar and coffee jars. There's a fly buzzing around, so I'll just pop them back on for you.' I guess she's so used to my need to have everything just 'so', that even though it's not second-nature to her, in my flat she automatically accepts my standards as normal. Her own place is chaotic and it's often hard to find a clean mug, let alone anything else. Most of her clothes are on the floor of her bedroom. I think of my closets, with everything on hangers, carefully sorted into sections for tops, skirts and jeans/trousers. This is making me feel worse, not better!

Anyway, changing the subject, it's been a very long time now since I heard from Mya and even Orrie hasn't paid me a visit. I'm beginning to wonder if, finally, I'm losing my 'sensitivity'. If you don't use it, you lose it. That suits me fine – it's bad enough thinking I might have an obsession and working on that, without having spirit problems to contend with as well!

When Dan and I met up in Brighton, I had a week to prepare what I was going to say to him. I thought it would be easy to acknowledge it was all over and that there wasn't really much point in talking about the past. I just wasn't prepared for the feelings that surfaced when I saw him. I felt different, things had moved on and I can't deny that, but there was still something there, between us. When we hugged it felt so natural and I found I had really missed the warmth and smell of him around me. But mixed in with this wonderful comfort were feelings of real, gut-wrenching disappointment. Gone was the confident, strong guy I fell for in the first place and what I saw was someone who was very different, he looked defeated. It was like he didn't know how to be with me, scared to say anything other than 'sorry'. I realise now I wanted, needed him to be the old Dan and say something funny to break the ice. At that precise moment I wanted him to say it would all be all right, that he was coming back to me and that realisation was a shock! Instead it was like he wasn't sure about us any more, not because of what he said, but strangely because of what he didn't say. When I talked about us both needing some personal space to think, he didn't disagree. When I suggested he come up to visit sometime, Lennie said she thought it was a good idea. Dan, I noticed, didn't say a word. I also wasn't prepared for the amount of guilt I suddenly felt, as I realised I had pretty much had things all my own way. I could see that Dan stopped communicating, not because of another woman, but because I was too busy organising our life to listen.

I guess my problem is, where do we go from here? Suddenly I feel a strong urge to let him know I'm thinking about him, so I pick up my phone. I'll text him, but what do I say? Well, here goes.

Hi Dan, just checking you're OK. Work's busy, off to a party tonight, one of the staff. Fancy dress, going as a pirate – women's lib and all that. Ha! Ha! Laurel x

There, I'm pressing send before I can start agonising over whether it's the right thing to do or not. It's time to get ready to party!

When Lennie and I pull up in front of the house, we're both seriously impressed. Lennie works with Steve, he's one of the doctors in the Intensive Care Unit and it's his thirtieth birthday. It's a three-storey town house on a new development and it's very stylish.

As Lennie introduces us, he kisses her on both cheeks and then grabs my hand. He leans in towards me, smiling. We make an odd group. I'm a pirate, Lennie is a lion (what else would she be!) and Steve is The Incredible Hulk – great outfit!

'Ah ha!' he says, 'so this is Laurel. Thanks for coming. I've seen you around, which ward do you work in?' Lennie hesitates then walks off, heading for the drinks table and Steve steers me out towards the conservatory. 'Bit quieter out here,' he says.

'Yes, great music though! I work in the General Medical Admissions ward, North Wing.'

'Oh yeah, I know Gary Brooks, one of the Consultants. You've recently had an infection alert there, didn't you?'

'Yes, C.diff. It's under control now, thankfully.'

'Nasty thing.'

'What's a nasty thing?' Lennie asks, as she hands me a very large glass of a weird blue-coloured liquid.

'Clostridium difficile,' says Dr Steve.

'Ah yes, well this punch would probably clear any suggestion of that nasty little bug in one go!' she says taking a sip.

'I'll leave you ladies to it, but I'll be back shortly, promise,' he says and gives me a wink.

As he walks away, he shouts across to the guy at the drinks table. 'Mike – easy on the blue stuff,' and he holds up his glass and points to it, grimacing.

'Wow,' says Lennie, taking a sip, 'so what did Dr Steve have to say?'

'We were just chatting ... about work.' Suddenly my phone bleeps and I scrabble around in my pirate pocket, which seems to reach down to my knees, to see who's texting me.

'Who is it? Anyone interesting?' Lennie asks.

'It's Dan. I sent him a text earlier, I was thinking about him.'

'Oh, what does it say, tell me!' I raise my eyebrows as I read his response.

That's crazy Babe, I've been thinking about you for the last couple of hours! Have a great party. Miss you, D x

'Not a lot, just a brief hello,' but she's not that easily fobbed off.

'C'mon. Hand it over.' She reads the text and smiles. 'See, he hasn't forgotten you, there's hope yet.'

'You're just an idealistic romantic. We're living separate lives so I can't see how a text is going to change anything.'

'Today a text, tomorrow a phone call, next week he's back in bed with you!'

At that precise moment, Steve appears with another guy. 'Lennie, Laurel – this is Pete, my next-door neighbour. So, who's been in bed with Laurel then?'

We all start laughing and instead of feeling awkward, I just join in the banter. Either the text from Dan has put me in a really good mood or this drink is making me feel *really* relaxed. Lennie and Pete sort of pair up and walk off chatting. Pete's dressed as Superman, but instead of the usual pathetic 'man in tights' thing, he looks really cute and I can see Lennie is impressed.

'Fancy a stroll outside?' Steve asks me and opens the French doors onto the lawn. It's a beautiful night, with barely a breeze.

'Sure.'

'You and Lennie seem really good mates, have you known each other long?'

'We were at school together, went to Uni together and both decided to go into nursing. I guess we've done pretty much everything side-by-side for the last fifteen years or so. Lennie's the sister I didn't have.' It makes me realise just how close our lives have been.

'She's a great girl, I'm really glad she decided to join the ICU. She's a breath of fresh air, sometimes you need someone new to come in to shake everybody else up and she's certainly done that! Anyway, sorry about just now, laughing and that. It was a bit indiscreet of me, I don't usually make a habit of listening to other people's private conversations. I think this "cocktail" might just have something to do with it.' He raises his glass, smiles cheekily and takes a gulp.

'It's OK. It wasn't how it sounded,' I can't help saying.

'Please, don't explain. I just feel bad now.'

'Honestly, it's fine. I broke up with someone a few months back and Lennie lives in hope we'll get back together.'

'Ah, I see. Sorry, even more of a guilt trip now. Sounds like it's not been an easy time.' He does actually look as if he's sorry.

'I'm surviving. Great party by the way. The big three-O then?'

'Hmm, bye-bye twenties. Can't say they were that great. Trouble is my mother is convinced that because I'm still single I must be either a closet homosexual or doomed to be left on the shelf, as she kindly puts it, forever.'

He's quite a fun guy to talk to and not what I'd expected somehow. 'My parents split up when I was very young so my mother is a bit anti-men. So I guess you just can't win with mothers! I thought I was in a really solid relationship and then all of a sudden things change, it's

106

hard. Finding the right person isn't easy,' I laugh but thinking about it, that was a bit heavy and I'm feeling a bit embarrassed now. Steve doesn't bat an eyelid.

'Splitting up with someone is hard. Sorry, is it something you don't talk about?' We look at each other and I can see he's giving me the option to change the subject if I want to.

'No, it is what it is. I thought it was his fault at first, but now I know I was at least fifty per cent to blame, maybe more.'

'I find that hard to believe,' he says and he sounds genuinely surprised.

'I'm obsessive,' I blurt out and he just laughs.

'Oh, obsession – depends on the particular obsession though as to how damaging that is!' There's a wicked tone to his voice and clearly he doesn't believe me.

'I think I've got OCD,' I say, flatly. Now he's really laughing.

'Oh yes, why?'

I shrug my shoulders and he can see it's a sensitive topic.

'Right, so you think you've got OCD. OK, listen to Dr Steve. You're going to come with me...' he grabs my hand and pulls me back into the lounge. The party is in full swing and we have to thread our way around some very energetic dancers. Lennie waves out and I can just see the back of Superman's head.

After four flights of stairs, well half-flights, we're both a little out of breath. He's still holding my hand and leading. 'Sorry Laurel, computer's on the top floor in the study. Just in here,' he opens the door and, although it's a modern house, it really has a sense of character and a den-like quality all of its own. Three of the walls have bookcases floor to ceiling. This is one well-read doctor!

He sits down at the desk, clicks into Google and types

in 'obsessive compulsive disorder'. He quickly scans down a long list of entries and clicks on one, opening up a page of information.

'Right. Pull up that chair and listen to this. And I quote – "While some with OCD perform compulsive rituals because they inexplicably feel they must, others act compulsively so as to mitigate the anxiety that stems from their obsessive thoughts. Compulsions include counting specific things (such as footsteps) or in specific ways (for instance, by intervals of two) and doing other repetitive actions, often with atypical sensitivity to numbers or patterns. People might repeatedly wash their hands or clear their throats; repeatedly check that their parked cars have been locked before leaving them; turn lights on and off, or touch objects a certain number of times before exiting a room; or walk in a certain routine way."' Steve pauses and our eyes meet, I see a glint in his eye and I feel like he's trying not to laugh at me.

'Don't say you have to go back and check you've locked the front door or the car, because I do that all the time too. Now, if you're saying you do that fifty times a day, then perhaps that's something we should discuss?'

I shake my head, trying not to laugh. 'No, I never check more than twice,' I say, trying to sound suitably serious.

'Right, so you don't spend hours each day doing the same ritual repetitively. You don't seem to have any problems holding down a busy, stressful job either, so that's a good sign. It means you aren't having to fend off feelings of panic or dread often felt by OCD sufferers.'

I'm trying very hard not to look directly at him, as he makes his point. We sit in silence for a moment.

'So,' he says, 'tell me exactly why you think you have OCD?' He's sitting there, quite seriously, staring at me in a very 'doctorly' way. I'm laughing, just a little bit too loudly, and I know the drink has gone to my head.

'OK Dr Steve. I'm a "cleaning freak" and a "putting things away freak" and a "plumping up the cushions freak" ... Perhaps I've invented a new disorder then?'

'On the contrary, you sound like just the type of woman my mother would approve of and my diagnosis is that you definitely don't have OCD.'

'But you can't possibly know that for sure, I could be hiding my obsessive traits and you w—' I don't get to finish my sentence because Dr Steve leans forward and starts kissing me.

To my utter amazement I find myself kissing him back.

Timing is a strange thing and just as the kissing starts to escalate, Lennie opens the door. 'I wondered where you two ... oh, sorry,' she shuts the door immediately, but we both jump up and then it's really embarrassing.

'Laurel, I'm so sorry, I didn't drag you up here to take advantage of you – please believe me. I just ... um ... maybe the cocktail went to my head a bit.'

'Steve, please don't feel bad – that was very, er, useful, really. I'd better go find Lennie.' We both head for the door and sort of collide, it's like a bad dream. Steve stands back and, in a very gentlemanly fashion, bows ever so slightly and indicates for me to go ahead. We both burst into hysterical laughter as we walk down the stairs and back into the crowded lounge.

Just as we start to go our separate ways, he pulls me back so he can lean in close to my ear, trying to talk over the din of the music.

'Look, I really would like to see you again sometime. Is that OK?' I smile and nod without really thinking about it, then move away quickly as I can see Lennie heading towards us looking very flustered indeed. He smiles back and we part company.

I don't know what's got into me tonight, but I think I've got some quick explaining to do now.

Sorry, men are off my agenda at the moment

To say Lennie is a little upset, is a massive understatement.

'What *was* I thinking!' she says, slapping her forehead. 'It's like throwing you to the lions, putting you in front of Dr Steve.'

'Lennie, I can't believe you said that. It takes one to know one,' I say, laughing as I watch her in her lion suit, padding back and forth in front of me. Fortunately on two legs and not all fours!

'No,' she hisses, 'you don't understand, he's irresistible and everyone falls for him. What was I *thinking*! Dan will so hate me now.' She's really distraught.

'Lennie, it's OK. The kiss was a mistake, it was the blue stuff,' I try to explain.

'So, like, I'm not kissing any strange men I've just met and I've drunk the same amount as you,' she says and her eyes can't hide how really annoyed she is. Oh dear!

'Look, I've been really wound up about this OCD thing since you mentioned it. Steve and I went up to his computer to look up the symptoms on the Internet. Steve's convinced me I don't really have a problem, I'm just a bit fussier than some people, that's all. He did me a favour, I was really starting to feel uncomfortable about it, seriously.'

'Oh great! Dr Steve has managed to heal you as well, now you're feeling grateful! Isn't there anything the golden boy can't do right?'

'Lennie, I think you've had too much to drink, what's wrong with you?'

It suddenly hit me and I didn't see it coming. 'You like him, don't you? I mean really, really like him.'

She's silent and turns her head away so I can't see her face. This is really bad. Lennie flits from one date to another and I've never known her to get 'serious' about anyone. She's so fussy and she always manages to find something wrong with them by the third or fourth date. My mind goes into over-drive, what has she said about him before tonight? I'm ashamed to say I haven't been as attentive recently as I used to be. My mind keeps going off at a tangent – even when I'm having a conversation with someone. She's mentioned him quite a lot – Dr Steve this, Dr Steve that. I totally missed the 'fancying' angle, I thought she was impressed with his skills, really. What a fool I've been.

I watch Lennie's lion's paw swipe across her cheek and she turns, a brave smile on her face. 'Sorr...ree, Laurel, honestly. It's just I've been so convinced you and Dan will get back together and I wasn't prepared for this.' Oh Lennie babe, I've no intention of breaking your heart over a guy.

'And we probably will. But I'm totally off men at the moment. That blue stuff was lethal and I feel very embarrassed now. God, I hope I never see Dr Steve again!'

She looks at me and brightens. 'Oh, right. Yeah, lethal booze. I've got a cracking headache already.'

'That's it then! C'mon, time to call our taxi.'

We manage to slip away quietly and the taxi drops Lennie home first. She's perked up quite a bit on the journey back and by the time we hug goodbye she seems fine. As I turn and wave out of the window, I'm feeling really awful. What sort of a friend have I become? Lennie obviously has strong feelings for Steve but does he realise this, I wonder? Why hasn't she told me about it – or did she drop hints and I was too caught up with myself to take it in?

What's wrong with me – alienating Dan and now I could lose Lennie? Then it hits me. When did I get so selfish? Why has everything suddenly become all about me? It stops *now*. I'm not the centre of the universe and I'm not a bad person. I don't mean to be self-centred, I've just forgotten how to care for someone else, in my obsession to be cared for.

Lennie has been the best sort of friend anyone could ever ask for. If I can only do one thing for her, it's going to be to keep away from Steve. I can't interfere, either something will happen between them or it won't. Whichever way it goes I know one thing for sure, I'll be there for her whatever happens.

Life has a funny way of tripping you up when you least expect it

I think I need to explain a few things. First meetings are always strange. I'd worked out in my head exactly how our first 'outside of work' meeting would go. Laurel and I would pull up in the taxi, knock on the door and Steve would be there, waiting. Steve and I would start chatting, I'd introduce Laurel and then she'd go to get a drink and some guy would start chatting to her. Steve and I would be so caught up talking, that the evening would fly by. Suddenly, when it was time to go, he'd suggest we meet up for a proper date. Laurel would be relaxed, a drink and a dance having helped her to chill, and we'd pile into the taxi, slightly drunk but feeling high.

It takes me back to the night we first met Dan. Laurel and I were in a nightclub having a laugh, when two guys walked in. They stood out a mile, not just because Dan was so tall, but they actually took our breath away. Laurel and I grabbed each other and both said 'Wow' at the same time. Except we were both saying 'Wow' about the same guy and Laurel never realised that. Ironically, he started talking to me first, when I was up at the bar getting drinks. He walked with me back to our table and as soon as he saw Laurel he was smitten – you could see it all over his face. I can't pretend I wasn't disappointed, gutted even, but I could see they'd just clicked and I was glad, for both of them. I can't even remember his friend's name now – he was very good looking but totally boring. I think I saw him twice and it fizzled out.

Dan always made me go ever so slightly weak at the knees, he was the sort of guy who's so cool he doesn't even have to try, it's all natural. He's deep, a thinker and he cares. If a guy ever treated me like he treats Laurel, I'd be in heaven. I can't understand what's gone wrong and why Laurel ever thought he was cheating. He never gave her any reason to think that, because he never looked at anyone else. He was besotted with her and sometimes, possibly, even a little bit afraid of her. That sounds disloyal, but Laurel is – well, a life-force. She never seems to run out of energy and there isn't anything she can't seem to do. It's not easy having a best mate who puts the rest of womankind to shame. But I love her to bits, she got me through my exams when everyone else thought I was going to fail, including me. She sat with me for hours and hours, patiently explaining theories that just seemed to go over my head at the time. She just wouldn't give up on me and then, miraculously, things started to stick and she gave me the confidence to believe in myself. Quite a few so-called friends had already written me off. It all happened during one of the blackest times of my life and she saved me, without really knowing the full story. That's what a real friendship is all about, you trust each other and you really care, but you don't judge.

I didn't know what to do tonight, when Steve carried on talking to Laurel after I introduced them. I panicked and then got landed with Steve's neighbour, Pete. I wasn't prepared for that or for the way the evening turned out. I'm so stupid, why don't I see these things coming? I badly needed to talk to Laurel and I was shocked when I walked in on them kissing. It was only an hour or two earlier that Laurel had received that text from Dan saying he was thinking of her.

The thing is, I *know* Laurel – really know her. The only 'secret' she's ever kept from me is that she can see spirits and talks to them sometimes. When she told me about it, quite recently, I was shocked there was something that big she hadn't shared with me. Then I realised that was her deep, dark secret. She had to tell me about it because of my 'visitor'. You see, one of her spirits had started visiting me and I didn't know that, only that weird things were happening around me. I would have been terrified if I'd known it was a spirit at the time, but looking back, what she said made sense and nothing's happened since. The thing is, she really didn't want to tell me, as if sharing it was acknowledging it, so I realised just how monumental it was for her to break her silence. She's a very sincere and caring person and when she said that tonight it was the drink, that the kiss was a mistake, then I know she was being honest.

Steve sort of asked me out once and I was so shocked I said I'd get back to him! He didn't mention it the next time we bumped into each other and of course I couldn't bring it up. He's got a reputation for a lot of first dates, but he seldom takes anyone out on a second date. Most of the single nurses adore him because he's got it all: he's intelligent, successful, easy to talk to (if your name isn't Lennie), funny and really cute. He's got short, curly hair, dark brown like his eyes, about five foot ten and a really fit body. So, I suppose it's true to say he could have anyone he wanted as a girlfriend. I'm short, medium brown hair that takes ages to straighten, athletic build – gym freak with small boobs – and sparkling conversation isn't one of my strengths.

Anyway, now I'm really confused. Pete asked me out tonight and I just couldn't answer him, I couldn't even think straight after everything that's happened, let alone answer questions. So we ended up playing this sort of 'game' and I told him I was married with six kids and I'd have to ask my husband first. However, my attempt at side-stepping the issue didn't work and he said he's going to ring me tomorrow. All I could think of was how did my little plan go so badly wrong and why couldn't I see it coming? On a nought to ten scale of monumental disasters, this is a nine point five, the only reason it isn't a ten is because I'm still just about breathing.

Lennie's dark secret

After the disaster at the party, I'd intended to have a heart-to-heart with Lennie. I thought if we sat down and talked about what was going on in her head, we could come up with a master plan. I had some good ideas about how to put things right. However, meeting her for coffee the next day, events had already moved on, but not in the direction I'd expected. I was already waiting for her in the coffee shop and I had picked a nice, quiet, corner table.

'Ooh, chocolate chip muffins, lush!' she said, sitting down with a clatter. 'God, I'm exhausted, have you been waiting long?'

'Five minutes, drink your coffee now or it'll be too cold. What kept you?'

'I was just walking out as a florist delivery guy walked into reception and asked for me by name,' she's looking at me and shrugging her shoulders.

'So?' I have to wait while she swallows a whole mouthful of chocolate muffin.

'So, Pete sent me flowers,' she shrugs again.

'That's good isn't it?' I'm looking for some sign as to whether Lennie thinks this is a good thing or a bad thing.

'No, not really. They are jolly nice though.' Well that's something.

'So what happened between you and Pete last night? Steve thought the two of you seemed to be getting on very well and whenever I caught sight of you, you had your arms around each other and were laughing.'

'Oh, it was great. He's quite a laugh actually, despite his story.'

'What story?'

She looks up at me, surprised. 'Didn't Steve tell you? His wife died, last year. It's really sad, he's got a one-year-old son and he has a nanny who lives in, to look after him.' I don't know quite what to say, Lennie didn't mention anything last night and neither did Steve. Well, I guess we were pretty well occupied talking about my OCD problem.

'Lennie, that's awful. He must really have enjoyed your company to send you flowers.'

'Yes, well, he asked me out,' she says, but she's got a guilty look on her face.

'Oh no, you don't like him! This just gets worse and worse, poor guy.'

'He asked me out and I didn't answer him, I just sort of left it.' She's very uncomfortable and I don't know why.

'Well that's all right, perhaps you needed to think about it. It's only a date though, you did say he was a laugh and you spent all evening together, so it can't have been too bad,' I say brightly.

'No, it wasn't that. It's just that I had last night all planned out and there wasn't anybody called Pete in my plan.' She's looking down at her plate and pushes the last of the cake crumbs around with her finger.

'Oh, I see. The plan was Steve. Oh, Lennie – it can still be a plan, last night didn't change anything. I honestly think that Steve likes you, but maybe he doesn't realise you like him back. I sort of felt that he'd invited Pete along especially to meet you, so I'm sure he did it with the best of intentions. Steve said some lovely things about you last night, he clearly thinks you're a great girl, but perhaps thinks you're not interested in him.'

'I suppose so,' she says but there's something up.

'Look, did it ever occur to you that the reason Steve started chatting to me straight away, was so that you would have a chance to chat to Pete? Not because he was instantly attracted to me? Steve said quite a lot about you so he obviously rates you. Are you sure he hasn't said anything to you before last night?'

She looks up and drums her fingers on the table. 'Well, he did sort of ask me out once.' She's embarrassed.

'And ... why didn't you say yes when you're clearly very interested in him?'

'Because I get tongue-tied when he's around and I end up making a fool of myself. I didn't know what to say and the next time I saw him he didn't mention it again.'

'Because he thought you weren't interested. God, Lennie, you can't go hurting someone's feelings by ignoring what they say, just because you might not be able to come up with a polished response. People get nervous and say daft things, it's always good for a laugh and that helps break the ice. So, what are you saying here exactly?'

'I don't know. In my head all I could think of was Steve, so meeting Pete was ... unexpected.'

'Lennie, that makes you sound really fickle. I think with what Pete's been through you need to at least be straight with him. So they've both asked you out and you haven't given either of them an answer.' Now she looks miserable.

'Yes but it's not that simple. It's not like I went to the party expecting to spend the evening with Pete, did I? I had this big conversation going on in my head, where I was going to give Steve an answer. Or at least drop hints about going out and then he was going to ask me out again and then I was going to say yes...' she limps pathetically to a halt.

'So, let me get this straight. You're at the party and you see Steve and me getting on and you're understandably

119

angry. Steve wasn't being mean to you, he thought he was there on his own, he didn't have the benefit of advance knowledge of your planned "conversation". So he thinks you're a great girl and if you don't fancy him, then his mate Pete deserves a great girl and the two of you might just hit it off. So, Steve's a really nice guy who hasn't done anything wrong, Pete's been through hell and it must have been quite a step for him to spend an evening talking with someone and getting on with them. Then I got drunk on some horrid blue stuff and had a meaningless snog. Does that just about sum it all up?' Now she's really uncomfortable.

'When you say it like that, it makes me feel stupid.'

'Lennie, people aren't mind readers. I know you'd mentioned Steve to me quite a bit before the party, but you should have explained what was going on. I went into that party not realising how you felt and how do you think that made me feel when I did realise? Not that I was making a play for Steve at all, it really was the booze. That was the first drink I've had in quite a while and it went straight to my head. Anyway, you need to think about your next step. You have to talk to both Steve and Pete.'

'I've really messed this up, haven't I?'

'Yes.'

'Laurel, I can't go out with Pete.' She's looking extremely guilty now and I wonder what she's going to say next.

'OK, so you don't fancy him. It's not a crime, you shouldn't feel guilty about that.'

'No, it's not that. Like I told you, he's got a baby.'

'If he didn't have a baby would you go out with him?'

She answers almost immediately. 'Yes, I would in a heartbeat.'

'Lennie, I know a baby is a huge complication, but we're talking about a date, not marriage.' Why is she making such a big deal of this?

'It's the principle, there wouldn't be any future in it.'

'You're saying you can't risk finding out if something could develop, because you wouldn't want to take on a baby? You're getting a bit ahead of yourself there, Lennie, date one might not be followed by date two. You might find you have nothing in common. I really can't see your problem. You were getting on very well, I know what you said, but if you were that distraught about Steve, you would have left or gone off sulking. You wouldn't have been laughing and dancing with Pete.' She's hanging her head and I can't see why.

'No, but if he knew me, the real me, he'd hate me,' her voice is flat and quiet.

'Lennie, you're losing me again – are you talking about Steve or Pete? What are you going on about?'

'You said once that sometimes a secret is so dark, a person doesn't want to acknowledge it?'

'When, when did I say that?'

'In the car on the way to Brighton to see Dan. We were talking about your "secret".'

'Oh, then. Yes, I remember.'

'And I said that I thought most people have something in their lives that they can't, or don't want to, face up to.'

'I thought you were trying to make me feel better.' But I can see in her eyes now that wasn't the reason at all.

'When we were at uni and I fell to bits, you thought it was just the pressure of the exams. Only one other person besides me knew the real reason. That was Nick Mills.'

'You dated him for a while, didn't you?'

'Yes, I thought I was in love with him at the time,' she smiles.

'Yeah, I thought you were as well. We were so young though, changing so much and everything happening at the same time.'

121

'More than you knew, at that time. I was pregnant.' She looks at her hands as she folds a white paper napkin in two, then four then eight. I close my eyes for a few seconds and suddenly everything slots into place. One moment she was doing well and she was happy, the next she was struggling with just about everything and she was miserable. Everyone thought she just couldn't cope with the stress of studying and exams. We spent hours going over and over things in textbooks, like she had to re-learn what she once knew, until gradually she settled back down. She literally had to claw her way back to being one of the top students. My mind is whirling with 'what if's' and I don't know what to say to her. I feel like a fool for not realising there was something much deeper going on then.

'My God, Lennie, you should have told me, I would've understood.'

'I hated myself. Nick just didn't want to know, for him it was easy. There was only one answer. I felt I couldn't tell anyone and I just went to pieces. The day I had the abortion I hated myself and I hated him. A part of me knew there was no way I would be able to cope with a baby on my own, but I also knew that I would always regret that decision. If I'd just told you or Mum or someone, perhaps there could have been a way around it, but I took the easy way out. The truth about last night wasn't that I was looking for you because I was upset Steve was with you, but because I needed rescuing from Pete. My fairy-tale story went right out the window the moment Steve introduced us.'

I'm speechless, my mouth is open and I'm totally stunned.

Gracie's very good friend, Lawrence

It's really odd that Grace should have mentioned telepathy, because I've just had a text from Laurel. It was like she could read my mind, because for the last hour or so I've been sitting here and reminiscing about 'us'. I was remembering the day we moved in together and how I carried her across the threshold – as if we were newlyweds! It was a major step and neither of us took it lightly. It was a full-on commitment, marking the next stage of our future life together. I don't often give way to nostalgia, I expect that's a bloke thing. For some reason though, today I've been having flashbacks, remembering the good times. It makes me realise that all of it was good, we only started arguing just before Laurel threw me out.

So, when Laurel's text arrived out of the blue just now, it was the oddest thing. If I was superstitious I might think it was a sign. I haven't heard from her since she came to Brighton, so I'm hoping this is a start and I think I might ring her in a day or two. Just to say 'hello' and see how she's doing. What's left between us is fragile, so I'm scared to make any assumptions, because if there's even a slight glimmer of hope, I don't want to blow it.

Everything else is going great at the moment and the money is rolling in. *Connections* loved my ad. No more 'lights off', grey, shadowy stuff that doesn't really show anything. We recorded some live footage courtesy of Cupcake. It's pretty insane watching the clips, recording things falling off shelves and smashing to the ground for no apparent reason. She seemed to enjoy it too, because she started acting up the minute the crew arrived. Perhaps she was an actress in her former life, who knows? She never shows herself though and still no messages for me to explain anything.

I'm just driving Gracie over to see her friend Lawrence, he does some sort of psychic research, but that's about all I know. Grace taps my arm and I realise I haven't said a word for at least half an hour.

'You're deep in thought. We need to park somewhere in the next road along, as Lawrence's offices are on this side of The Square.' It's a wealthy area and the houses are mostly Georgian, very grand and imposing, all expensively renovated. Not quite what I'd imagined, I suppose. I didn't think there was any money in this sort of thing. I pull into a parking space and Grace turns and looks at me, frowning.

'You've been in a world all of your own, Daniel,' she says and that makes me smile. From time to time she uses my proper name and I sort of like it, because it reminds me of my childhood and my Grandmother.

'I had a text from Laurel before we left and it was uncanny, as I'd been thinking about her all morning.'

Grace smiles. 'Funny, there are a lot of words we use casually to explain things we think of as coincidences, but Lawrence will tell you all about that,' she says.

'I'm in for a lecture then, am I?' I ask, cheekily.

'I'm rather hoping you will be pleasantly surprised. Don't be too put off by the way he dresses, though, he comes from money.' She says that as if explaining something that's going to be obvious. I'm not too sure how to take it, as we set off across the manicured gardens at the front of The Square.

Number 16 sounds like an ordinary house, but the reality is that this is a really grand residence. From the highly polished brass doorstep, to the beautifully repointed stonework, it's pristine. A row of bay standards in granite pots are lined up either side of the pathway leading up to the entrance. The exterior door is open and I lean forward to open the interior one, stepping back so Grace can go through. She leans into me for a second and whispers, 'We were an item once.' She giggles and I can see she's excited at the prospect of seeing Lawrence.

We're ushered in to Lawrence's office by a very professional young lady, immaculately dressed and with a very sophisticated accent. I'm surprised; it's not that I was expecting the hippy brigade, but this is so, well, formal. Efficient, business-like and wealthy.

Lawrence appears and his eyes light up the moment he sees Grace. He moves towards her gracefully, takes her hand in his and lifts it gently to his lips.

'So lovely, still so lovely,' he says, mesmerised. Their eyes are locked together for a brief moment and a thousand un-said words pass between them.

'Did she tell you we were lovers once?' he says, turning towards me and there is mischief in his eyes. She's pleased.

'Oh Lawrence, behave yourself. Daniel doesn't want to hear all that! It was years ago when I was a slim, sparkling little thing.' She's blushing though and I can see exactly how he could have fallen for her, she's certainly sparkling at this particular moment.

'Ah ha,' he says, stepping forward to shake my hand. 'Daniel, welcome.' His handshake is firm and his welcome is genuinely warm. He holds my hand for a few seconds and studies my face, as if looking for something, then moves away. 'Sit down, both of you, please.'

We're in probably one of the most expensively decorated rooms I've ever seen in my entire life. The room has huge proportions, with a high ceiling and beautifully restored architrave. There's a crystal chandelier that is probably three feet by three feet, gracing the ceiling of the sitting area. Lawrence is very well spoken, quite distinguished-looking, with a full head of grey hair. He's tall and wears his typical 'city' pin-stripe suit well, I bet he's got the bowler hat and brolly to go with it. I see he's wearing cufflinks. Actually, I've just realised he looks a bit like John Steed, from *The Avengers* in the 70s and, blow me, Grace does looks a bit like Emma Peel herself. She's still a very good-looking woman for her age and her skin and eyes are totally clear. Only her expanding waistline has turned 'sexy' into 'jolly'. I suddenly realise Lawrence has started talking.

'You're surprised, young man. Not what you expected?'

'If I'm honest, I don't know what I was expecting, but you're right, I suppose. This is all so very grand.'

He nods and smiles, clearly enjoying the surprise element. 'I'm a man fascinated by science. In my youth I was a neurosurgeon, relegated to running the practice now, of course, one of the frustrations that come with age, I'm afraid.' It certainly explains the grandeur.

'Oh Daniel, he's renowned world-wide. He's also such a great benefactor and he personally funds a scholarship through the Society of British Neurological Surgeons.' Grace can't hide her admiration for this man.

'Now, now, Grace. Daniel hasn't come for a consultation, no, he's more interested in my little hobby, no doubt.' I feel like a mouse sitting between two cats, so intent on watching each other's moves they keep forgetting I'm there!

'Hardly a hobby, Lawrence dear. A £5 million a year private grant is hardly pocket change,' Grace says and there's more than a hint of pride in her voice.

'I expect poor Daniel is wondering what is going on! So, let's get down to it. As a doctor I learnt at a very early stage that a large number of my patients were likely to die from their ailments. Some things are very treatable and sadly, others not so. Every specialist, doctor and nurse in the land will admit that whenever a patient dies, no matter how ill they have been, there is still an overwhelming sense of failure. Illogical, of course, because often it's a great release from weeks, months or even years of suffering. However, it is our duty to do everything we can to prolong life, so we battle on.'

Grace pours coffee from the tray of refreshments in front of us. I settle back on the Chesterfield, as I begin to realise that this is going to be much more interesting than I could ever have imagined.

'Grace is quite right, of course. I'm being cavalier when I talk about my little hobby. Of course it's more than that. I'm fortunate enough to have a private grant, funded by three very wealthy patrons. I shall just say that, having lost loved ones who were very dear, they have a vested interest in discovering what might lie beyond this earthly life. For me it's an interest that started the first time a dying patient grabbed my hand and asked me if it was all right to go towards the "beautiful light". So many patients close to the end, or those who have had near-death experiences, have talked about a tunnel that appears. Beyond it: the brightest, most comforting light. Many talk about a garden, a perfect place where they were happy to go, but were suddenly and inexplicably drawn back, into their bodies. Some talk about being brought back with regret, for they firmly believe what they saw and experienced was truly wonderful. Often, after their experience they look forward, without fear, to their final journey. And that change never fails to amaze me.' Lawrence pauses to take the cup Grace offers him.

'Thank you, my dear. Forgive me, Daniel, but I feel from what Grace has told me about you and your spirit visitor, that a little background information may be beneficial. Do, however, stop me if you feel at all uncomfortable.'

'No, please go on. It's all new to me and it's never even occurred to me that people in the medical profession get to see and hear things, afterlife stuff. My ex is a nurse but she never, ever talked about people dying. In fact, she hardly ever mentioned work at all. It must be tough though, when a patient dies and you have a real involvement with them.'

Lawrence sighs, a weary sigh. 'I've been privileged to share the final moments in the lives of some wonderful people. Many fortunate enough to have their loved ones around them and ready to take that final breath. I've also witnessed, sadly, some tragic and untimely endings. Where patient, staff and family fight for every precious second of life, only to feel the ultimate defeat. I've learnt to accept that there is a higher authority on this earth and when someone has been called, there can be a sense of peace in the final acceptance of God's will. Of course, I've also witnessed countless miracles. Cases where the prognosis seemed inevitable and then, against all odds, the patient survived. Those times were life-changing for all involved. Often we knew it was due to more than just our medical efforts.

'The reason that I'm telling you all of this is so that you can see there is a natural flow between life, death and what is beyond. As a doctor, my work ends when the last breath is taken, but as a scientist my interest, given what I have experienced, cannot end there.' We drink our coffee in silence for a few moments.

'There are so many things we don't fully understand, you see, Daniel. Auras for instance. Science is not happy to accept this concept, although we know each living creature emits gases, radiation and energy. So it's not a massive leap of faith, surely, to accept that these emissions, which are as unique as a fingerprint, can actually be seen by some individuals. Astral projection, another example, is something a lot of people have experienced. Usually when retiring at night and it can occur during deep relaxation, near-sleep or during sleep itself. It is sometimes referred to as an "out of body experience", where there is a sensation of leaving, or hovering above, the body. It often ends abruptly with a sensation of falling.' Lawrence pauses again to finish his coffee.

'He's good, isn't he?' Grace asks, reaching across and patting my arm. 'It's not too much for you?' I can see she's hopeful that I'm as fascinated as she is by Lawrence's informative talk.

'I'm amazed and I'm very grateful to you both, it's quite exciting actually.' And I really mean what I'm saying. I smile across at Lawrence and I can see he's pleased.

'It's a very wide topic and, of course, we must remember there is still no absolute scientific proof of life after death. However, we are spiritual beings and there are things that happen regularly to remind us that our "essence" is not bound to our physical body.'

I find this statement puzzling. 'What sort of things, Lawrence?' But immediately I ask the question, I realise where he's going with this.

'Intuitive feelings that come upon us from nowhere. Coincidences, déjà vu and, of course, people like Grace who have true psychic ability. But even those of us who are not gifted can experience feelings of "knowing". The feeling that something is going to happen, or sensing whether someone is fundamentally good or bad when we first meet them. I'm sure you have experienced this yourself on occasion. These are all simple examples of underlying psychic power. Telekinesis is believed to be a way of focusing our inherent abilities and using that energy, cultivating it, to make objects move. I'm not saying it's easy or that everyone has the potential to actually achieve this, but the point is, some do. We already know that thoughts in themselves are a type of energy.'

'I've never looked at it like that, but I understand what you're saying.' Actually he's blowing my mind!

'If you have a very close relationship with someone, over time it is very likely you will start sensing things before they happen. For instance, you suddenly think about telephoning a partner or loved one and as you go to pick up the handset, they ring you. You call it "coincidence".'

'Hey, that happened to me today with Laurel.' Some of this is beginning to feel very familiar. 'I was thinking of her and suddenly she sent me a text. We hadn't been in contact for a few weeks so I couldn't believe it!'

'Clever young woman, she's mastered something that's way beyond me, I'm afraid. I've only just started using my mobile phone to receive calls!' We all laugh.

'So, Daniel, your spirit visitor. Grace tells me you have a name for her?'

'Cupcake. Sounds daft, but it suits her. She's mischievous at times and, well, emotionally reactive if you like, outbursts when she's unhappy and she definitely exhibits jealousy.'

Lawrence raises his eyebrows. 'And Grace says she isn't known to you? You didn't know her in life?'

'Not as far as I'm aware.'

'Do you only see her when you are at home?'

'Mainly, but I sometimes feel her presence when I'm in the car, although it's very rare she'll be around me when I'm, say, at work.'

'I see, does anyone else see or feel her presence?'

'I'd say the answer to that is "no", but if she's moving things around and things get broken, then of course they become aware. I don't think she means to break things, it's not vindictive. I just think she isn't very good at it and it's her only outlet for communicating with me.'

'Well thought out, young man. Does she worry you?'

'She's not malicious in any way, she certainly gives out sympathetic and friendly vibes. I feel comfortable when we're alone together, because she seems more settled when it's just the two of us. However, when one particular friend of mine is around, it really unsettles her. Like she's jealous.'

'Ah, jealousy, that green-eyed monster. Bit of a human trait, I'm afraid, and it exists on both planes unfortunately.' Grace smiles at Lawrence and their eyes meet.

'So Lawrence dear, what are your thoughts about the little session I told you about in Daniel's flat?'

'An experienced medium like Grace here is able to pick up on what I believe to be energy that has become "stuck". To my mind, there are usually three main potential triggers. It might be the nature of their surroundings, for example when a life ends traumatically in a particular place, a murder or a fatal accident. Or sometimes they have a desire to put closure to something. For instance, a relationship that was very important to them and they may have what they feel is an important message to pass on. Finally there are those spirits who pass suddenly and don't know they are deceased – always a difficult one. You are an intuitive young man, Daniel, and that's instinctive. You are doing the right thing in talking to her and you may just need to give her time, be patient and hope that eventually everything will become clear. It might be that she just isn't able to pass on the message she wants to give to you, it takes a lot of energy to do just that. She may be young to the spirit world and it takes time to recover from the dying process. Especially if there was a prolonged period of illness beforehand, but as you didn't know her beforehand we cannot say for sure.'

There's a question I just have to ask. 'Lawrence, why do you think Cupcake picked me?'

He pauses for a few seconds and considers my question.

'Maybe she genuinely has a message for you alone. Not necessarily vital, of course, but if you weren't known to each other, it may be the turmoil that has surrounded

131

you that attracts her to you. The other possibility could be that the location is the link. You should be mindful of the fact that she may suddenly pull back at any time and find she can let go, move on with her journey.'

'That's a sobering thought. I'm kinda used to her now, I like her company.' As soon as I say the words, I think what a saddo I am.

'You realise that I am only the academic here, grappling with something virtually unexplainable, Grace is the truly gifted one. Of course, if this "contact" is telepathic, it could be mental activity generated by someone who isn't deceased.'

'You mean a living person? Why would that happen?' I'm shocked by his suggestion.

'Someone close to you may consciously or subconsciously be thinking of you, trying to help you through your troubles. They may not be aware of their ability and may just think they are being empathetic. You're not in any danger, you can be assured of that, but as usual with psychic phenomena, there are more questions than answers, I'm afraid.'

Grace reaches across and touches my hand. 'A lot to think about, Daniel,' she says and flashes an idolising smile back at Lawrence.

There's a lot more to all of this than I'd realised and I've enjoyed listening to every word Lawrence has said. The only thing is, I'm not sure what my next step should be, because for the first time I realise Cupcake might disappear as suddenly as she came. She's my confidante, my sounding board and I tell her all the things I could never tell anyone else. She literally is the one reason I've been able to keep going. If Cupcake moves on, I realise that it would be a positive thing for her, but I know I'd be lonely as hell and I'm not sure how I'd cope. Now, that really *is* the definition of a saddo!

When is a coincidence not a coincidence?

The visit with Lawrence has made me think seriously about what's going on. If Cupcake's presence is really 'empathetic telepathy' and the person is living, I ought to be able to narrow it down to some probable candidates. In the car on the way home I asked Grace to describe to me again the woman she saw when she visited the flat. It didn't prove to be that helpful really, but I went through a mental list of all of the females I know in their mid-twenties. The description actually ruled out quite a few of them and then Lennie appeared in my mind. Of course! She's always had a soft spot for me, Laurel always used to say she fancied me. Ironically for good old Lennie, she's always been our strongest ally. She once told me that Laurel and I renewed her faith in true love, so no wonder she's upset about the split. She arranged for us all to meet up in Brighton and I was just so grateful. I never stopped to think what a wonderful gesture that really was on her part. It hadn't occurred to me that Lennie too might have been deeply affected by what happened. After all, we were like her second family.

So, I'm sitting here in front of my Mac at work and, talk about coincidences, this next one is *huge*. Suddenly an email alert flashes on the screen. It's Laurel and she's asking me if I fancy a trip to London with her. It seems her parents have won two tickets for a show in London, with free accommodation and a champagne supper thrown in. They've given the tickets to her because they'll be in Italy. This is mega – Laurel wants us to spend some time

133

together! I realise it also solves my problem about finding out how things are with Lennie and whether it's at all likely that she could be sending me 'empathetic' vibes. I know what Lawrence and Grace would say, definitely psychic undertones going on here. Either way, I don't care, time with Laurel is time with Laurel and I'm up for that!

So, what IS the difference between a coincidence and fate?

Facing up to what I've done and who I am hasn't been easy. I guess I've been running away from things for so long, it's become second nature never to dwell on the past. Strangely enough, Laurel telling me about her psychic ability actually helped me in the end. Not at the time, when we were in the car on the way to Brighton to see Dan, but since I've met Pete. If you could have seen her that day though, the look on her face and her body language, as she reluctantly told me about her secret. It all said much more than her words. Then, when I finally told her the secret *I* had kept buried all these years, we both cried and held each other. She told me she felt ashamed of the fact that she couldn't embrace her gift. She felt guilty for not being able to cope with the receiving and passing on of the messages that came to her.

Shame and guilt are not emotions anyone finds easy to share and, although our circumstances were so different, once again we were united. Sharing our personal and deepest shame with each other has made us both realise that there really isn't anything we need to keep back from each other in future. That was strangely liberating in a way.

I don't know if I can ever truly forgive myself for the decision I made about the baby, but Laurel told me that I have to acknowledge my grief and try to find a kind of peace within myself. In the same way that Laurel has had to make peace with her decision not to be at the beck and call of her special ability.

It's funny, if someone had asked me if I could choose to be anyone else, who would I be? It would have been Laurel, without a moment's hesitation. Being on the outside and looking in, even though we were close, her life seemed so perfect. She had Dan, they knew where they were going together and everything was just so well organised and purposeful. After they split I needed them to get back together to prove to myself that true happiness does exist, that it really is attainable. To give *me* hope! It gets even more complicated, and I'm being *very* honest here. Every man I ever met, I compared to Dan and when they didn't measure up, I walked away telling myself I was disappointed. The truth is, that was just my excuse. Dan is lush, but of course there is only one Dan. I guess I really wasn't ready to bare my soul to anyone or face the truth about some of the decisions I made in the past.

Talking with Laurel and unpicking the big mess it had all become in my head was a huge relief because every little piece we unravelled, we analysed. Gradually this "huge" knot I had been carrying around inside me was broken down into small, manageable – although unpleasant – emotions. However, it gave me the courage to sit down with Pete on our third date and bare my soul to him. OK, perhaps I've skipped forward a bit too far and I need to explain how we got to date number three.

Pete turned out to be Mr Persistent. I think Steve and Laurel had something to do with it and conspired together, becoming go-betweens. Pete seemed to know my every move and whenever I turned around, he was either there smiling at me, or there was a bouquet of flowers, or chocolates or balloons being delivered. I knew why, so I knew he wasn't just freakily stalking me. It was like the moment Dan first saw Laurel. When Steve introduced me to Pete, I knew instantly and so did he. That magic thing just happened between us! That was why he told me straight away about his wife's death and about his son, Nathan. The way he did it was very matter-of-fact, this is what happened and this is where I am, sort of thing. He said I needed to know because he wanted me to feel I could walk away there and then. He actually said 'but if you stay, you can't hold me responsible if I make you fall in love with me'.

For the first time in years, I had met a man I didn't have to measure up to Dan. He was someone worth knowing in his own right. That was why I was scared and that was why I couldn't say 'yes' to a date.

Of course, once Laurel knew everything and, with Steve realising what this meant to his best mate Pete, I didn't stand a chance. I finally gave in and date number one was like meeting up with a long-lost friend. On date number two I met baby Nathan and my heart melted.

So, on date number three I wanted to bare my soul, to tell Pete everything about me, so that I could match up to his honesty and give him his chance to walk away from me. Instead of judging me, he compared my experience to having lost someone. He made me feel like I too was a victim, rather than just the perpetrator of a terrible deed. He made me see that when you make a choice, you can only do that based upon the options you think you have open to you at that particular moment. He also said that we all do things at times that we look back on and would change if we could. Thankfully, most are relatively minor in the grand scheme of things, but even if it's major, we have to get it into perspective. He said the world isn't perfect and neither are we, we just have to do the very best we can whilst we're here. It was at that particular moment that we both knew unequivocally that we were destined to be together. And I realised that, this time, I wouldn't be running away.

It had to be Breakfast at Tiffany's
– why couldn't it have been Grease?

Laurel loves the old classic films, in truth we both do, but I don't go around admitting that. She usually cries, but that's OK. As soon as she told me we were going to see the stage adaptation of Truman Capote's classic novel *Breakfast at Tiffany's*, my heart dropped into my boots. Silly, I know. What difference could any show make to the success of our first opportunity for a reconciliation? I just wish it wasn't a tear-jerker.

We rendezvous at London Paddington station and literally run towards each other as soon as our eyes meet in the crowd. I lift her up and swing her around, oblivious to the stares of people around us. Here is my Laurel and she wants to spend this weekend with *me*. This is it, this is the start of getting things back on track, man!

She's wearing skinny jeans and a long, pale grey jumper dress thing over the top. She wears her hair short now and it looks real cute. Her face is just one big smile. As I grab her suitcase and we start walking towards the tube, she nestles against my arm. Any thoughts of a jinx is left far behind, nothing can spoil this.

The hotel is one of the smartest in Knightsbridge. We're given a suite and there's a bedroom with two single beds (how ironic is that?) and a separate sitting room. The bathroom is huge, with a tub and a double walk-in shower cubicle.

The minute the porter leaves and shuts the door, I find

myself just standing here, looking at her. I can't believe we're together again, even if it's only for a short while.

'You're looking so good,' she says and she kisses my cheek, softly. 'The vitamins worked then!'

'Yeah, I'm fine now. You look delicious as always,' I say, and she laughs. I always used to say that and she had a standard retort, but she doesn't use it today.

'Thanks for saying "yes" to this weekend. It was a bit out of the blue and I didn't know if you'd feel awkward about it.' She's a bit uncomfortable.

'Hey, it's you and me. What's to feel uncomfortable about, Babe? We'll just take it a step at a time and have some fun.' I've obviously said the right thing, because she comes over and puts her arms around me.

'I've missed you, hunky,' she says and her voice wavers.

I've decided that I can't walk on eggshells all weekend and worry about every little thing I'm going to say. I'm just going to say what comes naturally and hope, really hope, I get it right.

'Hey girl, I missed you too. Getting together like this means so much, it's great of your parents, say thanks to them from me.'

'I think they've missed you too,' she says and I'm starting to feel choked.

By the time we unpack our things and sit and have a coffee, we're feeling much more relaxed. We sit out on the balcony and although there's a fair bit of noise from the traffic below, it's exciting. We're both buzzing, but trying to keep calm and keep our emotions in check. Getting ready for the show is awkward. Laurel uses the bathroom first whilst I kill time fiddling with the remote on the TV. When she finishes, I have a shower and by seven o'clock we're ready to be picked up and taken to the theatre.

I have to say, she looks totally gorgeous when she

eventually comes out of the bedroom. She loves dressing up for special occasions, it's usually the only time she ever wears a dress and this one is really sexy. Black with bare shoulders and slit to the thigh. She holds out a little white jacket and I help her into it. She's wearing her favourite perfume, the one I buy her every Christmas, and it brings a lump to my throat. What's wrong with me?

Steffy took my best suit to the cleaners and ironed a white shirt she found in my wardrobe. I can't even recall ever having worn it before. She also chose my tie. I can see that Laurel is really impressed and I must admit I feel really good. I've even put tissues in my pocket for the bit where Holly Golightly kicks Cat out of the taxicab – Laurel always cries at that point.

The show is actually a little more light-hearted than the film and, apart from the odd tear here and there, we laugh quite a bit. Laurel is really happy and chattering away just like old times. But I'm nervous. I don't really know why, perhaps it's pressure about making sure I do and say the right things, but it's making me awkward and I'd vowed that wouldn't happen.

Our champagne supper is in the main restaurant at the hotel and we slip up to the room to take off our coats, before heading straight back down to our table. The restaurant is full, but the tables are placed at a discreet distance to each other, so it feels very intimate and cosy. I nod to the waiter to let him know I can dispense the wine adequately myself and I think he gets the message. There's a bit of a silence and we're both clearly thinking about what we should say next. Our eyes meet and we suddenly start laughing at ourselves.

'It's like we're on our first date!' Laurel says, giggling.

'No, worse than the first date. I already had a few beers under my belt before I started talking to you that night!'

She laughs, but realises I'm serious. 'I couldn't take my eyes off you,' she says.

'Ah Babe, you're only saying that to make me feel better,' I say and the old banter seems to be coming back to me.

'So, what've you been up to?' She raises her wine glass to her lips and looks across at me, for a second I can see that her hand is shaking, ever so slightly.

'Work mostly. It went from not getting paid at all, but having to work all hours because we were desperate, to getting paid loads of money and having to work all hours to keep pace with the demand. Same difference really, just everyone's in a better mood these days.' I'm trying to make light of it, to disguise the ongoing feelings of guilt I still have.

'You still sharing with Karl?' she asks, but I can see as soon as she says it that she regrets it. I realise she's being cautious too.

'Yeah, Tony moved out so it's just Karl and me now. I suppose at some point I need to decide what I'm doing next – not sure if Brighton's really where I want to be. I'm back to working from home most of the time, so I could be based anywhere more or less, within an hour or two's drive.'

'Sean and Chris made it up for good this time then?'

'Yeah, I think this frightened them. They realised they would lose everything, including their homes. I think there was family pressure on them to turn it around. Sean's been great, he blames himself for ...' I've led myself up a path I don't want to take, so I take a big gulp of wine and Laurel diplomatically changes the subject.

'Lennie's doing well, I've got some news you just won't believe.' It's strange but I haven't had a moment to think of the things I'd actually planned to say to Laurel and one of them was to ask about Lennie.

'I don't think I could be surprised at anything you say about Lennie. She's not the most predictable person we know, is she?' We both laugh. Lennie can be described as whacky sometimes, overly-sentimental on occasion and frequently stubborn. All that rolled into one person! The more I think about it, the more convinced I am that she's Cupcake, even if it only comes from her subconscious thoughts.

'She's seeing someone. Not sure of the exact number of dates they've had now, but they're well into double digits.'

'No! You're kidding! She never goes beyond date number three! What's the catch?'

'No catch. His name is Pete and they just hit it off. He lost his wife last year to ovarian cancer and he's got a little boy.'

'Wow, that's pretty full-on for Lennie. This is the same Lennie we're talking about here, is it? The little Miss-I-can't-commit who seems to always pick the, well, weird ones.'

'Yeah, it's Lennie all right and you probably wouldn't recognise her any more. She's changed a lot lately, matured. I guess everyone gets there in their own time and it just took Lennie a little longer than most.'

I'm really surprised. Particularly because, if she's really involved with a guy, she's unlikely to have been spending much time sending me kindly telepathic thought waves!

'So, how's she feeling about us now?' I'm not sure that came out as naturally as I hoped it would, but it's too late now. Laurel looks at me and I see a slight frown.

'How d'you mean?' Oh. Not so smooth then.

'Um, you know. She was upset. We were like her second family, you know.' Good thinking, Dan! That was a smooth recovery.

'Yeah, you're right. She was a bit "off" for a while, but

her feet haven't touched the ground lately. She's so good with Nathan, Pete's little boy, and they spend every spare minute together. I haven't seen her for probably three weeks now, but I speak to her on the phone most days.' Laurel looks a bit sad and I realise she might actually be feeling a bit lonely.

'So, work busy for you at the moment?'

'It's been OK. A friend is helping me trace my family tree and I found a relative who's living in California, who Dad didn't even know existed. He's been very excited about it.'

Two waiters appear from nowhere and take away the appetiser plates. With a flourish, they place the main course in front of us. All I can think of is, why does Laurel always change the subject when I try to talk about her work? I realise she always did that before, like she doesn't want to share that part of her life with me and, for the first time, I feel a bit annoyed. We both make the appropriate sounds in response to the beautifully presented food and the waiters finally leave us in peace.

'I didn't know you were interested in genealogy, you never mentioned it before,' I say casually.

'No, it was just one of those things that someone mentioned in a conversation and I thought, why not? I've got time on my hands at the moment and it's fun. Lots of skeletons in the cupboard – no, I'm only joking,' she says, putting her hand on my arm and she gives me one of her beaming smiles.

'So, your friend is an expert or is it a hobby?' For some reason she doesn't seem to like that question and she pretends to be finishing off some food before she answers.

'Sort of a hobby, it's just something he enjoys doing.' She takes another fork full of food and we both eat in silence for a few minutes.

'I see. Meet him at work?' Now it's awkward.

'Not really, we met at his thirtieth birthday party. Lennie was invited and asked me to tag along. He works with Lennie, he's a doctor.'

'Oh, right. Sounds like a very clever guy.' Laurel puts down her fork and looks directly at me.

'Look Dan, I'm not going to feel awkward. I think we both need to talk about what's happening in our lives at the moment and Steve just happens to be a friend. I don't want you to get the wrong impression, that's all.' Wow, this *is* awkward.

'Hey Babe, I wasn't grilling you and I wasn't trying to imply ... I'm cool, I understand.'

She picks her fork up again and levels a question at me. 'So, there are always plenty of females around you – what's been happening?' I can't tell her about Cupcake or Grace, because she'll think I've lost the plot. The only female around me at the moment is Steffy and I don't *want* to talk about her, but I've got no choice.

'You know me, I've been burying myself in work. Usual boring stuff. This old friend from uni turned up and just happens to be Sean and Chris's niece. Small world. She's still a pain in the ass though, like the annoying kid sister you'd prefer not to have around too much.'

Laurel laughs. 'Not the Goth? The one you told me about, who nearly got you thrown out of university after she was caught climbing in through your dorm window?'

'Yeah, the very one, Steffy. Except she's changed a bit and it's not for the better. She's even more outlandish now. She's going through a gay phase at the moment.' We both burst out laughing and the awkwardness starts to melt away again.

We end up talking about the past, bringing up stories that make us both laugh until our stomachs ache. I'm not sure we impressed the waiters and I'm not sure how much of it was down to the champagne and the wine. Heading

144

back to our room, we're both just a little bit tipsy and it isn't until we're inside the room that we both realise there's a decision to be made here. Laurel leans back against the door and looks at me, raising her eyebrows as if to say 'what now?' I want to kiss her, but I don't know if that's what she's expecting.

'Look, Babe, it's been a while. I'd love to jump into bed with you just like nothing's happened, but we'd be kidding ourselves. I was so made up about spending time with you, I haven't thought this all the way through. Guess you're not surprised, that sort of sums me up, doesn't it?' She's looking at me with those mesmerising, pale blue eyes of hers and, as usual, I have absolutely no idea what she's thinking.

'I hoped it would all fall into place and we'd just know what we wanted to do,' she says and I can hear the disappointment in her voice.

'So, I guess I've blown it then: if we have to talk about it, then perhaps now isn't the right time?'

'Guess so,' she says and I can't tell if she's disappointed or relieved. Heck, for that matter, am I disappointed or relieved? The answer is that I'm too nervous to say for sure. For some reason though, I decide to kiss her anyway and she just melts against me, there's no resistance. Oh, this is going to be *so* difficult!

'C'mon,' I say, 'we'll push the beds together and snuggle up. It's good we don't want to make any mistakes – there's too much to lose, but I need to be close to you tonight.' Her answer is so soft and quiet, I have to lean in real close.

'Me too, Dan, me too!'

We lay in the dark, facing each other. Suddenly we're both very sober.

'Things have moved on a bit, haven't they?' I whisper. I can just about see her face in the gloom.

'I guess we should have expected that. Are you disappointed?'

Somehow it's easier to be honest in the dark. 'Yes and no. If something hadn't changed, then I realise maybe we wouldn't still have a chance, but it's like I don't know the real you any more, Babe.'

'Hey, that's exactly it! I feel scared to think you have a life now that I don't know anything about and it feels wrong somehow. Am I really so different?' she asks.

'More than I think you realise. You've always been so sure of everything, you never hesitated and Lennie and I just followed along behind you, in awe.'

She sighs. 'But that's just it. No one ever thought to stop me, to challenge my direction, to make me stand back and think!' There's a real sadness in her voice and anguish too. It's painful to hear.

'But I thought you were happy, Babe, and you were the strong one, that's who you are. You like things to be done in a certain way and what's wrong with that? You keep the rest of us in line.'

She sits up and puts her head in her hands. 'Listen to what you're saying, Dan. You're telling me our relationship was based on you doing exactly what I told you to do. Didn't you mind that? Don't you have ideas of your own?'

She's getting this way out of perspective, but I don't know how to say that without making her feel I'm downplaying it.

'That's it Babe – I liked the way we were. You organised me, you had the vision for both of us.'

'And look how that ended! Lennie held something back from me for years just because she was scared I would judge her. She thinks I'm perfect, that I can't do anything wrong. That doesn't make me feel good. Dan, it makes me feel shut out.'

I sit up next to her and put my arm around her

146

shoulders. 'You're the centre of our lives, Laurel. You kept us going even though both Lennie and I were struggling with our own demons. We don't have the vision of the future that you do and without it, it's hard to know what the next step should be.'

'But no one realises I'm *not* strong, not underneath it all. I need my life to have routine and be organised, because that's *my* coping mechanism. That's how I keep moving forward. People assume that means I'm in control, but I'm not, not really. It's isolated me – that's why Lennie held on to her problem for years, too worried to share it, in case I thought less of her. That's why you couldn't talk to me about work and being broke. You both felt you were letting me down in some way, but I'm the real failure here. Suddenly I stood back and I realised I was like a train thundering along to its destination, oblivious of everything going on around. I never stopped to ask myself whether where I was heading was really where I wanted to go.'

I make a move to hold her closer but she gently pushes me away.

'No, listen to me, please. Hear me out because I can only say this once. When my Dad walked out on my Mum all those years ago, she had no choice but to put on a brave face and cope. When you have a young baby and you're suddenly on your own, you do what you have to, in order to survive. She became this person who took the knocks, but never let it touch her, inside. She hated men because she thought that all of them, including her own father, had let her down. She was my role model, so I thought you had to develop this "driven" approach to life, to make it all work. But underneath I wasn't making conscious decisions, I wasn't evaluating what was going on. I had it in my head that I would have a different life than the one I had as a child. I would make a relationship work and be happy. I would have a family of my own. Can you hear the problem with all this? It's all "I" or "I would", there never was any "you" in any of it. I never asked you what you wanted, because nothing could get in the way of my goal.'

Now I'm horrified. 'Laurel, what are you saying exactly? Are you saying you didn't love me or you didn't really need me?'

She realises her words have stung and I can feel her mood soften slightly.

'No Dan, I fell in love with you the moment I first saw you. It's just that, the reasons we worked as a couple were the wrong reasons. I told you what to do and you did it. You were like my big, strong protector and for the first time in my life, I had a man around me who I could really trust and who trusted me implicitly. But you trusted me too much and you just handed over your life, as if there was no way I could do anything wrong or hurt you in any way. When I saw your strength crumbling away, I knew things were going badly wrong somewhere, but I couldn't ask and you couldn't tell me. That was how our relationship worked. Then, when I started to feel this absurd anger with you for failing me, it was because I felt that all I had ever asked of you was to be strong and there you were, just falling apart. Except the reality was, I'd asked everything of you and you'd given me everything in return. When you really needed something from me – compassion and understanding – I told you to get out.'

The sudden quietness is almost like a humming in my ears.

'But I didn't ask you for anything, Laurel, so how can you possibly say you failed me? I failed you because I was running away from everything instead of facing up to it.'

'You still don't get it, do you? As depressed and afraid as you had become, you were more afraid of admitting

148

it to me. That's not how a relationship should work, Dan. In fact, a lot of people would say, that was no relationship at all.'

'But Babe, I love you and I don't care about any of that. We can learn from what we did wrong – both of us. As long as we both feel the same.' My voice is wavering, I sound like I'm begging and all I want to do is grab her and show her how I feel.

'I think I still love you too, you know. But this fairytale family life I thought I wanted so badly, suddenly seems like the last thing I need at this particular moment. I thought I needed all that to keep me safe, to give me security, so I wouldn't get hurt and the future would be all neatly mapped out. Now I know I can't go down that route, until I'm certain that I won't make the same mistakes again. I've got to find myself and my own strength. I've got to learn that it's OK to make a wrong decision and if, for the moment, it only affects me, then I might have a chance. I don't want to turn into my mother, blaming men for the way her life has turned out. I can see now that she was a big part of the problem. Dad and I have been a lot closer recently and I realised something that hadn't occurred to me before. In all the years, with all the bitter remarks Mum has thrown at him, he has never ever said anything critical to me about her. I know he wasn't around very often when I was young, but looking back now I can see why. Mum didn't make him welcome, so he kept his visits brief. That's no way for a child to grow up and I can't risk history repeating itself. I won't risk you ending up leaving me just because I pushed you too far.'

'I think I need a drink,' I say sadly. I hold out my hand to her and we both walk into the sitting room. I reach for the switch on the side light, but she stops me.

'No, let's get a drink and go out onto the balcony,' and

I can just about make out a watery smile aimed in my direction. I grab some miniature vodkas and a can of tomato juice from the mini-bar; Laurel grabs two glasses and some ice, and we slide back the glass doors. Outside the air is sultry. The sky is like a swathe of deep navy blue fabric and the stars look like someone has thrown diamond dust all over it. How can we be here, so unhappy, beneath this magnificence, I ask myself?

'It's lovely, isn't it?' she says softly, looking up at the heavens and we put down our drinks and hold each other.

It's like we're two completely different people that I don't even recognise and I'm frightened. Everything I thought we had and everything I hoped we were going to have, is suddenly turned upside down. My brain is buzzing as I'm trying to work through everything she said, but my body is holding her as if my life depends on it.

'It's not over, Babe, we just gotta start again. From the beginning and make it right this time. You said yourself you think you still love me. That's a good starting point, isn't it? Some people search all their lives for someone to fall in love with and it just doesn't happen, so fate must have put us together for some reason.'

'I never thought about it like that. I'm sorry – I didn't mean to just pour it all out. It's all been going around in my head for weeks and weeks, but it was jumbled. I guess I'm as surprised as you really, some of the stuff I said was buried really deep. Can we just get drunk and go to bed?'

'Now that's an offer I definitely can't refuse!'

The night was only just beginning and, don't get me wrong, it was great! But I had this niggling feeling in the back of my mind, like I'd signed up for something without understanding the terms and conditions. Does that sound as absurd to you as it does to me?

The turning point

Reaching a 'turning point' in your life is an awesome moment. The stage at which things really do change, for ever. The weekend away was that sort of a moment for Laurel and me, the start of moving forward. We decided that we're gonna ring each other every day at seven o'clock and we're gonna talk – tell each other the highs and lows of our day. Share things. Laurel is coming down at the end of the month so we can spend the weekend together and pick up where we left off.

I'm happy, very happy, course I am. It's just that, when I told Laurel I liked our relationship the way it was, I meant it. See, I think we split up because I don't cope with stress well. I'd been working so hard just trying to keep things going, it was easy for me to ignore the reality of the situation. Yes, I was on the brink of losing my job and yes, I was virtually broke because Jupiter Live weren't able to pay me, but none of that was Laurel's fault. And not talking to Laurel about it wasn't because I felt I couldn't, but because that was me just being me! When she started to pour her heart out in the hotel room, she said our relationship wasn't working and that came as a shock. I thought our split was because Laurel was sick and tired of me being moody and constantly working, so obviously I hadn't been giving her the attention she deserved. Suddenly, I find that's not what it was all about and now she wants to become this whole new person, so she can live her life in a different way! I keep going over some of the things she said and she threw in that I was 'scared of her'. Potentially everyone's a bit scary when they get angry and lose it, aren't they? Actually, I *am* scared now, because what if she changes beyond all recognition? It's like I've finally found what I've been looking for, but now I've got it, I don't really recognise it any more.

Our weekend started out well and ended well (too well in fact). The middle bit confused the hell out of me and I'm not sure how relevant or important that is. I've decided to give Lennie a ring for a casual chat and see what Laurel told her about the weekend.

'Hey girl, what're you up to?'

She shrieks in my ear and I have to hold the phone at arm's length until she stops. 'Dan! It's you! Oh, I wish you were here, so I could hug you! Have you just spoken to Laurel?'

'No, not until this evening, why?'

'She was just telling me about your sexy weekend. She's so happy, I haven't seen her like this for a long time! She was going to see how you felt about Pete and me dropping in on you both at the end of the month, when she's down with you. It would only be for a couple of hours, but I *really* want you to meet Pete and Nathan.' She's babbling on so fast, I have to listen really hard to keep up.

'Sure, yes, congrats! Wow! So, Laurel had a good time then?'

Lennie laughs and splutters. 'Ye...ssss!! She didn't tell me everything of course and the drunken bit at the end was a bit hazy ... but she's got her glow back again and she can't wait for the end of the month!'

Seems like everything is fine then, perhaps I'm panicking a bit – looking for problems because it all looks so promising.

'Great. I must admit I can't remember everything myself, 'cause it did get a bit wild there for a moment.' We both laugh and I can hear a real, honest happiness in Lennie's voice.

'Welcome back, big guy – not before time! Anyway, you'll love Pete – he's so ... perfect!' She's on a high, but the word 'perfect' just sets me off thinking about some of the things Laurel said. According to her, 'perfect' is not good, so is this something I should worry about for Lennie? Anyway, there's something else I need to ask while I've got the chance.

'Can't wait, looking forward to it. Lennie, do you believe in telepathy?'

'That's an odd question to ask. Not really, so much easier to pick up the phone and it's quicker! Why?'

'Nothing really. I've missed you being around to talk to, like we used to do. Just wondered if you'd felt like that at all?'

'Softie. Course I've missed you like mad and course I've thought of you loads, more than you realise. But Laurel's needed a lot of support and then meeting Pete – I haven't had a moment to catch my breath for ages. And then work's been chaotic, but I didn't mean to lose touch after the Brighton thing, honest.'

'No, no it's not that. I meant to say a really big thank you for arranging that meeting, after all, it led to this! Speaking of work, I hear Steve's helping Laurel trace her family tree – sounds like a clever guy!'

'Yeah, he's the one who introduced me to Pete. Actually, it was at Steve's thirtieth birthday party – I went with Laurel. Steve's OK, his Mum thinks he's a closet homosexual because he isn't married!' She giggles, as if it's a joke everyone's privy to.

'Is he?' I ask, hoping she's going to say 'yes'.

'No, well – I don't think so. He dates a lot, but I'd say he was a classic commitment-phobe. Definitely the bachelor type, likes his own space, but a great mate. He came out with us girls on a hen night last week!'

'I thought men weren't allowed on those things?'

'Oh, we treat him like one of the girls, nobody minds. Laurel's really grateful, because all this family tree stuff has given her something to share with her Dad and they're getting on really well because of it. Her Mum doesn't know though.'

'Glad you said, just in case I put my foot in it!'

'I think you could get away with just about anything at the moment ... hey, what was that noise?' Lennie hears a loud bang down the phone line.

'Just a door slamming, I'd better go – I need to go and shut the bedroom window. Wind's blowing up here. Great talking to you, girl. See you in a couple of weeks.' I put the phone down with relief.

'Cupcake – did you have to do that?' There's no window open, I lied. Cupcake has been playing up all morning. The noise was the door in the hallway slamming shut – it's the third time in the last hour and it's driving me nuts. I've been trying to work, but she obviously wants my attention and I don't know why. She was quiet for most of last week and there was no sign of her at all when I was in London. Since I've been back though, it's a different matter. Last night when I rang Laurel, I actually sat in the car so I was sure I wouldn't get any interruptions.

Talking to Lennie just now was the right thing to do, I'm worrying about nothing – it all feels good. It's not easy for me to relax at the moment and I'm beginning to see that's mainly down to Cupcake. She does sort of fit with Lennie's over-exuberant and chaotic style and I'm wondering if the last day or two is reflecting all of the emotions Lennie is finally letting out. On the phone she sounded like she'd OD'd on coffee or something! Another door slams shut and I jump. No wonder I can't relax.

'Cupcake, I don't know what you want, but you're driving

me mad! I'm going out to post some letters, try and get a grip before I get back please. I've got a lot of work to do this afternoon.'

I leave the flat thinking I've got to be mad, talking to an empty room. It must have been the right thing to do though, because the afternoon is fine and as I pick up the phone to call Laurel, I'm pleased with how much I've managed to get done.

'Hey Babe, it's me.'

'I've been sitting here, next to the phone, daydreaming about you! How's your day been?' Laurel sounds happy.

'Good, actually. I rang Lennie and we had a chat, like old times. I popped out for a bit of fresh air and walked up to post some letters. I bought you something, saw it in a shop window.'

'Oooh, what is it? Tell me!'

I laugh, she sounds so happy and upbeat and it's good. 'No, you have to wait. I've done really well this afternoon and I think Sean will love something I've put together for this new Art Gallery launch. I'm really in my stride, I've got a creative flow going on. That's all down to you, Babe!'

'Awww ... I wish I was there with you.'

'How about you?'

'Morning shift today and we were busy. We had eighteen day surgeries, small operations so they're in and out the same day, so it was all go. I had to take the car in for a service and while I was waiting, I called into the bookshop and bought this really cool book for recording family events. A bit like years ago when everyone had a family bible and at the front they'd write the history of the family as it happened.'

'You're really hooked, aren't you?'

'It's fun actually and Dad loves it. He's the last male on his side of the family and if I get married there's no one to carry on the name. I'm doing this for him – it's my gift to let him know I care, after everything that's happened over the years.'

'Oh Babe, that's so good to hear you say that. I always wanted to talk to you about your Dad, but your Mum just hates him and I didn't want to upset you. Whenever I saw him I always thought he was a decent bloke and he was just trying to get close to you. Everyone makes mistakes, but even I could see he loves you, no matter what went on before.'

'Do you realise we never, ever talked like this when we were together? I wonder why.'

'I guess we ended up taking each other for granted. It happens. We had our wake-up call and we're doing something about it.'

'Yeah, I suppose you're right. I miss you so much now, it hurts not being with you.'

'Same here, Babe. But you know what they say.'

'What?'

'Absence makes the heart grow fonder!'

'Was that "absence" or "abstinence"?'

'Heh, heh, behave yourself, Babe. Three weeks to go before I get my hands on you again.' She sighs. I've been worrying about nothing and it really is getting back to normal between us.

When I put the phone down and turn around, I suddenly feel very cold and slightly nauseous. Something is definitely in the room with me. I swear I hear words, softly spoken and I'm straining to listen, but I just can't make them out. I get goose bumps – like something is crawling over my skin and I feel it from my head right down to my toes. The hairs on my arms even feel weird, like static. I realise I'm feeling very uncomfortable being alone in this room, but just as I'm deciding what to do, Steffy bursts in.

'Hey Dude, I've come to cook you a meal.' Usually I'd be groaning, but today I feel like she's saved me – but from what exactly, I really don't know.

My big sister

When I was very young, I couldn't understand why Mya always got to do the new stuff first. When I was five, I clearly remember walking to school holding Mum's hand, but Mya was allowed to walk on ahead with her own friends. I asked Mum why I couldn't do that and Mum said it was because Mya was ten years old and a big girl. She said when I was ten, I too would be allowed to walk to school with my friends.

In my head I worked out that there was a five-year difference between us both and I was very excited, because I thought I would eventually catch up. But when Mum explained that Mya would *always* be five years older than me, I was really upset. I remember saying, 'What's the point of me growing up if Mya's always going to be five years older than me?' At the time, that realisation seemed so unfair, although I can't for the life of me see why now. But that was then. Mum simply laughed, tweaked my nose and said, 'Ah, but when Mya's old, you'll still always be five years younger!' As if that made a difference. She went on chuckling as we walked, but I was distraught. For the first time, I saw that I would *never* get to be the first one to do *anything*. And that really hurt, it made me feel like I would never be important, ever.

Of course, no one around me ever stopped to think about the way a younger sibling's mind works and throughout my childhood and teens I always felt like I was walking in Mya's footsteps. Nothing I ever did seemed to surprise anyone. Oh, I had my fair share of 'well done' and 'what a clever girl', because I did well at school. But I never seemed to be able to find anything to do that was unique, something the family would acknowledge was especially my achievement. Silly isn't it? I suppose that's what the phrase 'sibling rivalry' means. Oh, there was a bit of hair pulling when we were very young, but we never really quarrelled much. Actually, my teens weren't too bad either, because Mya had been the one testing the water and trying to push the boundaries our parents established. So, by the time I was at that tricky point in my development, the curfew was already set and things were sorted. As long as I obeyed the rules, which I did, we all had a quiet life. I didn't have to battle for anything like Mya had done and I came to see that there was a benefit in being the youngest after all!

There were a few years when it still rankled a bit and I wondered what it would be like to go and do something totally off the wall. Just to get that little 'I did it first' badge. It didn't happen of course, because out of the two of us, I was always the quieter one. Making trouble just isn't in my nature. Also, I couldn't complain, because Mya was simply very good at being a big sister. She looked out for me at school during the years when we were both at the same school. So, when I was one of the littlest ones in school, I had the luxury of a big sister in one of the top classes who made sure nobody picked on me. I know some of my friends used to envy me that advantage, but I guess I never really appreciated her in the way that I should have done. I never really acknowledged her support.

I was seventeen when Mya met Sam. It was Mya's first really serious relationship and they were together for about three years before the accident. She was driving home from work one day and suddenly it happened, a car ploughed into the back of her when she was waiting to make a right-hand turn. It was a fast road, it was raining and it was dark. The driver who hit her was taking avoiding action, because a cyclist had hit a pot-hole in the road and fallen in front of him. He didn't hit the cyclist, but he did collide with Mya.

We received the call that she'd been taken to the local Accident and Emergency centre and that she wasn't badly hurt, just very shaken up and a bit bruised. She had been lucky. She had a stiff neck, which they said was mild whiplash, a painful bump on the side of her head and a sprained wrist. They did a CT scan just to check that the bump on her head wasn't anything more serious and she was discharged with some pain medication.

I remember the relief when we all arrived home. Dad drove Mum and Mya back and I followed in Sam's car. I burst into tears as soon as I got inside his car and he was great. At the age of twenty I hadn't experienced any real traumas before and the shock was enormous. He just talked to me very calmly and by the time we were walking into the house, I had it under control.

I think we all said a little prayer of thanks when we saw the state of Mya's car. She was lucky to be alive. Except that, as the days went on, we all started to get concerned. The hospital had given her a list of symptoms to watch out for and if she experienced any of them she was to go back immediately. Mya thought the tiredness was just a reaction to the shock of the accident and then she insisted her headaches were because she wasn't sleeping well. She suddenly became very poorly and Mum and Dad ended up rushing her back to A&E late one Friday night, about a month later.

It's not easy to recount all that's happened, because a lot of it is based around horrible sounding medical terms that don't mean a thing to most of us. Mya was diagnosed as having a 'chronic subdural haematoma'. The Consultant explained that this sometimes happens after a head injury where there is bleeding, but the blood collects slowly. It wouldn't have shown up on the first CT scan. By the time Mya was admitted to hospital she was drowsy and confused and we were all terrified. They rushed her in for another CT scan and the Consultant spoke to Mum and Dad in a side room. Afterwards they told me that Mya was going to have an operation, but that the Consultant was very optimistic everything would be fine. They didn't tell me until later that the operation involved actually drilling some holes in Mya's head where the bleed was, to allow them to remove the blood. The holes were then closed up using stitches.

Mya seemed to be recovering well, although she had a permanent headache for several days after the op. But she was bright and chatty, so we were all just really thankful. We were told she would probably be coming home some time in the following week, if she kept up the good progress. Then Mya started to feel unwell again, but this time she had a very high fever, chest pain and a cough. She kept getting the shakes and it was horrible to watch. They told Mum and Dad that she had developed bacterial pneumonia – it had some long fancy name – but that they expected her to respond quickly to strong antibiotics.

The day I got the phone call I was in work, training one of the new recruits on how to enter data onto the system; it was an ordinary day. Dad told me to go straight home. I knew from his voice something bad had happened, but everyone had been so positive the night before, I couldn't believe it was going to be really bad news.

As soon as I walked into the sitting room at home, I looked at Sam, Mum and Dad and I thought, that's it – she's dead! It was exactly eight months and one week ago.

A *twilight world*

We all drove to the hospital together in Dad's car. Mya had been moved into a special unit attached to Intensive Care. We stood around her bed as the Consultant explained things to us and the reality hit as soon as we saw her that day. This was different. Before, she had been talkative, even through the pain and the high temperatures, the coughing and the chills. She always knew we were there next to her and we talked about normal things, to get away from what was going on around her. Suddenly, it was like this patient wasn't my sister Mya at all. It looked like her, but she wasn't 'there'. No activity inside. Like watching someone when they're asleep and you know the familiar shape of their face, the shape of their hands on top of the bed cover. It isn't until they wake up that it's really them and they smile and laugh and do all the things that make them who they are. But I still couldn't believe what he was trying to tell us.

'Mya has lapsed into what is known as a vegetative state. It's not a coma and there is hope of a recovery. We will be maintaining her care and joint mobility and we will be continually assessing her level of consciousness. Sometimes it's the body's way of resting, to aid recovery. Mya has been through quite an ordeal and we are still very happy with the results of the surgery. The latest CT scan shows no sign of any further bleed into the brain. The pneumonia is responding well to the antibiotics and her breathing is much improved. She has become a little dehydrated, so we are giving her intravenous fluids at the moment, but that drip will come out later today. Are there any specific questions you would like to ask?' We stood there like wooden statues, hardly daring to breath and break the silence. I looked at Mya and just couldn't believe what he'd said.

'But her eyes move sometimes, I saw it, just now. She could just be asleep, she was so tired yesterday. You said she's been through a lot, you could have made a mistake.' Mum came up and put her arms around me. Mr Whittaker gave me a sad little smile that said it all.

'I know how it must appear to you. She looks conscious, sometimes she will open and close her eyes as if she has a sleeping cycle. She is breathing on her own, her circulation is stable and you can expect her to move occasionally if her limbs become stiff. Our specialist nursing staff will ensure she is comfortable, they will turn her so she doesn't develop any sores. What you have to accept is that her mind is not functioning properly at the moment and she's not exhibiting signs of discriminative perception. For instance, she doesn't smile when you walk into the room and this indicates a lack of recognition. She can't reach out for an object or respond to a question. She is able to make a range of spontaneous movements, but at the moment those movements are not a meaningful reaction on Mya's part. We are hopeful that this may be a transient state, that once the infection is clear and Mya has had the chance to recover fully from the effects of the operation, her level of responsiveness will gradually increase. However, there are no guarantees and we can only take this one day at a time. One of the specialist nurses who will be looking after Mya will come in directly to speak to you. If you have any concerns I am always happy to come along and talk to you at any time.' He shook Dad's hand and left. We all stood around in shock, everyone looking at Mya as if she was suddenly going to wake up and things would be back to normal.

I remember very clearly that the nurse who walked in had a lovely smile. It lit up the room. It was almost a relief in a way, because the atmosphere had been so tense that it felt like someone had died. I think we were all thinking the same thing – that really there was no hope. Mya had just gone downhill over the past few weeks and it seemed like it was all going in the wrong direction. As soon as the nurse entered the room, all eyes were on her, she represented hope.

'My name is Leanne, but everyone calls me Lennie. I'll be overseeing Mya's care while she's in an ICU room. Mr Whittaker will have explained that Mya isn't in an actual coma, but this is where we look after patients who are suffering from various levels of reduced consciousness. I understand this is a lot to take in and do please remember that I can sit down and talk to you as a family or individually at any time. You can expect Mya to make sudden movements and at first this can be alarming. One mother told me that every time her son made a movement, however slight or involuntary, she thought that was the second he was going to wake up. Please prepare yourself for that. Always remember, a great number of patients do gain full recovery and eventually go home, able to pick up their lives where they left off.

'Please don't feel you have to be quiet when you are around her and I would encourage you all to make short, frequent visits, rather than prolonged "vigils". In the past, patients who have recovered have indicated they were aware of having family members around them. Sometimes even recalling parts of conversations. It's been compared to being in a dream, where you are convinced everything is real – except in this case it is real, although the patient has limited abilities. We encourage visitors to sit and chat, to hold the patient's hand, if it's something they would normally expect you to do. Treat them as if they are awake, but just unable to talk to you for the moment. We'll be ensuring Mya has all of her medication, we'll be managing her hydration and feeding, as well as using passive joint exercises. With your help in talking to Mya and letting her hear your voices, we hope this will give her the very best chance of recovery.'

Lennie represented a little ray of sunshine, in what had been one of the worst days in the life of our family.

Visiting Mya

We all quickly settled into a visiting routine. Mum goes into the hospital for a couple of hours in the morning before going to work. She likes to help the nurses with Mya's washing and dressing, brushing her hair and little things like that. Being involved with the practical things helps to make her feel useful and that's good. Dad calls in on his way home, late afternoon and he sits and talks to Mya for about half an hour. It's tough for him because he hates hospitals and he misses her so much, they always shared everything. I tend to talk more to Mum, simply because we're both so alike – quiet and a bit reserved. Mya takes after Dad and they're both more outgoing, more noisy – it's a bit of a joke in our house that Mum and I like being on our own sometimes just to get some peace!

Sam and I go in and visit most evenings. Sometimes he comes to our house straight from work and Mum cooks for us all, then we go to the hospital together in his car. Occasionally we meet there, if he's working late or has to pop back to his flat first. It's not easy visiting someone who isn't really aware that you're there with them. If it wasn't for Sam, there would be times when I just wouldn't be able to do it. That makes me feel ashamed, but it's true.

At the weekend, Mum and Dad visit together every Saturday and Sam and I visit on Sunday. We can spend a bit more time and often get involved in Mya's exercises – helping to keep her muscles supple and in working order. We always talk to her while we follow the strict regime of massaging, stretching and flexing.

The lead nurse, Lennie, told us we mustn't feel guilty about having time to ourselves. It's hard though to walk out of the hospital and leave Mya there, then try to pick up your life as if everything's normal. I feel guilty if I find myself laughing and joking around, or if I go out for a few hours and I don't think about Mya at all. It's like, if I forget her – even for a little while – she'll know and she'll think I don't care any more. I couldn't bear that, I just couldn't bear it.

Each visit follows a sort of 'set' pattern, as the weeks turn into months. We spend hours holding her hand, talking to her about the past, watching her face for the slightest sign of a change. I can see the weight she has lost just by looking at her face, but when we help with the muscle exercises it's tough to see how thin her legs and arms have become. Strangely though, her skin still seems to glow and she doesn't look ill at all, she just looks like a doll really. Perfect and little and unreal. Mum is always very particular with her hair and her clothes. She's always buying new things to take in, so Mya always looks lovely.

I remember one visit in particular. Something had been bothering me all week and I needed to say it, but I wasn't sure when would be the right time. I knew that if I didn't do it soon, I probably wouldn't do it at all and living with the guilt of that would have been worse.

'Mya, we all love you so much, everybody loves you because you're so special. You know that, don't you? It's just that, in case you were wondering, it's OK to let go, if you have to, that is.' I remember watching her face and there was no movement, nothing to say she had heard the words I had spoken. A part of me hoped she would hear and realise how hard it was for me to say those words. That she would then make some monumental effort to communicate something back to me. I remember Sam leaning in towards me.

'Sadie, I don't think you should say that,' he half-whispered and I could see that he wasn't angry, just sad.

'I have to,' I said, wiping the tears that were falling down my face. 'Someone has to say it, Sam! Imagine hanging on when you really desperately want to go. It's supposed to be peaceful on the other side and we've got to understand it's up to her, only Mya can decide whether to let go or battle on. We could be holding her back rather than helping her. Don't you see that?' I looked at him apologetically, but I felt better for having had the courage to say what I felt, deep inside.

'I know, Sadie, I know. But we must stay positive.' He put his hand on mine and we sat in silence for a long time afterwards. It was even harder than usual to hug her and leave that day.

The light at the end of the tunnel

I'm meeting Sam now, it's seven-thirty on a rainy, dreary Wednesday evening. I'm hanging around at the hospital entrance, our usual meeting place when Sam's going to be late. We always meet here and go in together. We both realise why, but we haven't acknowledged it, not in words. It's just that, if the day comes and we walk in and she's not there...

I can see him parking his car, he looks tired as he walks across the tarmac towards me, dodging an ambulance on its way out of the car park. He gives me a weak smile and I smile back, trying to look more cheerful than I feel tonight. Must be the weather making everyone feel a bit down.

'Hi Sadie. Are you OK?' He kisses my cheek and I'm glad he can't see that I still blush when he does that.

'I'm good. And you? You look a bit tired tonight.'

'Yeah, didn't sleep too well last night again. Let's go see our girl then!'

We tiptoe into Mya's room – I don't know why we do that, it's not like she's asleep. She has a room of her own still and at this time of the evening they turn off the overhead lights and turn on the wall lights. They give a soft glow that bounces off the ceiling and it makes the room feel much cosier than it does during the day. The overhead lights are harsh and daytime feels much more clinical and cold. Sam moves two of the visitor chairs from the corner and puts one each side of her bed. Karen is the nurse on duty at the moment and she waves out as she walks past the glass partition.

169

'I see Karen's still here,' Sam says, sitting down. I slip off my coat and take the other seat opposite him. We smile at each other. Each visit starts in exactly the same way, there's an awkwardness – not between Sam and me – but in disturbing the heavy silence. Like we'll wake her up by talking in front of her and she'll be cross because she really is just resting. We're fine once we start and I look at Sam, he's good at breaking the ice. It's our pattern, the one we've followed all these months.

'Hi Mya, it's Sadie and Sam again!' He always takes her hand in his, just for a few moments and then gently places it back on the bed. It's the only time he actually touches her, because when we leave he just blows her a kiss. He settles back into his chair and smiles at me, it's always a nervous smile, like he's shy. Always the same.

'Hey, Mya, me again. Nightmare traffic out there tonight and it's raining. That horrible drizzly rain, fogging up the car windows. I look like I've had a perm 'cause my hair's gone so frizzy!' Sam laughs and this time I can see he's beginning to relax.

I always start with something light-hearted. It's so difficult to know what to say, it's not like having a normal conversation, you see, we're searching for the 'key' that will unlock her brain. The months have taken their toll on all of us and we're jaded, exhausted, all out of fresh ideas. There's nothing left to say, but we continue trying and live in hope.

'I saw Melanie at work today, Mya, and she sends her love. She asked if she could pop in to see you, so I thought I'd ask Lennie next time I see her. What do you think, Sadie?' Sam asks.

'I think Mya would like that. I bet she's bored silly with the rest of us! I know I would be! Mel could call in with Mum and Dad at the weekend – see what Lennie says first though.' Sam and I share a look – we're thinking about visitors and infections. We're both paranoid about using the antibacterial wash when we arrive and leave the room.

'When Mya gets well, I've been thinking we should have a party. So many people sending you their thoughts and wishes, Mya, everyone's missing you.' He's trying to sound upbeat, but the tiredness has drained him and I can see he's struggling. Mya moves her legs, shifting her position, but that's all.

We both hear a noise that breaks the heavy silence and turn to see Lennie, standing just inside the doorway. Sam and I exchange a nervous glance, I'm not sure why.

'Hey guys, I've just come on shift. How's Mya doing tonight? Karen tells me she had a very good day. Mya mumbled something just after your Mum left this morning. Has she been quiet since you've been here?' Sam nods and Lennie walks over to check Mya's pulse. Her hands must be cold because Mya suddenly flinches.

'Sorry Mya,' she says, moving her hands away immediately, 'it's quite cold out there now.' She turns to me. 'It's OK, Sadie, you shouldn't feel guilty. No one knows what to say, not really. Mya knows she's loved and I'm sure she knows you're here with her and that you'll all support her, no matter what!'

'Thanks Lennie. It's just that sometimes I feel that I should know what to say because I'm her sister and if it was me in that bed, then Mya would know the right things to say and do.'

Sam reaches across and pats my hand. 'I'm not sure that's true, Sadie, but as Lennie says, I'm sure Mya knows we're here with her and that's what matters most.' He gives me a smile of encouragement and I see in his face just how very tired he's feeling. Mya suddenly moves her head and we all watch her.

'My heart stops every time she moves,' I say.

'I know,' says Lennie. 'But she's moving much more often now, so that's a good sign. She's going to be reassessed tomorrow because we're beginning to see the very early signs that she's regaining some elements of recognition. Look how instantly she reacted to my cold hands just now. Why don't you play some music for her?'

Sam rifles through the stack of CDs on the side table, all Mya's favourites she kept in the car with her. Her collection is eclectic – she loves the old music Mum and Dad used to play a lot at home, as well as James Blunt, Robbie Williams and even a lot of classical stuff.

'Oldie or newie do you think?' Sam asks us.

We both say 'oldie' at the same time and Lennie gives me a wink. Sam puts on the Beach Boys and suddenly we're all tapping to 'Good Vibrations'. We're all laughing and start singing along softly when I look at Mya. Her eyes are open and not just for a second, she's not closing them! Lennie is brilliant. Sam and I just jump to our feet and stand there, not sure what to do. Lennie kneels down right next to Mya and leans in to her.

'You remember the Beach Boys, don't you Mya? Sam made a good choice, didn't he? Can you squeeze my hand, or move your finger? Let me know you can hear my voice.' We watch, our eyes glued to Mya's hands, looking for a sign she can hear what Lennie said. The seconds tick by, half a minute, a minute. Suddenly the index finger on her left hand lifts, ever so slightly, she holds it there for a few seconds and then lets it drop back onto the bed.

'Oh, my God!' I say and I realise I've been holding my breath. 'Mya, Mya, it's Sadie, I'm here with you.' I move forwards and drop down onto my knees on the other side of the bed. I take her hand and gently let it rest on my own. There's a slight movement and I look up at Lennie, amazed.

'Well,' she says, 'I'd say that's pretty good for a start.

172

Wouldn't you?' We all start laughing as the Beach Boys strike up 'Do it Again'.

'Brilliant choice, Sam,' says Lennie, beaming at him, 'brilliant choice!'

When Sam and I eventually walk out of the hospital that night, the reality hits home and we hug each other and start crying. We stand in the chilly air, under the canopy to avoid the rain and just hug for all we're worth. It's like all the tears we felt we couldn't shed before just come flooding out. All that anger and frustration – why Mya? why our family? – finally out. The release is strangely draining, but we realise that we're also crying because, at long last there is some real hope. Before, it felt like crying would be accepting defeat, giving up on her as if it was already a foregone conclusion. That might sound ridiculous, but that's how it felt. People are walking past us while we hug and cry, but we're oblivious.

'I didn't think she'd make it, Sadie!' Sam whispers quietly into my ear.

'I guess I didn't either. Part of me had already started saying goodbye, but there are things I needed to say to her that I haven't been able to put into words. I really want to have her back and let her know what a brilliant sister she's been all these years! That's my dream and it's going to happen, she's going to make it happen.'

Mum and Dad are ecstatic when we get home and tell them the news. It's the sign we've all been waiting for and they want to head straight out for the hospital to see for themselves. Lennie already told me to tell them that it was best to let Mya rest tonight, but perhaps they should both pop in first thing in the morning. And she is so right, because when they get there at nine o'clock the next day, Mr Whittaker is there with Mya. Mum phones me as soon as they leave to tell me what is happening.

'Darling, it's the best of news! Mya smiled at Dad –

173

actually smiled! Mr Whittaker did some of the response tests while we were there and she reacted to her feet being touched. She managed to move her hand when he asked her to, it's marvellous. I can't quite believe this is happening at last.' Mum's crying and laughing at the same time. She gives the phone to Dad.

'Hi darling, it's true! Mr Whittaker is going to get a specialist physiotherapist in to start doing some more intensive exercises to encourage Mya to push herself a little. He's not sure how quickly the improvements will happen, but he thinks she's turned the corner at last.' He can hardly contain himself, I can hear the pure joy in his voice. It's like I've got my Mum and Dad back, as well as Mya.

It's felt like living under a shadow since Mya has been in hospital. I don't think any of us have done more than 'exist' for months now. You can't take pleasure in anything, it sucks the joy out of life and living. You fail to notice the good, because you're so caught up in the bad. I realise now what a privileged life we all had before and how little we really appreciated it. Seeing someone you love sink into oblivion is the most painful thing ever. We watched her, wondering what was going on inside her head, what sort of thoughts did she have, was she aware of anything happening around her? A counsellor came to see us once and told us that many of her ex-patients who had survived being in a similar position had amazing stories to tell. She said that nothing was proven, scientifically or otherwise, but that they often spoke of having vivid dreams in which they were contacting people. Dreams where they did have some form of involvement and could often recall things that had gone on around them while they were in their 'deep sleep', as many seemed to refer to it.

Stranger still was the secret that Sam and I kept from

Mum and Dad. A young woman knocked on our door one day whilst they were at the hospital. She said her name was Laurel Prentis and she had a message from Mya. It was surreal. She seemed genuine, but she was very nervous and she didn't want to talk really, just literally pass on a message. Sam and I were stunned. We didn't know what to say. I realise people get messages from the dead, and I suppose we did think that Mya's chances of survival were getting slimmer and slimmer as each day passed. But Sam and I didn't really know how to react. She knew my name was Sadie and she also knew Sam was Mya's boyfriend – but I had never seen her before and she certainly wasn't one of Mya's regular circle of friends.

Laurel's visit was a really weird coincidence, because for quite a while both Sam and I had been feeling that Mya was around us sometimes when we were at home. Mostly at the weekends, when Mum and Dad were at the hospital and Sam would come and spend the day with me at home. We'd sit and chat, watch videos, that sort of thing. I suppose we were comfort for each other, because we could relax a bit and both understood the pressure we were living under. Friends just didn't fully realise how bad it was living as we were, constantly dreading the phone call that would send us all into a spin. It was just easier to keep each other company, so we didn't have to make an effort if we didn't feel up to it. Living on hope is exhausting and sometimes leaves you feeling empty inside. You have to experience it yourself to know that feeling.

We'd begun noticing Mya's cat, Parsley, acting really weirdly. Like he could see something that we couldn't see. He would stop and stare at it and sometimes actually walked around it in a circle! But there was never anything there that we could see.

I'd also done something really silly just a little while before and Sam wouldn't support me on it. I went to a séance. Even worse, it was being filmed live. That part was something I didn't really give any thought to though, it was just a friend at work told me about this medium, Grace something or other. She was supposed to be really good but she doesn't do private sittings. I managed to find her on the Internet on a website for a programme called *Connections*. They do live filming and I managed to get an invite to a ouija board session. I didn't know a lot about it, but I had this feeling that I should see someone psychic, in case there was a message waiting for me. Something I couldn't pick up on myself. I have absolutely *no* idea where that thought could have come from – so I took it as a sign.

Spending hours and hours with Mya, just sitting there, all sorts of things go through your mind. I felt that she really wanted to tell me things, I don't know why, because she wasn't able to give any signs at all. It was just this feeling. So strong at times I think even Sam, on occasion, commented that he felt some sort of 'vibe'. So, I went to this live séance session and I didn't tell anyone, except Sam of course and he dropped me there and then picked me up when it was finished. Afterwards we had to go for a drink, because I was so spooked that I couldn't stop shaking. While I was there someone touched me! I felt the pressure of a hand on my shoulder, there was a warmth and then I screamed. I think it was Mya. It sounds totally illogical, but I was convinced. So convinced that when I repeated everything to Sam, he believed me and that was *such* a relief. I thought he would think I was imagining it, because the awful thing is, if it had been the other way around I think I would have thought just that!

Anyway, Laurel just came to tell us that Mya was OK,

just like that and out of the blue! Mya *knew* I had gone to the séance and the message was that Mya didn't want me dabbling with that sort of thing. I was amazed – how could she have known that? Actually I was relieved to hear Laurel say that, because it wasn't exactly a good experience.

Sam and I discussed whether we should mention it to Mum and Dad. We both agreed that wasn't a wise thing to do, although the guilt of not telling them was dreadful. What if it actually was a message from Mya and she wanted them to share it? But on the other hand, how could anyone believe that someone in a 'vegetative state' could pass a message on to someone they didn't even know? But how did this Laurel person know anything about any of us, anyway? I can't begin to count the number of times Sam and I sat and discussed this after that day. Every time we came up with the same conclusion, it wasn't right to tell Mum and Dad. My dabbling had caused the problem and, while we were both secretly just a little bit happy to have met Laurel and heard what she had to say, we were also sceptical of giving it any credibility. Daft, isn't it? A bit like wanting to have it both ways at the same time!

There was one other thing. This is something I didn't share with Sam and for which I feel very, very guilty because it was meaningful. Laurel said Mya had told her something that would prove the message came from her. She referred to '*the* kiss'. I don't think I did a very good job of hiding the fact that it meant something to me and that the message suddenly became something much more important. It's just that only three people in the whole world knew about '*the* kiss'. It was at a time when Mya was spending lots of time in her bedroom with her best friend Kate. All they would do was talk about boys and clothes and things. They wouldn't let me join in and I used to hate it. Being five years younger was such a pain and I felt like a baby. This one time I walked in and found them kissing each other. Mya pulled me into the room and made me promise not to tell anyone, especially Mum and Dad. I sort of blackmailed her into giving me something – I think it was all the sweets I could eat for a whole month or something silly like that. She explained that they were practising for their first kiss with a boy and they had no intention of being called bad kissers behind their backs! I actually thought it was a good idea but, of course, I wasn't going to admit that to Mya. For the first time I felt like I had some real power and I was enjoying it.

The thing is though, how on *earth* did Laurel know about that? I didn't talk to Sam about it after Laurel left, because he didn't ask. We were both in shock at the time, as it had never occurred to either of us that Mya could actually communicate her thoughts. It was a real pity that Laurel wasn't willing to talk very much, we could see she felt awkward and although Sam tried to ask a few questions, once she'd given us the message she just wanted to leave. It would have been wonderful to know a bit more about how it all works and about Laurel herself. She wasn't anything like Grace from the séance, who was much older and that experience had been very spooky. Laurel just knocked on our door and how she knew where we lived, we just didn't know. Sam did give her my telephone number and I asked for hers. She didn't want to give it, but I promised I wouldn't bother her, only in an emergency and I've kept to that. But it has been hard because there are so many things I desperately wanted to ask her.

Sam and I have had a chat about it recently and we don't know if I should ring her to let her know the good news about Mya. After all, it must be so hard to be able to receive messages from people you don't know and it was so brave of her to come to see us that day. If I was in her shoes, I don't think I could have got involved. Imagine being pulled into other people's misery – that's not a gift, it's a burden.

Sometimes a hill feels more like a mountain

When you have a goal, you often spend so much time concentrating on achieving it, you never really get the time to think beyond it. That was so true for all of us once Mya was out of her deep sleep and everything ahead was unfamiliar.

It hadn't occurred to anyone that Mya would need to re-learn things that she used to do automatically. Eating, walking, catching up on what had passed her by in the months she was in her twilight world. At first she found it hard to talk for more than a few minutes at a time, she tired easily and she was often confused. It was a shock to her to be told that she had been asleep for so long and you could see the fear in her eyes, fear that she would never get her old self back. Mr Whittaker told us we needed to give her gentle encouragement and that everything would just have to happen gradually. Each step was a milestone to start with. Each visit now had a focus. Whether it was reading to her, encouraging her to eat or helping her with her short walks from the bed to the door and back. We weren't prepared for how exhausted everything made her or how anxious and frustrated she felt at not being able to do more. She was different and I supposed we too feared she would never be the same again.

The first time she looked at herself in the mirror, she cried. I was with her and I held her hand. I cried too, as the realisation hit me that she had changed so much, she almost didn't recognise herself. We had all grown used to the changes in her, but Mya was devastated by the pale, gaunt face that stared back at her from the mirror. Her slender body now gave the appearance of a girl, rather than the young woman she remembered. Mr Whittaker had warned us that Mya would need a long period to adjust, to get well and become strong enough to feel she had her life back under her own control again. He said we would need to understand her frustrations and be patient and gentle with her.

Mum would often cry when she arrived home at night after a long session at the hospital. There was no routine to our visits any more, we just took it in turns to spend as much time as possible at the hospital. Mya needed our support now even more than before. She would often hold my hand and sit and weep with anger, because her legs weren't strong enough yet to do what she wanted them to do. She hated being in that room and she longed to come home. For the first time we held a family conference and decided to speak to Mr Whittaker to suggest she come home sooner rather than later. We would all be active in her rehabilitation and do whatever it took to make it work. He ruled that out immediately and explained that it wouldn't be in Mya's best interests. She was going to need the constant support of a physiotherapist and a counsellor, who between them would facilitate the healing of the body and the mind. He told us it was early days and we just needed to let Mya settle into a routine and that would help her to feel more in control. He was very firm and we backed down. But it was hard to accept, we just wanted her home and that was where she longed to be.

What was particularly distressing was Mya's reaction to Sam. He was there every day, just like before, but as the days went on he often didn't stay very long. It was as if what had been between them just wasn't there any more. He was really upset about it – he didn't say anything to anyone, but Mum and I could see it. We'd grown to know him so well and to Mum he was like the son she never had. To me ... well, I can't think about that. Before the accident, Mya and Sam were always together, always sharing something, like couples do. He tried so hard to offer her help, but it seemed he always managed to say or do the wrong thing at the wrong time. They never touched at all, not even to hold hands and the worst thing was, I could see Sam accepting that what had been was now lost. I couldn't understand it though; he was upset and felt excluded, but he wasn't devastated. It was more that there was this big hole in his life where Mya had been and, since the accident, that hole had been filled, ironically, by me. I tried not to think about it, even when Sam's visits started to tail off. Instead of every day, he'd visit every two or three days and then once a week. Then his visits stopped altogether. Mya didn't seem to notice or care. But Mum noticed and she also noticed that it was breaking *my* heart.

The days go on and I'm hiding from it. I'm hiding from the emotions I didn't even realise were there. I won't let them surface because I can't go there. I've learnt that keeping busy means you don't have to think and that's how I'm surviving at the moment. I've got my sister back and that's all that matters. I'll be by her side for as long as she needs me and I'll never, ever let her know that I fell in love with Sam while she was 'away'.

Mum tried to talk to me about Sam yesterday, but I changed the subject. When Mya eventually comes home, she may want to pick up where she left off and that might include her relationship with Sam. I don't know what's going to happen and I don't even know what Sam's doing any more, he's shut himself away from all of us. All I do know is that what I feel isn't really important, because my sister is alive and my family is healing, we all are. Things will get better and for now, it's still one day at a time and no more.

Each week we see an improvement and Mya begins to smile more than she frowns. We sing along to her favourite music and I read her the jokey texts I get from friends on my phone. We play board games and cards, Mr Whittaker says it's all a part of helping Mya increase her stamina and improve her dexterity. They have a mobile hairdresser who visits the hospital and Mya has had her hair cut into a new style. It had grown so long and she hated it. She's asked me to take in her make-up and tonight we're going to have a girlie evening, face packs, the lot! I'm taking in some treats – Mya loves strawberry cheesecake and I've got her favourite one to take in.

When I pull up in the hospital car park, Mya is waiting in the entrance and waves out. She's wearing jeans and a jumper and she looks so excited. It's the furthest they've let her walk so far and to her it represents a freedom she hasn't had for a long time. I've got several bags of things to carry, but I still run the last little bit because I can see she can't wait, she's full of excitement.

'Mya, it's too cold for you to be out here! Quick, come on, back inside!' She leans across to try to take one of the bags, but I brush her away lightly.

'No, no, no. Walk ahead, I just want to see how you're doing.' I laugh but the real reason is I don't want her to tire herself out and the bags are heavy. She walks ahead and sashays, as if she's on a catwalk.

'Very sexy,' I call after her and a guy walking towards us does a wolf whistle. He doesn't know her, doesn't know our situation. He just sees a beautiful young woman, full of fun. Mya looks back at me over her shoulder and whispers.

'I guess I haven't lost it totally then?' She's beaming. She's the Mya I used to know and she's beginning to see for herself that the progress is real.

'You idiot! You haven't lost anything at all. Except you need to eat a few cheesecakes to get a little bit of fat back on you and then you'll be unbearably perfect!' She laughs, but I notice she's walking a little bit slower now and I hope she hasn't over-done it already. She's still in the little room on her own, but now it's full of cards and things from home to make her feel more cosy. She holds open the door while I manoeuvre in with the bags and I'm relieved to be able to put them down.

'Right,' I say, 'take this cheesecake first and put it over there. Mum sent plates, forks and glasses. I've brought some tropical fruit juice so we can have a party. Shall we do the face packs first?'

'Mm. Cucumber and mint, sounds edible – are you sure we put this on our faces?'

'Yes and it's going to feel so good.' I take off my coat and plonk down on the bed next to Mya. She turns and gives me a big hug and it's just the best feeling in the world.

'You're a brilliant little sister, did I ever tell you that?' It's only a comment but it hits home. It brings back memories of things I want to tell her, but now is not the time.

'Course I'm brilliant, I learnt from the master,' I say laughing and lie back on the bed.

We plaster on the cucumber and mint goo and sit on the bed with our bright green faces, eating cheesecake. We laugh and chat for a while, then go into the en-suite to wash off the masks. As we're drying our faces, Mya suddenly looks at me, as if she's making a decision about something.

'What's up?' I ask. She's stopped messing about and

seems hesitant. I wonder if she's not feeling well and whether our sudden burst of activity is too much for her at the moment.

'I'm good. Don't look at me like that – leave the worrying to Mum, it's her thing, not yours! I need to ask your advice, that's all. Let's go and sit down.'

'OK, I'm listening.'

She chews her lip for a bit, a habit from her childhood and I realise she doesn't know how to start.

'C'mon, just spit it out!' I say and she laughs.

'The counsellor, Jayne, she comes in to see me every day,' she stops.

'Yeee…ssss and?'

'You haven't met her, you all saw her predecessor. Anyway, she keeps asking me questions about what I can remember since I've been in hospital.'

'Oh, I see. I don't suppose you can remember much so that's a bit redundant then!' I can't see where this is going.

'Well, it's like this. I do remember, quite a lot I think. I'm not sure if it all actually happened though and I don't want to tell her about it. Do you think that's awful of me?'

I'm surprised and I'm not really sure what to say. 'Look Mya, she's the expert. Obviously it's her job to get you to talk and it could help you, you know, with any issues you might have about what's going on in your head.'

She laughs and leans across to ruffle my hair like I'm ten years old. 'You don't change, kid, do you? Doesn't it ever occur to you that sometimes you have to go with your own gut feeling on things? Yeah, it's hard waking up to the reality of having lost a chunk of your life and seeing everyone you love worn down and worried sick. But I'm on the mend now and what's in my head is my business. I certainly don't need a shrink, I need a detective.'

I'm shocked at the way Mya is looking at this, but actually it's the old Mya coming through – very strongly.

'But Mya, there are times to be cavalier and times to listen to the professionals. Don't you think this is one of those times when you should be listening?' It worries me that she doesn't realise how damaging it could be if she doesn't work through this properly, but hey, what do I know? I feel like saying she should ask Mum, but it's so nice to feel my opinion is worth having.

'Yes, but do you want to know what happened or don't you?' She looks at me and the mischievous Mya is back, full on.

'Course I'm curious, I spent hours next to you just wondering about whether you could actually see or hear anything at all. We all tried to say things that would trigger memories, remind you of the life waiting here for you. It would make a difference to know you didn't feel alone.'

'Ah ha! I knew it! But you have to promise not to repeat any of this to Mum and Dad or anyone from the hospital. Say you promise.'

'OK, I promise.' She settles back and I glance at the clock: it's only six thirty so the nurses won't come in until after visiting time finishes at eight o'clock, at the earliest.

'I thought I'd died, Sadie, really. I know I had pneumonia and I can remember thinking every breath was going to be my last, it was so hard to breathe. Suddenly I saw this really bright light. There was a path, a bit like a tunnel really, that seemed to stretch ahead of me. I was curious. It felt safe and I wanted to follow it. I could see in the distance something that I instinctively felt was good and welcoming. A bit like being on a bridge where one side is winter and the other side is summer. That's the best comparison I can give you to explain how it felt. I wanted to go on – I didn't want to stay where I was. I felt like

186

I was free of my body, free of the pain and I was heading straight into the light.' She stops to judge my reaction.

'It sounds like a nice memory, but even I've seen stories about people having near-death experiences and seeing the light. You don't think that could have been in the back of your mind and you were just dreaming?' I can't think why she wouldn't want to say this to Jayne, unless she felt it was all too predictable.

'Oh, it gets better than that! That was the predictable bit. It's just that you have to understand the impact of that so you can get the full picture. You see, as far as I was concerned, I was dead.'

'Sounds morbid to me,' I say, sadly.

'Oh shut up and listen! I didn't stop "feeling" or "having thoughts" after the light experience, it was just that everything was suddenly different. I had no idea about time or place as there was absolutely nothing I could reference. At first it was like being in a totally dark room, no noises whatsoever and lying there thinking. All of the activity was inside my head, contained. I felt relaxed and there was no pain, but I couldn't understand why I was so alert if there wasn't any point to it. If I wasn't attached to my body I couldn't actually *do* anything. Then I started seeing this person and her life going on around her. Not only was I able to see what was happening, but I could speak to her – mind to mind but having conversations. I asked her questions and she answered.'

Now I'm seriously concerned. 'Look, Mya, I've got to stop you there – this really is something you need to talk through with Jayne. You were in bed in hospital the whole time, so anything in your head was a dream, even if it was complex. If you feel it was real, then you really do need professional help.' I think I might have to break my promise and talk to Mum about this. Find a way for Mum to get Mya to talk to her next.

'Sadie, just for once forget about worrying. Just sit and listen to me with an open mind. If, when I'm done, you think I'm even remotely mental about this, I'll speak to Jayne. OK?'

'OK.'

'So ... where was I? Ah yes, Laurel.' It was like someone had slapped my face. It suddenly occurred to me, what if fate had a hand here and if so, for what reason would Mya and Laurel's paths cross? I felt a prickle, like a small shock making the hairs on my arms stand up.

'So, she was a friend, someone you knew before?' I just had to ask the question, although I could see that Mya didn't really want to be interrupted.

'No, I have absolutely no idea who Laurel is, but I'm going to find out.'

'Why?'

Mya's eyes widen as if I should have guessed the reason. 'Because I need to know what happened after I couldn't contact her any more. You see, I realised that the reason I was suddenly involved in Laurel's life was because I was meant to mend her relationship and get her back together with her soul mate.'

'How d'ya know that? Mya, it was just a dream.' I can't believe that Mya really believes she was involved in Laurel's life in some way. Perhaps I talked to her about Laurel when she was in the hospital – although I seriously doubt I would have done that intentionally. Sam and I had agreed it would stay between the two of us. She might have overheard me speaking to Sam, though, I don't know. Laurel obviously has a gift and can see things others aren't able to, but is it possible that Mya's state gave her some sort of psychic ability? I shake my head, I need to go away and think this through.

'It wasn't and I can prove it.'

'Mya, it's going to look like you've lost your mind. Do

you realise how this sounds? You were here, you left your body and you followed someone you don't know and watched them living their life? You weren't dead, you were just in a state of reduced consciousness. What's happened to you is like a – like a hallucination. Bits of things floating around in your subconscious that you've read or heard and together with your imagination and your state of consciousness, it makes a sort of story. That's all, babe.'

She looks at me and closes her eyes. I'm expecting some sort of angry rush, but instead she gives me the most brilliant smile.

'Babe,' she repeats softly and sighs, a happy sigh.

'Mya, this really is something you need to talk through properly with someone who can give you knowledgeable advice, not just your sister.'

'You promised, so you can't go back on that. If you tell Mum I will never, ever trust you again.'

'You know I won't. But Mya, please think about telling Jayne. She won't think you've lost the plot and she will understand. She may even be able to explain exactly how it can happen, so that you'll be able to see I'm right, it was all just a very complicated dream.'

We hug, but I can feel that she's cross with me. The trouble is, I need to talk to someone about this and I can't talk to anyone here and I daren't mention it to Mum. I'm going to have to ring Sam and I don't know how I feel about that.

It's breaking my heart, but I need to talk to you

How many times I pressed the numbers on my phone and stopped before the final digit, then pressed the cancel button, I don't know. Six, seven, maybe eight times? Talking to him is the last thing I want to do and yet the first. I want to hear his voice, I want to know how he's doing. He's broken my heart and I can never tell him and I wouldn't want to. Even if it's over between Mya and Sam, there was so much history before the accident, it makes anything between Sam and me impossible. Anyway, I've always been just Mya's little sister to Sam, never anything more.

I've got to speak to Sam, even though it's like pulling a scab off a wound that's beginning to heal, because he and I know that there must be something in what Mya is saying. I know that when I hear his voice, I won't be able to say any of the things I'd like to say and I can't let any of my feelings slip out. I've got to do this for Mya, so I've got no choice. The phone rings and rings but no one answers. In a way, I'm a little relieved.

It's been an exhausting day and I'm here on my own, so I run a bath and take a book and a glass of wine into the bathroom. I light some candles and add rose essence while the tub is filling. The bathroom becomes a retreat, somewhere to hide where I feel safe. As I slip into the water and start to relax, I begin to feel sorry for myself. Then I feel ashamed and then I feel guilty. It's like a pattern I've fallen into recently, because I feel like I've lost my way. I've been swamped by everything going on around me and now the fear of losing Mya is fading, I just don't know how to slip back into my own life. I know Mya won't want me around her every minute of the day when she goes home, but I've lost my confidence. The phone vibrates on top of my book and I have to grab it quickly before it slides into the bath. I press the call button in error and I hear Sam's voice. Shit! I'm in the bath, but he's talking to me and he doesn't realise it's awkward. Deep breaths, deep breaths, be cool Sadie.

'Hi Sadie, sorry I missed you. I feel I've been a bad friend, I've been meaning to ring, wanting to ring actually, but I know you're all tied up at the hospital still. How's life treating you?' He sounds normal, he sounds very cheerful actually and I suddenly wonder why I dreaded hearing his voice.

'Fine. You wouldn't recognise her now, Sam, she's almost the old Mya again. It will still be a little while, but it's nice to hear everyone laughing again and feeling positive. We all miss you.' I feel like I just want to tell him about all of the emotions welling up inside me – not just about how I feel about him, but about Mya, Mum, Dad, the lot.

'Has Mya asked about me at all?' I wasn't expecting that and I hesitate for a few seconds. 'No,' he says, 'I thought not. Don't feel bad about that, Sadie. Life moves on regardless of the tragedies we have to deal with. If Mya hadn't had her accident there's a chance we wouldn't have made it anyway, it happens. Not your fault.' Ah, he's trying to make me feel better, that's so typical of Sam!

'Actually, I was ringing to ask your advice.'

He chuckles, I think he's pleased. 'Not sure I'm much good at giving advice to other people, but you can try!' he says amiably.

'Laurel Prentis, you remember?'

'How could I ever forget? Weird, really weird.'

'It's going to get weirder. Mya is convinced that when she was "asleep" she was watching Laurel, involved in her life. She could "speak" to her through thought and she thinks the reason she could do that was to save Laurel's relationship.'

'Crikey. Obviously she picked up the name from one of us, we must have been talking about Laurel when we were at the hospital. Little things trigger the subconscious and before you know it, you've got a dream. Déjà vu is a bit like that, I hear.'

'I knew you'd common sense it. It's just that I'm pretty sure we never mentioned Laurel in the hospital. Think about it. Whenever we talked it was usually at home on Saturdays, when Mum and Dad were out visiting. Mya won't talk to her counsellor about any of this and she seems to feel she's on some sort of a mission. She talked to me about it because I think she's expecting me to help her. What do you think I should do?'

He pauses for a few minutes and I try desperately not to make any splashing noises, so he won't realise I'm in the bath. I could die of embarrassment.

'Sadie, I wish I could tell you to gloss over it and hope it will go away, that Mya might lose interest. But I think you've got the same feeling that I've got. Thinking back, we were both pretty impressed with Laurel. She wasn't asking for anything, she didn't really want to be there, delivering that message, and we haven't heard from her since. As far as I can see, she had nothing to gain. So why did she contact us unless she really did believe she had a message from Mya? Did Mya seem to know her from before?'

'No, I asked her that and she said definitely not. It's too much of a coincidence though, isn't it? There's something going on here, but I don't think Mya should get involved. She's only just getting her strength back to allow her to do normal things and I don't want to encourage her to get involved with things that aren't natural. Am I overreacting do you think? I'm sorry to burden you, but there's no one else I can confide in.'

'Sadie, girl, I'm always here for you. I think you're doing everything I'd do, if Mya had confided in me. Trouble is, she's headstrong so all you can do is play it down. I've still got Laurel's number. She seemed like a caring person, should I ring her and explain that we need to know how she received that message? After all, there could be some other explanation.'

'Like what?'

'Well, we weren't with Mya every second of the day. Perhaps Mya woke up and spoke to – I don't know, the lady cleaning the wards. People go home at night and talk to their family about what happens at work, even if they don't give names. There could be a logical explanation or it might be wishful thinking, but if one of us doesn't ask the question, we'll never know for sure.'

'I knew you'd think of something. You're my rock, do you know that?' The moment I finish speaking I'm mortified, it sounded like I need him and I'm relying on him, which I am. I'm so cross with myself I nearly drop the phone and, shifting position to grab it, the water sloshes up over the side of the bath.

'Sadie – are you in the bath?' I can't help it, but I start laughing. 'I think I'd better go,' he says, sounding very embarrassed. 'I'll call you tomorrow after I've spoken to Laurel. Night.'

Oh my God! He's going to think I'm such a twit. How uncool was that? But wasn't he brilliant?

Sam called while I was on my way home from work and just about to pop in to see Mya. I stood outside the hospital chatting to him and trying not to sound nervous to be speaking to him again.

LINN B. HALTON

'Well, I phoned Laurel and it just seemed simplest to meet up with her. I think this is something we need to talk about face to face, I hope that's all right with you, Sadie?'

'Sure, good idea. Did you tell her anything?'

'No, I just said things were getting complicated and although we're sorry to have to bother her, there are a few questions we have to ask. She said she understood. She did mention there wasn't a lot she would be able to add, because she hadn't had any further contact with Mya.'

'When are we meeting up?' I ask and I don't know whether I'm excited about talking to Laurel and finding something out, or about the thought of seeing Sam again.

'Can you call into my place after visiting Mya? About eight-thirty?'

'Of course, I'll see you later. Thanks, for everything.'

'You're welcome. Tell Mya I'm glad to hear she's doing good.'

'I will, bye.'

OK, so now I'm a believer

When I arrive at Sam's, Laurel is standing in the hallway and I'm glad about that. It means I only greet Sam with a 'hi' and we don't have the awkward 'do we hug or do we kiss?' decision. It's been a while and I'm nervous. He takes our coats and ushers both of us into his sitting room. I'd never been to Sam's flat before and it's a bit of a surprise. He has a lot of art, mostly paintings and a few sculptures here and there, but they are all real statements, edgy stuff. Apart from that, it's comfortable and reasonably tidy, not quite the bachelor pad I thought he might have. Strangely, I can't see any sign of Mya. None of her touches, she loves soft furnishing and she definitely wouldn't have chosen those curtains or the sofas! I suppose they spent most of their time together at Mya's flat, which is bigger and very stylish.

Laurel and I both say 'yes' to a glass of wine and Sam disappears into the kitchen, returning with a tray. He pours out three glasses and places a bowl of crisps on the coffee table in front of us. We exchange smiles and all pick up our wine glasses at the same time. Sam raises his in the air slightly and says, 'To Mya'. Laurel and I do the same, but Laurel looks uncomfortable.

'She's doing very well at the moment,' I say to Laurel by way of explanation.

'Sorry? Do you mean your sister Mya?' I look at Sam and he looks back at me, puzzled.

'Well, yes. She's on the mend, I've been to see her tonight actually.' Laurel places her glass on the table and sits back in her chair. She looks embarrassed.

'I think I've made a terrible mistake! The message I passed on was from someone in spirit, they had recently died – didn't I make that clear? I've given you a message that wasn't meant for you at all! I'm so very, very sorry.' She's really upset now.

'No, it's OK. You knew where we lived, you knew Sadie was Mya's sister and you knew who I was. It's been hard to accept, but we really believe it was a message from Mya.' Sam is trying his best to make Laurel feel at ease, the last thing we want is for her to walk out.

'Laurel, we've only asked to talk to you as we're trying to help Mya. She has some strange "memories" from the time she was "asleep".'

Laurel picks up her wine glass, takes a big mouthful and swallows with a gulp.

'I think you'd both better fill me in on exactly what's been happening, because when I came to see you I was under the impression Mya had died.'

Sam and I look at each other in amazement – that had never occurred to us. I suppose we'd assumed that Laurel understood all about Mya's condition, because she'd had contact with her, but apparently not!

Sam tells Laurel the story of Mya's accident and everything that's happened up until he stopped visiting. I notice he doesn't mention anything about his relationship with Mya having changed. We can both see from Laurel's reaction that this all comes as a bit of a shock. Amazing actually, because we'd assumed we would be the ones in shock, listening to Laurel and what she was going to reveal – not the other way around!

'Oh my God, if only I'd said something – made it clearer. It's just that I hardly ever use my "gift" now, but Mya isn't someone you can just walk away from, is she?' We all laugh and that really breaks the ice.

'You seem to have got the measure of my sister. You can imagine the hard time she's giving me now, because she wants me to find you!'

I tell Laurel all about the conversation I had with Mya yesterday about her dreams. I repeat exactly what Mya had told me, virtually word for word.

'I'm speechless Sadie. I'm used to handling spirits, but never anyone in a coma or, as you say, a similar state. I can't think I've ever even heard of messages being passed unless it's from the afterlife. This is all new to me. It's funny though and I actually said this to Mya, the link we had was very different from anything I'd ever experienced before. She wasn't with me all the time, but when she was it was full-on. She was shocked to think she'd died and I didn't know any different, so I treated her like I would any spirit. Except that we talked in my head and not out loud, but it was a proper two-way conversation, not just garbled words or even just "images".

'She was hard work at times because she was constantly trying to figure out a point to everything and she saw every little bit of information as a clue. I must admit I felt way out of my depth and the only reason I came to give you that message was because it meant so much to her. She told me you'd gone to a séance – there's a whole story I could tell you about that, but perhaps now it's best to keep this fairly short. The point is, even Mya was convinced she was dead. She wanted me to tell you she was OK because she didn't want you going to any more séances, she could see it scared you – she was there.'

Sam tops up Laurel's glass but I shake my head, I need to have a clear head. We all sit, looking a bit stunned.

'Crikey,' he says, 'I guess this psychic stuff isn't nonsense after all.'

'I think there's something else I should share with you both now,' I say. 'When you said that Mya gave you a piece of information to validate that the message was from her, you mentioned "*the* kiss".'

'I forgot about that,' says Sam. 'You never said anything about it afterwards, Sadie, and I forgot to ask.'

'Sorry, it was a lot to take in at the time and I didn't know what to do for the best. Truth is, it did mean a lot to me and only three people in the whole world know about that little incident.' I recount the tale and both Sam and Laurel start laughing. I blush, because it makes me feel like the childish younger sister again and not a young woman. It's not the way I want Sam to think of me. Oh, there I go again! Let it go, girl, let it go!

'Look,' says Laurel, 'there are people who would just love to get hold of all this – sorry, I don't mean the "kiss" story! Seriously, we're going to have to be very careful here. Are you both looking for explanations or is the focus helping Mya? If we're helping Mya, are you trying to cover this up or get to the bottom of it for her?'

'Good point,' says Sam. 'I think that's rather up to Sadie and what she thinks is best.'

'You know what Mya's like, Sam, sometimes she's so stubborn she just won't let go of things. Her real concern isn't her sanity, it's what happened to Laurel and her "soul mate". Mya feels involved, but actually it's not anyone's business and it's unfair to Laurel that Mya wants to know about her life. Does it make you feel uncomfortable?' We both look at Laurel.

'I haven't really thought about that. I can sort of understand it. I must admit, from the little I know of Mya she isn't the sort to just let things go if she's curious. If she remembers everything that we shared, then she will probably ask you at some point about my visit, because she knows I saw you both. I didn't actually tell her very much, only that I gave you the information she'd asked me to. I was trying to encourage her to stop thinking about the past and prepare herself to move on in the afterlife. I thought she was just getting bogged down and that once you heard that she was OK, then she could stop worrying about her family. That's often how it works with spirits, which is what I thought I was dealing with.'

Clearly, there isn't an easy solution to this.

'Laurel, would you be prepared to meet Mya?' Sam asks the question, straight out. It was on the tip of my tongue, but I just couldn't say it. I could have hugged him.

Laurel takes her time, has another gulp of wine and a couple of crisps. 'I'm glad I had a lift here,' she says, 'I'm feeling a bit light headed with all this wine!' She takes a deep breath, as if accepting the inevitable. 'It breaks all my rules and I really don't tune in now to anything by choice, but I suppose Mya is going to need closure. I haven't been through a very happy time myself recently and spirits often pick up on the raised energy levels that surround people dealing with problems and stress. What I can't understand, is *how* and *why* Mya linked with me in the first place? It doesn't make any sense now that I know she never was a spirit. Perhaps that's something Mya can clear up for me, I'd be interested to know the reason. So, yes, I suppose the easiest way is for us to get together.'

Sam and I are both relieved, as we know Mya isn't going to let this go, so there's no point in pretending. Also, I've been feeling very uncomfortable about knowing things that I haven't shared with Mya. Even if, by the sound of it, Mya knows most of it anyway!

'Great, that's great, Laurel. Sam and I both appreciate this. Oddly, Mya believes that all of her "dreams" are real and mentally she doesn't have a problem accepting any of it. She won't talk to her counsellor, because she says what's in her head is her business. She has no intention of revealing anything. But she did say she wanted me to do some detective work and find you. Actually, she also said something about being able to prove she wasn't dreaming. I wonder what she meant by that?'

'Well,' says Sam, 'I think the three of you should get together and find out.'

Laurel looks across at Sam and raises her eyebrows. 'You're not curious Sam?' she asks.

'It's not that, it's more that I don't feel it's my place any more.'

'Oh,' says Laurel, 'sorry. I didn't realise things had changed.'

'One of those things, don't worry about it. We didn't break up as much as things just moved on around us. I'm sure Mya and I will always be friends and anyway, Sadie's still my best mate.' He smiles at me in a strange way, but it makes me feel just like a kid again and I can't pretend I'm not disappointed. I smile back as if everything is totally fine and we finish our drinks.

I offer Laurel a lift home and she accepts. As we leave, Sam gives Laurel a brief hug and kisses me on the cheek. I've missed the smell of him and it makes me feel sad, because I don't know when I'm going to see him again. In the car Laurel tells me that she's a nurse and suddenly I realise she works in the same hospital where Mya is a patient. We're both astounded we hadn't thought of a potential link through work. Laurel says she's never worked in that part of the hospital or on the Intensive Care Unit and usually avoids the corridors around it. I'm surprised and I must have shown that, because she immediately explains that it's because she sees spirits. The worst place of all, she tells me, is being close to an area where people are in a critical state, because many don't make it. As spirits they aren't always prepared to leave and hang around, desperate for answers. I bet that's really distressing.

She works on a general ward where people are having minor operations and are often only day patients. They all get to go home and she's fine with that.

I feel really sad as she tells me that her mother also had the 'gift', but rejected it at a very young age and eventually it's possible to shut it out completely. She said that whilst she didn't want to encourage it, sometimes she just got caught up with the people, their lives, their families. She explained how guilty it made her feel when she started to push it all away, but how much more peaceful her life is now. She told me she honestly felt that she should never have received this gift. She felt sad at wasting an opportunity someone else could have chosen to develop, but she has now accepted that as the price for her own well-being. She was moving on and away from it, with no looking back.

It made me realise what an act of kindness it had been, coming to our house that day and also agreeing to meet up with Mya now. We arrange to meet at the coffee bar in the hospital on the following evening at seven o'clock. Laurel isn't working tomorrow anyway. She said it was just easier not to be seen visiting the unit, in case anyone started asking who it was she knew there. That made sense and I also thought it would nice for Mya, she loves getting out of her room and we often go across for a coffee when I visit. So, tomorrow we'll piece together the puzzle of Mya's twilight world.

I think you've already met...

I decide not to tell Mya that Laurel is coming and I know that's a big risk. I have two reasons. The first is that I don't want her to be disappointed if Laurel has second thoughts about turning up. That's possible, especially given the chat we had in the car. This is all happening in Laurel's working environment, with people around that she has to see every day and who may not understand her situation. The second is a sort of test, which might sound a bit thoughtless, but if Mya instantly recognises Laurel it will give all of us a real sense of validation. As unbelievable as it sounds to Sam and me, Mya and Laurel seem to be saying much the same thing. That's very good news, because it means there's nothing wrong with Mya's memories, or her mind, for that matter. The fact that it then presents us with an enormous leap of faith about something that can't physically be proven is another matter entirely. I'm feeling very guilty about Mum and Dad though, because if any of this gets out I know they won't be happy with me, or Sam for that matter! I'll accept that though, because Mya has chosen to put her trust in me and she must have done that for a reason.

I rang Sam in my lunch break to tell him about tonight and about Laurel working at the hospital. He's absolutely stunned by that bit of information, in much the same way as I had been, when Laurel casually mentioned she was a nurse. I didn't tell him that Mya doesn't know Laurel will be there tonight, because that's my judgement call and I don't think he'd understand.

Surprisingly we chatted quite happily for at least twenty minutes before I had to dash away, but it was like old times. Easy and familiar. It made me realise that I also miss him as the close friend he has become. When you think about it, we shared some of our darkest moments and through it all we used each other as support. I guess that, as the baby of the family, I always had the constant attention of Mya, Mum and Dad. Suddenly everyone was too busy to notice what was happening to me and I'm not complaining, just saying how it was. Sam stepped in and became the replacement for the people I loved who were temporarily occupied. Perhaps I'm not 'in love' with him, I just love him for what he did for me? But that's something I need to think about, because it really does feel like heart-wrenching love to me at this moment. Perhaps it will pass.

My brain is buzzing with so many thoughts and I realise I'm nearly at the hospital already. I've driven the whole route on 'auto-pilot'. God, I hope I didn't go through any red traffic lights! How can I not remember the journey? I've got to stop doing that and concentrate a bit more in future, I've seen the result of one accident and that's more than enough.

Mya jumps at the chance of walking over to the coffee bar for a chat. She's really bright again today and tells me she thinks Mr Whittaker will let her go home soon. I steer her into a corner table opposite the entrance, so I can keep an eye on the door. I go and fetch our drinks and when I get back she immediately starts talking about our chat the other day.

'Thanks, can you pass the sugar? So, you've gone all quiet about my twilight zone, you are going to help me – aren't you?' I know she's anxious because she's playing with the packets of sugar in the middle of the table. I've got to try to change the subject somehow, just until Laurel gets here.

'Maybe. Oh, I've got a message for you. I bumped into Sam and he said to tell you he's glad to hear you're doing well.' I put an upbeat spin on my voice to encourage her to talk about him, but it's hard.

'Oh, great. Is he well?'

'Yeah, looking good. I was a bit worried about him for a while there. He wasn't sleeping and he looked really hanging at times.' She's still fiddling with the sugar packets, rearranging them.

'I know what you're trying to do,' she says, looking directly at me.

'What?' I'm trying to keep an eye on the door without making it look obvious.

'Trying to get me to talk about Sam. I don't really have anything to say and you know that, Sadie, without my having to spell it out.' I stop looking around, there's an edge to her voice that suggests I've missed something.

'What do you mean?'

'You like Sam. I saw it the first time I saw you both together after I woke up properly. And Sam likes you!' Wow, I didn't see that coming, but suddenly I notice Laurel has just walked in and she's heading our way. Mya is still nervously fiddling and doesn't look up until Laurel is almost at our table. Her reaction is instant and unmistakeable. She jumps up, surprising both Laurel and myself and throws her arms around Laurel.

'It's you, it's really you! Sadie, you're the best sister *ever*! I thought you'd never get around to it.' We all sit down because everyone is suddenly looking at us, wondering what all the commotion is about. 'Why do you think I had that little chat with you? I knew you'd get in touch with Laurel for me,' she squeezes my arm and then turns to Laurel.

'You're the reason I can't pick up with Sam where we left off,' she says, matter-of-factly. Laurel hasn't said a word and looks like she needs a stiff drink, but all I can do is buy her a very strong coffee. When I get back, Laurel seems to have settled down and they're laughing together.

'What's funny?' I ask.

'Oh, I asked Laurel what Hohokus means, she was going to Google it for me,' and they both laugh as if it's a really funny joke, but I don't get it.

'So what does it mean?' I ask, puzzled.

'It's Red Indian for Red Cedar Tree actually,' Laurel says and it starts them off again! Mya wipes the tears from her eyes and attempts to calm down, because heads are turning in our direction.

'Seriously, Laurel was just telling me what hard work it was talking to me.'

'She used to give me a headache,' Laurel says, rolling her eyes.

'Poor you. I'd hate to have Mya inside *my* head, talking to me all the time. No offence, sis, but you're like a whirlwind.'

'Am I? Do you still think that now?' I realise Mya's asking me if she really is getting back to her old self.

'You engineered this without me realising it, didn't you? And I didn't even suspect for one second I was being manipulated. Clever stuff, sis!'

'Oh, it was just the quickest way to get some action. You know I hate just talking and talking about things, I'm a decisions girl at heart. Besides, I knew you'd talk to Sam and I wanted you to start doing that again.'

'I'd say you were very much back to normal, if not a bit sharper if that's at all possible. We'd all better watch out now. Have you got any sisters, Laurel?' It was just something I said without thinking about it. A throw-away comment, making conversation really. I wasn't prepared for the response.

205

'No, I'm an only child and I hated the fact that it was just me, because it was hard when my parents split up. But I've known my best friend Lennie since school and she's just like a sister to me.' And there it was. Just like that. The last piece of the puzzle. Laurel looks first at Mya and then at me – it's a 'eureka' moment and we can't hide the impact.

'When I woke up – properly and could focus on what was going on around me – I saw this nurse. She was talking to me as she was tidying the bed and I thought, I know you! I even recognised her appearance and her voice, although I realised I was actually meeting her in the flesh for the first time. It was Lennie and I knew who she was and that she was your best friend. I had this mental picture of her, chilling out with you in your flat and it was then that I knew everything in my head was real. I don't know how, but it was. I knew then that I had nothing to worry about and I was totally in control of my mind. I haven't said anything to her, there's no point in her knowing about all this, is there?'

We sit together for over two hours. I listen as Mya and Laurel tell their own versions of 'the story' of what they have shared. It would be totally beyond belief if this wasn't my sister corroborating what was being said. I realise that they now have a friendship that neither will walk away from, just because 'the story' is over. It's also sad to hear about Laurel's life with Dan, he sounds a really great guy and Mya is so happy they are giving it another chance.

'The reason I can't pick back up with Sam is because having seen you and Dan together, it made me realise that Sam and I had slipped out of love and into friendship. That tingle we had at the start had just mellowed away and watching you made me realise it's worth waiting for the fireworks.'

'There aren't any guarantees for me and Dan, but we're

talking every day now and I'm spending the weekend with him at the end of the month. You're going to have to meet him some time, he doesn't know about any of this though. He doesn't know about my psychic abilities. Actually, I need to ask you about that. Did you "persuade" Lennie to get Dan and me together?'

Mya immediately colours up. 'Ah. Yes. Look, you've got to understand it was all so very frustrating because I couldn't control anything, but I could see it all so clearly. I wanted to show you what you couldn't see – how much Dan was hurting and how desperate he was. He stopped communicating because he just shut everything out and you'd stopped listening. It was crazy and neither of you could see that. I didn't make actual contact with Lennie because I wasn't able to, I just moved a few things so she'd start thinking in the right direction. It took an old picture of you and Dan to do the trick, but it was exhausting because she ignored it at first. Eventually, after probably five attempts, she saw it as a sign and got in touch with Dan.'

'So, Lennie didn't know it was you at all? Nothing she could have picked up on while she was with you on a day to day basis in the hospital?'

'No. She may have talked to me when she was looking after me, I think everybody seems to have spent hours talking to me, but I can't remember any of that specifically.'

'It's so typical all of this. Nurses just don't talk about work outside of the hospital – if she had just once mentioned you, things would have clicked into place. I wonder where it all would have gone from there? She did tell me about her "weird happenings" to explain why she'd interfered between Dan and me. It was a shock when she admitted we were calling in to see him on the way back from our holiday in France. She said she felt she was being "told" to get us back together and she did it with the best of intentions, so I couldn't be cross with her. I remember thinking you were probably to blame, but I didn't say anything because I didn't want to pull Lennie into it! I did end up admitting to her that I see spirits, because she was so unsettled by it all and I thought it would make her feel better. That was awkward, because she didn't take it very well that I hadn't shared it with her before. She accepted it was something I didn't want to talk about.'

It's all such a lot to take in, harder for me because this is the first I've heard any of it. Whereas Laurel and Mya are really just comparing notes and filling in the gaps.

'I was counting on Sadie finding you and bringing you to me. I know my sister and she'd do anything for me! Actually, before I forget, there's something else I need to confess and you're not going to be happy about this either.' Mya's looking very apologetic and dreadfully guilty.

'I don't think now is the time to be holding anything back,' Laurel says encouragingly.

'After I lost touch with you, I had no control over what was happening – like most things, I was just reacting to the situations I found myself in. For some reason, I wasn't with you any more, I was with Dan instead. But it wasn't just the odd visit, it was like I was almost living with him.'

'But Dan never said a word about anything. You told me yourself that you'd seen him just before you left. I remember that, but I didn't think much about it at the time.'

'He wouldn't have. I couldn't talk to him like I could talk to you. All I could do was watch him, be around him. I couldn't read his thoughts and he had no idea who or what I was. He wasn't freaked, even though the only way I could try to communicate was by moving things. I didn't do it very successfully, because we aren't talking about bits of paper or photographs here. Hey, I was new to all this and I didn't really know what I was doing, only that he was very unhappy and very near the end of his tether. I had to try to do something to get him to focus and pick his life back up. I thought I was observing him for a reason and that reason had to be to try to do some good.'

I've been holding my breath, waiting for a reaction, but Laurel and Mya both start laughing.

'Poor Dan, I bet he didn't know what was going on! You do know he's been working on a ghost programme – I bet he thought it was something to do with that. We've never talked about spirits, he thinks I'm not at all interested in the subject. I always avoided having any conversations because I thought he would be horrified if he knew I saw dead people. I thought he'd feel freaky about spirits being around me at home. It's not something to be exactly proud of and I certainly don't advertise it. I'm not sure what to do now, because it's going to be very hard not to talk to him about this. What worries me most though, is that we thought we were really talking through everything with each other. You've made me realise that isn't the case, we're still keeping things back and I'm not sure how I feel about that. Why don't we feel able to share our most intimate thoughts? We used to, a long time ago.'

There's an awful silence and I can see that Mya is desperately trying to find something positive to say, but she can't. I can only imagine how she feels now, hearing that Laurel still has doubts about her relationship, despite all of the effort Mya has put in to making it work for the two of them. I'm just an observer, but I feel uneasy and I have a horrible feeling that Mya isn't going to like where all this is going. But I could be wrong and this could make all the difference. It could make them stop and think at the very least. Laurel isn't the sort of person to ignore warning signs. Hey, but what do I know?

Life just keeps getting better and better

They say every cloud has a silver lining and I guess it takes a bit of getting used to when you actually find it! After all the grief, the heartache and the stress of work, I'm finding it just a little bit scary how well everything's going.

Steffy left yesterday for a new job, in Japan of all places. She's just that kind of girl and I don't think she'll ever put down roots in any one place. Unless of course, she can find someone sufficiently interesting, who can manage to tie her down – not literally, although it makes me laugh because that's just up her street!

I've also left Jupiter Live. I don't feel I owed them anything, because things are going great for them now. Although Sean says I'm his number one, they have a great bunch of guys there now with a lot of talent. The psychic programme *Connections*, that I've been doing the graphics for this past year, offered me a job. I get on very well with the producer, Bill, and all of the technicians who do the live shows. They made it plain it was because of me that they didn't pull the contract with Jupiter Live when things were falling apart.

It's an exciting opportunity because I'm shadowing Bill as well as running the graphics side of things. This is a real break for me because it's always been my dream to get involved with production and they do studio recordings as well as live feeds. I've been talking to Bill about an idea I've had and it's all thanks to Cupcake. We actually have film, which we use in the adverts for the live programme, of Cupcake doing her thing at my place. The whole team were amazed when they were filming it and she did a pretty good job. It gave me the idea that there must be a lot of people out there who have had similar experiences to mine and who might be prepared to sit down and talk about it. It wouldn't be so 'in your face' and dramatic as the live shows. It's quite a radical change in their usual programme format, so Bill's thinking of calling it 'Real Connections' or 'Connections Up Close'.

We're talking about starting with two or three one-hour programmes each featuring different interviews. Real people, real experiences and, as they say, up close and personal! He's asked me if I would also take part and talk about Cupcake and I'm thinking about it, I don't know at the moment. The thing is, Cupcake left. It was the day she just couldn't settle and her activity was really getting on my nerves. I know the exact moment she left, because it was the only time I ever felt scared by what was happening. I suddenly felt very sick and suddenly I understood exactly what was meant by the phrase 'feeling like someone had walked over my grave'. Even the hairs on my arms and neck stood on end, it was a horrible few minutes, which passed and then I was fine, but that was the last of her visits. It has left a hole, I can't deny that. I probably shouldn't have spent so much time talking to her, but I realise now it was very healing in its own way. She made me talk about the things I had buried and that funny old saying, a trouble shared is a trouble halved, I found actually has a lot of truth in it. The comforting thought was, I could speak openly and honestly for the first time ever in my life, in complete confidence and without being judged, because I was talking to a spirit.

So, what else is happening? Lennie rings regularly and we chat, or rather she chats. It's funny, but Lennie has this great presence, she lights up the room when she walks in and she's just so good to be around. Not many people know that she's had her demons, she only let the mask slip once with me and I saw a hint of some sadness she wouldn't share. I don't know what's happened exactly, but I'm assuming Pete and baby Nathan have just made her inside match her outside now. She's got a tough job, which can be pretty depressing for her at times, I should imagine. Laurel always said she could never work on Intensive Care and it took a very special sort of person to cope with it. But if there weren't people like Lennie around, the world would be a sad place and I wish there were more like her.

I'm counting the days now until Laurel's down for the weekend. She's arriving Friday night and then Lennie, Pete and Nathan are stopping off around lunchtime on Saturday for a few hours. They're off to Pete's parents for the weekend and I think it might be to tell them they're planning to get married. I haven't been told officially, but Lennie keeps dropping hints. I suspect Pete's told her she can't tell anyone until he tells his parents, but I think they've already told Lennie's parents. I hate going to weddings and doing the suit thing, but I'll be glad to make an exception because Lennie deserves the fairytale.

I've made a special effort with the flat and Karl will be away all weekend, so that worked out well. He's a bit happier now that Cupcake isn't around, he never fully understood what was going on. He smokes weed a lot and sometimes things just go over his head, although there were times when he got really uptight about all of the breakages and strange noises. When I started my new job this week, I told him I'd be moving out soon. I haven't said anything to Laurel yet, because it's nothing to do with us seeing each other again. I just need to have my

213

own space. Don't get me wrong, I was more than grateful to share when I came to Brighton after Laurel chucked me out. I was broke, so I needed something cheap and, looking back now, it wouldn't have done me any favours to be on my own too much then. I'm not saying I was suicidal or anything, but I was definitely on the edge of something and it was probably Cupcake that brought me back to reality. How funky is that? Having had the experience was an eye-opener and certainly has helped me with my ideas for my new job. Trouble is, I miss her like I would miss a friend who suddenly goes away. Now that *is* worrying, so I'm going to skip over that quickly.

I'm really nervous about this weekend and I don't really understand why. I haven't spoken to Laurel since Monday, because she's away on some sort of training course to do with work. At the end of each day they have an assessment and she needs to study each evening so she's really prepared for the next day. It sounds tough, but she seems to be really focusing on her career now and she's enjoying it. I've bought something for her and I had it gift-wrapped. I'd been out walking, it was the day that Cupcake was playing up and it was the day she ended up leaving. I'd gone out to post some letters just to get away from all the noise – she was banging doors that day. I ended up strolling along the beach. It was a crisp day and the wind was whipping up the sea into a foamy spray. It was quite dramatic walking along the shoreline and I love that sort of weather. At the end of the beach there's a little promenade that runs off into some small alleyways and I found a little gift shop there. I stopped to look in the window and there was this crystal pendant. Laurel has always collected crystals, she's obsessed with them! Every room in the flat has one hanging in the window, she says she loves the way they catch the light. I thought it was a bit too girly personally, but hey, I wasn't going to upset her about that.

When I went inside the shop there was this really delightful old dear. She looked about a hundred, although she was surprisingly agile. She took the pendant down for me and I said it was perfect, could she gift-wrap it for me. She was quite canny, I don't suppose she gets many customers at this time of the year and she noticed that something else had caught my eye. She smiled at me, lifted it out of the window and placed it on the counter. It was a small square wooden box and the lid was covered in tiny pink shells. I could hold it easily in the palm of my hand, so it wasn't a very useful box, but it would hold something small like earrings or a ring.

'Caught your eye, didn't it?' she said as she wrapped Laurel's present.

'Yeah. My girlfriend would hate it, but it reminds me of when I was a kid and looking in gift shops then – they all sold boxes with shells on them. Gone out of fashion now, everything has to be designer or minimal, different world out there now,' I said.

She nodded sadly, agreeing with me. 'Shame. It's very pretty though,' she said. Somehow, once I'd picked it up, I just couldn't put it down and I felt a bit daft. It wasn't expensive, but I couldn't think of any real reason to buy it, other than it seemed the right thing to do. How odd is that?

'I'll take it anyway. I expect I can give it to a friend, Christmas or something,' I mumbled feeling like a bit of an idiot. Do men usually get fascinated by little shell boxes? Not the most macho moment I've had in my life. Anyway, she asked if I wanted it gift-wrapped, but I said to just put it in a bag and I shoved it into my jacket pocket. I picked up Laurel's beautifully wrapped little parcel and carried it home very carefully. I knew she'd be over the moon with it, it's a pear-drop shaped crystal on a very fine silver chain and it's beautiful.

Friday night doesn't turn out to be the romantic get-together I'd planned. We walked into town for something to eat and end up seeing a bunch of the guys from work. They insisted on dragging us both to a club. Laurel looked tired when she arrived, but she was buzzing from the course and she went straight into party mode with hardly a pause for breath. I found it harder because I was set for a chilled evening, but eventually we were both on the dance floor giving it our all. We didn't get back to my place until the early hours and we just collapsed into bed, I think we both regretted drinking the Tequila chasers – I won't be doing that again in a hurry!

We had a lie-in this morning because we both had trouble 'coming to'. A shower, toast and coffee and we're both reasonably presentable – just as well, because we're due to meet Lennie down on the beach in just over an hour's time.

There's something about a walk on a beach ...

Laurel isn't quite as relaxed as I'd hoped she'd be and I think I know why.

'You're quiet this morning, Babe. How's your head?' She looks up at me and the wind catches her hair, obscuring her face in a blonde haze.

'I'm fine, it's just been a long week and it probably wasn't such a good idea drinking so much last night!' She grimaces.

'Yeah, sorry about the guys. It wasn't a part of my plan, I promise. Sorry about the flat too – it isn't exactly glamorous is it? It takes me back to my student days. I'm going to move out soon, I'm thinking of buying a house, you know – an investment now things are going well.' I'm testing the water to see what her reaction is to that.

'Hey, that's great. Will you stay in the same area?' It's just a question, I don't think there's any motive behind it.

'Yeah, probably. I love the beach and there's a lot going on here, close to town. I'm working with the *Connections* team permanently now. It's a good opportunity and Sean understood it was time for me to move on and chase my dream.'

Laurel stops walking and gives me a hug. 'I'm so pleased for you, you deserve a break. You've worked so hard and it's nice to see you so relaxed for a change.' I hug her back but there's something missing today, although I don't know what exactly.

217

'Ouch … what's this?' she pulls a small, crumpled bag from my pocket and looks inside. She takes out the shell box that I'd forgotten was still there. I pull out the small, gift-wrapped jewellery box from my inside pocket and take the shell box from her.

'That's something I just picked up, *this* is for you, Babe,' I say.

'Thank goodness,' she says, 'I thought for one awful moment you'd bought that for me. Sorry, it's lovely of course, but so *not* me.'

She unwraps her gift excitedly. 'Oh Dan, I *love* it, I absolutely love it!' she beams and I can see she's immediately embarrassed.

'What's wrong?'

She puts the crystal pendant back in the box and places it in her coat pocket. We start walking again in the direction of the beach huts, where we're going to meet Lennie in about forty-five minutes' time.

'The shell box,' she says, 'you bought it for someone else.' I'm puzzled now.

'I bought it without really thinking about it. It reminded me of the past, I think, you know, looking in gift shops when I was a kid on trips to the seaside. Why? It's just a trinket, Babe.'

'I've just realised what it represents,' she says and she's suddenly looking really sad.

'It doesn't represent anything.' This is crazy, I don't know what's going on, but Laurel's suddenly going really cold on me. I feel like I've done something wrong and it's serious.

'Dan, can we sit down for a while? There's something I need to tell you.' I look at her and I have no idea at all what this is all about. I can't believe a little box could upset her so much.

'This sounds heavy, Babe. What's going on?' I ask the

218

question teasingly, but Laurel looks at me and I'd say she's a bit tearful. We wander along in silence until we find an empty bench, looking out to sea.

'Over to you,' I say lightly as we sit down.

'I don't really know where to start, because it's a long story and not easy to explain. Here goes then. You know I like crystals? Well, it's because they promote physical and emotional wellbeing. They give protection. It's not unusual for people with psychic ability to recognise the power given off by things nature gives us for free.' I look at her to see if she's joking and this is a wind-up. Where's all this coming from? She glances at me, but doesn't give me time to collect my thoughts and say anything, before she continues.

'Why didn't I tell you before? Lennie said the same thing when I told her recently, for the first time. I only told her then, because she had an encounter and she needed reassurance. I wouldn't be telling you now, except that it changes things. I suppose I had two real reasons for not telling you both, even though you are two of the closest people to me. The first is that I was scared you would be spooked to know that I saw spirits, could talk to them and that they were often around me. That includes when I was at home with you. The second reason was that after spending most of my childhood and teens thinking things would never change, I've spent the last five or six years trying to distance myself from the spirit world. I can't live with it and that may be selfish, but I have to have my life back. I didn't choose this "gift" and I just can't handle all of the intense emotions that spirits bring with them.' She's looking at me and expecting some sort of reaction, but I'm numb.

'Laurel, Babe, I just don't know what to say. It's a shock, but what does it change? I wish you'd felt comfortable enough to confide in me obviously, but I can see why you didn't.' What's she expecting from me, I wonder, am I just disappointing her all over again?

'There's more. Lots more. This young, female spirit came into my life. It wasn't the usual sort of contact, not through my spirit guide or as a physical presence. She talked to me in my head, she was watching me and watching you. She was involved in our lives and that's something that had never happened to me before, ever.' She pauses, but I realise it's just to collect her thoughts and I can't interrupt.

'Her name was Mya and she was bewildered. She was aware she'd been suffering from pneumonia and she remembered going towards the light. Then the next thing she knew was that she was a part of my life, indirectly. She wanted explanations and I didn't have any I could give her. She thought the reason everything was happening, was that she was supposed to reunite you and me. She had this romantic view of us representing everything she wanted from a relationship. I don't want you to tell Lennie this, but she managed to give Lennie some pretty scary hints about getting you and me to meet up. That's why Lennie rang you and arranged our meeting on the way back from France.'

'I think she might have visited me as well,' I say and Laurel smiles knowingly at me. 'Oh, you know then,' I say and I start to see the bigger picture.

'Don't rush me, I have to tell you everything so you'll understand.'

'OK, it's just a bit coincidental all this, isn't it? But I know two people who say there's no such thing as a coincidence and I'm beginning to think they've got a point.'

'Yeah, there are a few ways of looking at it – fate, coincidence or part of a greater plan? Who knows for sure? Anyway, back to Mya. Suddenly, I found Mya wasn't in my life any more. You and I weren't in contact and our lives were going in different directions. I only found out about her contact with Lennie after it had all happened. You never mentioned anything, but then we weren't in touch, so why would you? Did you think it was to do with the programme you were involved in?' She looks at me quite calmly, as if everybody has this sort of conversation.

'I suppose I did, although in the end I was convinced it was Lennie. Telepathic sympathy, would you believe! At first I thought I was hallucinating and that wasn't exactly a shock, because I was acting a bit strange at the time. I was really stressed and I was so worried about money and letting you down. One moment I was happy and everything was fine and the next it was all slipping away and I didn't seem to have any control. I felt like a failure, like everything I touched ended up turning bad. It wasn't the best time in my life, so what was one more odd thing happening, in the overall equation? She was good company, actually. I think she saved me from going mad. She never talked to me or appeared, just broke most of the ornaments and slammed doors really.'

Laurel grins and sits there, pulling strands of hair out of her eyes as the wind continues to play around us.

'That's what I always loved so much about you, Dan, some things just don't faze you at all. You just take it all in your stride, unquestioningly.' We smile at each other and it has a gentleness, a rush of mutual sympathy.

'Mya was trying to guide you through and she found it frustrating because it was almost impossible for her to directly influence anything. But she tried hard and I think she actually achieved a lot with all of us, don't you?'

'Yeah. Must be scary though, being dead.'

Laurel clears her throat. 'That's just it. She isn't dead.' We both look out to sea at the same time, as if there's something in front of us that suddenly catches our attention.

'Why did I know you were going to say that?' I ask her.

'Because you bought that shell box for her. And deep down, you sensed that one day you'd be able to give it to her in person. I've just come down this weekend to tell you where she is. She has no expectations, because she never thought beyond the idea of having passed into the spirit world. It's funny, she spent so long trying to get you and me back together just to keep her own dream of what love can be alive. And it was actually something she said, when we met up recently, that made me realise that you and I have come to the end of what we once had.' I realise she's crying and suddenly my eyes well up because I realise it's true.

'It just didn't feel right, Dan, although I desperately wanted it to be. Mya said that when she first saw us, she saw the passion and the fireworks between us. She knew then, that was what she'd always been looking for herself. When Lennie and I went to France, I was still trying to get over all that had happened between you and me. I was walking on the beach one day, when I suddenly understood that if Mr Right wasn't out there for me, it wasn't the end of the world. I could survive on my own, but that had never occurred to me before.'

That hurts, even though I know in my own heart that we're over, it still hurts.

'So I'm not Mr Right then?' I ask but it's not really a question at all.

'At first I would have said yes, but I now know that the reason it worked for me was because I was insecure and I saw you as my big, gentle protector. You shielded me from things while I was battling with my own demons and for that, I will always love you. But I'm not in love with you any more and I don't think you're in love with me now.'

I can't say it, I can't say those words. I don't need to.

'Hey Babe, it was good when it was good. What can I say? Did the crystals really help?'

'Yes, I really believe they did. I wish I could have explained to you about it, you must have thought it was odd but I needed, really needed, the power of the healing they gave out. Which is why it's such a coincidence that you bought me this beautiful crystal, because it's like a going away present. I think the shell box is your future.'

'Wow. I'm not sure I believe that, but I guess I know deep down that we're going in different directions now. I just can't believe I'm saying it. You've been such a part of me for so long and letting you go is the hardest thing I've ever had to do.' We both scuff our feet on the sandy concrete beneath us. On the wind we hear a cry and I look up to see Lennie, Pete and Nathan in the distance, waving out.

'What do we say to Lennie?' I ask.

'Nothing. It's a big weekend for them, they're going to tell Pete's parents they're getting married. I'll tell her later, next week probably. I don't want Lennie to realise she was the one who linked Mya to us. I think she talked to Mya while she was nursing her and I think she just talked about what was worrying her at the time. We were her major concern and she was just trying to encourage Mya and ended up talking about us. Please don't say anything about Mya, it's over for Lennie and there's no point in making her feel responsible, please promise.'

I look at her and our eyes lock. It's like all our past memories flash by in front of us and there's an overwhelming second filled with the 'magic' that was 'us' for just a while.

'I promise. It was good though, wasn't it?'

'Yeah, the best, hunky.' We hold hands and stand up. Walking towards Lennie, Pete and Nathan it seems like a dream. They're so caught up in their own happiness, there's absolutely no way Laurel and I can be sad. Life is full of so many good things happening all the time and we both know there are lots of good things ahead, for both of us.

Pete's a great guy, I knew he would be. Firm handshake and no nonsense approach. He's got his feet firmly on the ground, probably because of the tragedy he's had to live through. Nathan is a little ball of activity. He's got these huge blue eyes that seem to just draw you in. I'm not really a baby fan, never had any real experience of them, but he's real cute. Lennie dumps him unceremoniously into my arms.

'Nate, meet Uncle Dan. He's going to take you for a walk along the beach while we all get a coffee. I'm freezing!' she says and they all walk off, waving. My first reaction is panic, but then I turn to the little guy.

'Right, little man, it's just you and me. Ever seen a seagull before?' As we walk along the water's edge, I talk to him and point out the waves, the birds, even the clouds. He follows my finger when I point and he seems to like it. He gurgles, then says something that I can't even guess at. He smiles at me though, so I guess we're mates. When he looks at me, his eyes just seem to get bigger and bigger and suddenly I get this overwhelming feeling of déjà vu. I've been here before, with Nate in my arms, showing him the sea. So real and intense is the feeling that I have to shake myself and make myself move on. Dan and a baby, on the beach in Brighton, who would ever have thought?

Close your eyes and hold out your hand

Laurel and I still talk regularly and neither of us feels strange about that. I guess we're both very comfortable, being just friends seems the right thing for us now. In a way it's a relief from the strain of trying to make 'us' work. We'd fallen out of love, don't ask me when exactly because I couldn't say, it was a gradual thing that just crept up on us. For different reasons, we'd both become dependent on each other and I guess the truth is, we were both scared of going it alone. It's a tough world out there with no guarantees that you'll find someone to share your life with.

Laurel's doing well though, she's working hard and hopes to become a midwife. Her relationship with her Dad is coming along nicely and her Mum seems to have accepted it. She's arranged for Mya to come down to Brighton, so that the two of us can meet. She's given us both very strict instructions – that's so like her! We have to meet on the beach and I have to give Mya her present there.

So I'm here on the beach, waiting. I must admit I'm nervous. We'll probably feel really awkward, after all, we don't really know each other. I don't even know what she looks like. The shell box is in my pocket and if I don't give it to her, Laurel will want to know why. I wonder what Mya will think about it though; she'll probably think I'm nuts.

I thought we'd have a walk along the beach, grab some lunch and then I'd show her around the studio at work.

She might get a kick out of seeing where *Connections* is filmed. After all, she's got a bit of an insight into the psychic world and if we can't think of anything to say to each other, it'll pass the time until she heads back this evening. I don't know why I let Laurel talk me into this, but I suppose I am curious. Mya was important to me at the time, because I could talk to her and feel everything I said was safe. Now I feel really exposed, to think I've bared my soul to someone I really don't know. I suppose the reason I want to meet her is to see if I trust her, you know, that gut feeling you get for a person the first time you meet them. That makes me sound a bit paranoid, doesn't it? I'm probably overreacting, but even with Laurel I never totally opened up. But I feel bad when I compare what I was going through to what Laurel told me about Mya's experiences. She must have been terrified – I know I would have been! I think I'm worried that Mya won't find me as interesting in real life – does that sound strange? It also occurs to me that she's probably just as nervous and suddenly this doesn't seem like such a good idea after all. This could be a disaster!

It's a great day though, really sunny and the sky is totally clear. There are lots of kids running around and people taking advantage of the sunshine. I'm sitting on the bench where I sat with Laurel, the last time I saw her. Every time I see something move out of the corner of my eye, I look up. If I see a woman on her own, I watch her to see if she's coming in my direction. There've been a few, but none where I felt any sense of recognition at all. I'm beginning to think she isn't coming, so I walk up to the kiosk to get an ice cream and join the queue of noisy, excited children.

Suddenly something brushes my arm. I spin around, expecting one of the kids to have bumped into me and I see this girl. Mya is slim, about 5' 4" by the look of it, she has long, dark hair and she's a stunner. She has a scar about two inches long on her cheek, which I guess is from the accident. It draws the eye, an angry blemish on an otherwise perfect face and it makes my heart thump in my chest.

'Hi,' I say, 'just in time for an ice cream!' She laughs and she has a little movement she does with her head, sort of tilting it to one side, that's really cute.

'I'll let you in on a secret,' she says, 'I've been watching you and waiting for you to get in the queue. I thought this has got to be worth the price of an ice cream at least.' Sense of humour too, I see. I laugh and we nervously look into each other's eyes, searching for something, but I'm not sure what. Some sort of recognition, familiarity maybe? She indicates she'd like to walk and chat, so we head off along the beach front.

'So,' she says, 'it's really you! Shall I get the apologies out of the way first?' She's teasing me and I like it, it's friendly and it's breaking the ice.

'OK, sounds like a good start to me.' She's fun, let's see what she's got to say for herself.

'I am sorry about all of the breakages. Under the circumstances, I'm sure you'd agree that it would be very unfair of you to hold me responsible. Anyway,' she says, laughing and tossing her hair away from her ice cream, 'you'd have to prove that it was actually me. Unless you're recording this conversation, I'll deny all knowledge. Agreed?' I look at her and raise an eyebrow, she's caught my interest.

'Agreed.'

'Good, a man who's reasonable to deal with. This bodes well. I didn't mean to freak you out. I didn't mean to listen to things you might not have wanted to tell me, if you'd known my real situation. I guess we were both dealing with something that wasn't what we thought it was. So, don't feel embarrassed about anything please, because I feel just as awkward about what I was doing. So that sort of makes us quits, doesn't it?' She's refreshingly straightforward. I suppose, in a way, I'm not surprised.

'How about the door slamming stuff?' I give her a stern look, I'm not going to let her off the hook that easily.

'Yes, seemed like a good idea at the time. You have to understand I was sort of limited in the things I could do. What would you have done?'

'Depends.'

'Depends on what?'

'On what I was trying to achieve.'

She looks up from under her eyelashes, she's interested and, damn it, she's interesting me.

'Everything I did, I did with good intention but, yes, I'm very sorry for all of the disruption and the noise. You ought to say sorry to me now.'

I stop and glance at her, with a look of surprise on my face. 'Why?'

'All of a sudden you've turned into this guy who doesn't say a lot. Don't forget I know you pretty well and from my experience of you, you never had a problem talking at all! Ah, I suppose it's different now I'm here and you can actually see me. Is that it? Anyway, it might have skipped your memory, but you shouted at me when I was only trying to give you clues to get you going in the right direction,' she says plainly.

'That's below the belt. Is this something you think you're going to hold over me forever now? Well, I have to say I know something about you too. Maybe you didn't speak to me with words, but I know what makes you react and that gives me a real clue about the sort of person you are. I know you're passionate about things – that sort of emotion is something you can't hide. I'm sorry I shouted at you though, but you were a real pain in the ass at times.'

She looks at me and contemplates.

'OK, I can accept that. Laurel wanted us to meet so that you could see I'm a thoroughly trustworthy person and that I'm harmless. Does that make you feel better?' Ice cream dribbles down her chin and she laughingly holds her hand out to catch it. I put my hand in my jacket pocket and pull out a tissue to give her, at the same time I feel something in a paper bag.

'Oh yeah, I've got something for you, you're going to think I'm mad. I bought this for you, or at least, with you in mind. I thought you were a spirit, so it was silly buying it really. Laurel says I should give it to you anyway, because it was meant for you in the first place. Does that make any sense at all?' I hold it out in front of her.

'What is it?' she asks, not taking it, just staring at the package in my hand.

'It's a present, take it and have a look.'

'I don't take presents from strangers,' she says but her eyes are smiling mischievously. She looks at me for one long, drawn-out moment and I see a whole range of emotions flit across her face. It's like I'm asking her to reach out to me and not just the gift. We're connecting and this is just a symbol of that connection, this is the point of no return. I feel that what we say to each other now is important, but I'm not totally sure why.

'Ah, but we're not strangers. Are we?' I say and she acknowledges that with a nod of her head.

'What if I hate it? I'll be embarrassed, I'm not good at hiding disappointment.' I can see that would be true, she doesn't hold back.

'Take a risk. I've got a feeling it'll be all right.'

She throws the remains of her ice cream in the bin and wipes her hands on her jeans. She takes the bag and pulls out the box. Mya holds the little box up in the air, so that the shells sparkle in the sunlight. She moves it back and forwards, like a child probably would.

'It's perfect, it's totally perfect! Thank you, Dan.' It's the first time she's said my name and I like the way it sounds when she says it.

'So I'm forgiven for shouting at you?'

'Yes, I wasn't really upset with you. I am sad about you and Laurel though, seriously. She said she's told you everything and you must think I'm a meddler. It's just that it struck such a chord with me, when I saw how hard you were trying and what you were battling with – all that worry. Sorry, I honestly didn't mean to start dragging up personal things and make you feel awkward. It's all behind us now. It's really nice to meet you finally and I hope you're not disappointed with me.' She's so direct, it's a bit overwhelming.

'No, no – not at all. I didn't really have a picture of you in my head, you were more like a feeling. You became my comfort zone, which I know sounds totally daft, because all you really did was listen to me ranting on and break things in return. Actually, you sound like a woman a man should run away from, not towards!' Now we both laugh.

'Okaaaaay, so I guess I deserve that. I hear you're involved with a psychic show yourself?'

'Yeah, at first I sort of thought you were something to do with that. Not that I felt uncomfortable about any of it. I did talk to Grace about you, she's the medium on the show.' I hear her laughing and turn to look at her.

'I know, Dan, remember I know everything.' I like that she's making fun of me, that she feels comfortable enough to do that. It's personal without being heavy.

'Hey, are you hungry, 'cause I know a great little place for lunch? This is turning out to be quite a day, bit of a surprise really.'

'I think you meant to say that I was a bit of a surprise. Yes, I'm starving and I need a drink!' she says and I can see we're going to get along just fine.

We head into town and find a little wine bar. I order some tapas dishes and two blond beers.

'So, here's to the future. May it be full of good things for all of us,' I say as we chink glasses.

'It's strange sitting here with you, in the flesh,' she says, smiling to herself.

'Yeah, I know what you mean. I thought we'd pop into the studio where we film the live *Connections* shows. I sort of assumed you have an interest now in that sort of thing, but say if it's a really bad idea. I don't want to be insensitive if it's something you're not happy with, or if you have to rush back.' I'm giving her an option to back out if she's already bored with me.

'No, I'd like that. I've got a lot of questions about my – sorry, our – experience. At some stage I'd like to try to seek out some answers. There's not much information out there about people who've been through this, but it won't have been the first time. It's a bit isolating, though, so it's been great being able to talk to Laurel, and to you, of course. I feel like I've been on a long journey to a place no one else has ever been. In an obscure way, it was exciting and I have to find my way back to a very ordinary life by comparison. I don't really have much to do with my time at the moment, which doesn't help. I'd like to start working again soon, but things have moved on where I was before and I want to start afresh. Somewhere where no one knows I've had an accident and there's no history. It's amazing to think I can talk to you so easily, someone who doesn't really know too much about me. I suppose we've shared quite a lot really. You accept what happened and you're not obsessed with finding answers – you don't really mind either way, do you?'

'I suppose I am curious about some things. I have to say that I started to look at things very differently after Grace took me to see Lawrence.'

'In what way?'

'It's like the shell box. Why did I have to buy it when I knew Laurel would hate it? Why did I go into that gift shop on that particular day, the day you disappeared? Why did Laurel see it and realise that the two of us were over and we needed to move on? All because of a little box I suddenly felt I had to buy. I can't believe I'm telling you all this, it sounds a bit irrelevant, trivial.'

'I think we both know it's not. So much happened during that time, it's not possible for me to tell you everything. I realise, though, that sometimes the little things people leave out or don't think to mention, can actually mean an awful lot. What does stick in my mind is seeing you on a beach, Brighton probably. I saw you as a child walking along the water's edge, with your parents walking hand in hand alongside. You were happy. Then I saw you all grown up, walking on the beach with a baby in your arms. I don't know what any of it meant, but that little shell box just seems to be a link, a reminder. Perhaps the box should stay with you, but I'd kind of like to keep it myself really, if you don't mind that is. I suppose it represents a part of my "dream", let's call it, so it does mean something to me. I wasn't unhappy during that time, just frustrated because I really wanted to help you. I sympathised with you. You were hurting.' She suddenly sounds unsure and there's a look of vulnerability, as if she's scared she's said too much. It makes me want to hug her.

'Mya, whatever we shared, I don't think it should just end there, not if we don't want it to. We've shared things that a lot of people who've been together for years don't always get to share. Please don't go distant on me, I'm being as open with you as you're being with me. I think that's a good start, don't you?'

When she smiles, her scar turns a pale colour, rather than a livid red when her face is still. She's someone very special, one of those people – a lot like Laurel – who, when you meet them, you feel so comfortable that you forget yourself. You start to let your barriers slip and they get to see the real you, the person you usually hide from the world.

'You're so kind, Dan, in the most genuine way – you're real, I like that. Don't worry about me, I still get a bit tired at times. I'm also nervous. I guess that makes two of us.'

We have a great lunch and then head off to the studio. No one knows who Mya is, they just think she's a friend come to visit me. Everyone takes to her, she's easy to chat to and asks intelligent questions. I'm impressed. I take her to meet Grace, who's just come out of a meeting with Bill.

'Hi, Gracie, come meet my friend Mya.' Mya holds out her hand for Grace to shake, but Grace moves past her hand, and gives her a hug.

'My dear,' she says, 'I think we're way past shaking hands. I'm so delighted to meet you at last.' Mya and I both stand back and look at Grace in awe. 'You didn't think I'd pick up on it? Really, you two, I wouldn't be very good at my job if I didn't know, now would I?' A look passes between us all.

'I've got some questions, perhaps some time we could have a talk?' Mya says to Grace.

'It would be my pleasure, my dear. I have a very good friend, Lawrence, who would also be very interested to meet with you.'

'I know,' says Mya and she gives Grace a special smile. I take Mya back to the train station and wait with her until her train arrives. We go into the news kiosk and I pick up some chocolate and a magazine for her. As I queue to pay, the background music changes and it's a song by Lou Reed, *Perfect Day*. We look at each other and we both know it's a sign. The words say it all.

Mya boards the train and we both feel mixed emotions. We hug as if we're parting for a long time, instead of just a little while – and that's something about which I have absolutely no doubts whatsoever.

'It really has been a "perfect day", Dan,' she says. 'I hope it's been perfect for you too.' I take her hand and kiss it, gently.

'One thing I haven't said, that I really want to, is a "thank you" from the heart. You saved me from myself, when I was capable of doing something really silly and I know that you're just as aware of that fact as I am. It's pretty decent of you not to have brought it up. Perhaps all of this is a part of our fate and some things really do happen for a reason.'

'I'd like to think that was true, Dan. You will ring me, won't you?' she says and a brief hint of hesitation registers on her face.

'Just try and stop me,' I say. 'I'll call you in the morning.'

The train pulls away, Mya leans out of the window to wave and call out to me.

'It really was a perfect day, thank you, Dan,' she says and suddenly, deep down inside me, I get this feeling. It's like everything in my life has suddenly clicked into place. At last I feel like I'm exactly where I'm supposed to be and I'm happy, really happy.

Grace's Epilogue

Life holds some wondrous surprises

I have been a medium for almost as long as I can remember and that's a lot of years! I have seen more than my fair share of sadness, tragedy, happiness and joy. I have always felt it was a privilege to help people however I can; sometimes I've made a difference and sometimes, regrettably, I haven't been able to.

Lawrence was the first love of my life. He's also the last, although he was not the only one. When we first met it was fate, kismet – there are lots of words to describe something that was destined to be. Except, in those days, a young lady of my tender years was still very much under the control of her parents. We are talking about a different age, with different rules and standards, very little freedom for the majority. My father thought Lawrence was very unsuitable, not least because some of his family were traders and that just would not do. It was a world where people were measured against a very strict code that now seems almost laughable. Lawrence's parents were offended and after a whirlwind courtship, we were made to part and it broke both our hearts.

We met again, more than forty years later. Ironically my family has more or less disowned me because I chose to follow my 'calling'. And it was my 'calling' that reunited Lawrence and me. He married only a year after we were parted, his father had a business acquaintance and Lawrence married his daughter. He told me he had a happy life, although they were never able to have children. I too would have liked children but, unlike Lawrence, I never married. Somehow I just never seemed to meet anyone who fulfilled my expectations.

Lawrence and I were reunited at a Psychic Symposium. Lawrence was there in connection with his private research work into the afterlife. Meeting up was a very pleasant surprise and we had fun catching up on the detail of our separate lives. His wife died several years before and, like most of us more mature people, we have both found that life can be very lonely at times. Incredibly, the spark we had experienced all those years ago had never diminished and all the years just melted away. Age does mellow the emotions in a lot of respects. After all, I wouldn't really want to be reacting now as if I was still eighteen years old, but some emotions stand the test of time. Although we live apart still for professional reasons, we spend a lot of time in each other's company.

It's as if life has gone full circle and, while we weren't given the opportunity to share a large part of our lives, God has given us the final years to see out together. For that we are both eternally grateful and I am thankful for each and every day we have together.

Throughout my life, a mere handful of people have left a lasting impression on me. Lawrence will, of course, always be my number one, because I never forgot him, even for a moment. When I first met Dan, I felt such a rush of strong emotion, it made me breathless. It was like his soul was crying out in anguish, he was lost and he was needy. It was painful to watch and I felt helpless, because all I could do was befriend him. It wasn't my destiny to be the one to save him. When Cupcake arrived in his life, I genuinely believe she saved him. Life has a path, but on that path there are choices and sometimes a choice can change everything. Dan was on a dangerous path and I could see an end ahead of him that made me despair. Cupcake, or Mya, as I now know her to be called, was sent to guide him to the destiny he was supposed to fulfil. The fact that she also turned out to be his soul mate is what life is all about. You can plan, you can make your choices, you can think you have total control. But who controls the paths that converge and who decides which moment in a life is a truly defining one?

I think there's an even greater reason why Dan and Mya were destined to be together. As their future unfolds, I am convinced I will be proven right. They are going to help a lot of people in a way that is totally unanticipated by either of them at the moment.

Lawrence and I both believe God is instrumental, as far as he can be, given that we all have minds and wills of our own. We also believe that when loved ones pass on, they still watch over us. At times they send us healing and energy to help us accomplish things we couldn't achieve without their help. Of course, people believe all sorts of different things and who can ever claim to be an expert in something that cannot be proven? But there again, who is to say that what we believe isn't true?

All I know, beyond a shadow of a doubt, is that when I see Dan and Mya together – hugging and kissing, laughing and talking – it gives me the most wondrous feeling. If I could choose to do one thing that's impossible, I would choose to take the 'feeling' that their love creates, and bottle it. It is the very essence of the purest form of love – giving, selfless and true. Many search all their lives and never attain it. You see, it's really only about 'the giving' and not 'the receiving' and some people never fully understand that.

For those still searching, never give up, because no one really knows what might lie ahead and we must all live in hope that eventually our turn will come. I'm living proof of that and so are Dan and Mya.

After all, isn't everybody just searching for their own happy ending?